Grave Expectations

Rob Johnson

XERIKA PUBLISHING

In memory of Tom Doyle.

Thanks for the *craic* and all the laughs.

ACKNOWLEDGEMENTS

I am indebted to the following people for helping to make this book better than it would have been without their advice, technical knowhow and support:

Penny Philcox; Colin Ritchie; Dan Varndell; Nick Whitton; Heidi Woodgate; Patrick Woodgate.

And last but not least, my eternal gratitude to my wife, Penny, for her unfailing support, encouragement and belief.

COVER DESIGN BY PENNY PHILCOX AND PATRICK WOODGATE

Special thanks as always to Penny Philcox for the cover artwork and to Patrick Woodgate for the original design.

1

There wasn't a snowball's chance in a crematorium furnace that we were going to turn up at a funeral with "JUST CROAKED" scrawled across the rear window of the hearse and a whole bunch of tin cans and balloons tied to the back bumper.

I mean, what sort of sick bastard would do something like that on the day of somebody's funeral? What sort of sick bastard? Well, I know exactly what sort of sick bastard would do that, and his name's Edgar Shithead Ackroyd. Not that his middle name is actually Shithead, of course, although it sure as hell should be. He and his two gormless sons, Ray and Roy, had been plaguing us for weeks over what might be called an undertakers' turf war, and was one of the main reasons that "Max Dempsey and Partners: Funeral Directors" was once again struggling to make ends meet.

That's me, by the way. Max Dempsey. My real name's Simon Golightly, though, which was absolutely fine when I was a bank *manager*, but didn't sound right at all when I was embarking on my subsequent but short-lived career as a bank *robber*. And even when we'd taken over Danny Bishop's undertaker business about seven months ago, I decided to stick with Max Dempsey, mainly because I just preferred it.

Anyway, back to the turf war. "Edgar Ackroyd and Sons" were the only other undertakers in the area apart from us, and they'd stop at nothing to damage our business and steal our clients. Their usual trick was to do something to the hearse to make sure we were late to the funeral service, such as letting its tyres down or boxing it in with two other vehicles to stop us getting out. The latest "JUST CROAKED" ploy was a new one, but fortunately it had only been done in some kind of chalky paint, so it didn't take long to wipe it off. What took a lot more time was untying all the tin cans and balloons.

I suppose you might reasonably expect that a turf "war" would involve at least two sets of combatants, but that's not exactly the case if I'm being totally honest. Turf *massacre* might be a more accurate description. The thing is, you see, we wouldn't have dared to retaliate, whatever the Ackroyds threw at us. For starters, rumour had it that Daddy Ackroyd had some pretty close connections with a few of the more unsavoury members of the criminal underworld. Names such as Billy "The Butcher" McNally, Jack "Hacksaw" Higgins and Tony "Psycho" Vincenzi had been bandied about from time to time, and I hadn't the slightest intention of testing out whether the rumour was true or not. And then there were the junior Ackroyds, Ray and Roy, who were twins, and although not at all identical, were both ugly as fuck in their own particular ways. More to the point, and where they were very much alike, they both had far more muscles than brains, and each had done time for some rather nasty cases of grievous bodily harm.

As for our side, I'm late forties, a pound or two overweight and have a long-standing and deep-rooted aversion to pain. Other than me, though, Alan and Scratch looked as if they could handle themselves perfectly well if it ever came to any physical unpleasantness. On paper at least. Alan, for instance, had been an "almost champion" weightlifter in his younger days but had had to retire due to a serious neck injury, or so he claimed. The upshot was that he frequently resorted to wearing a padded neck brace, which he reckoned excused him from most forms of manual labour or a common or garden punch-up.

On the other hand, you might well assume that Scratch was more than capable of holding his own in a scrap. Well above average height with a powerfully muscular physique to match, the shaved head and busted nose made him look like a right thug, but appearances, as they say, can be deceptive. He'd cross the road to avoid stepping on so much as an ant, and I'd never seen him even swat a fly in all the years I'd known him. This proverbial gentle giant also had almost every allergy known to medical science. Whatever it was, if you could touch it, smell it or swallow it, it was odds on that Scratch would come out in a rash. Hence the nickname.

His driving abilities, however, were second to none, and these were precisely what we needed right now as we finished untying the last of the tin cans and piled into the hearse. Scratch floored the accelerator, and we shot off up the street with the screech of rubber on tarmac. If we were going to make it to the bereaved family's home in time, we'd need to be breaking a few speed limits.

'This is crazy,' said Alan, who was sandwiched between me and Scratch on the bench seat at the front of the hearse. 'We can't keep letting Ackroyd and his lads get away with this sort of shit.'

'Oh yeah?' I said. 'Any suggestions?'

'Well, how about we hire some heavies to give *them* a bit of grief? Get 'em to back off and stop poaching our customers for a start.'

'Heavies, eh? And pay them with what? We're borderline skint, as you very well know.'

'Which is at least partly down to the Ackroyds, as *you* very well know.'

It was a fair enough point, of course, but even if we could afford to, I could only imagine what the repercussions might be if we escalated our side of the turf war, so I didn't respond. Nor did Scratch, who was presumably too busy concentrating on the road ahead as we hurtled along, turning quite a few heads at the sight of a hearse racing past at fifty miles an hour in a thirty zone. Possibly that, or more likely he didn't have any answers either.

2

The funeral had gone off OK as it turned out, but the fee we'd got was a piss in the ocean as far as our financial crisis was concerned. In fact, the outlook was so bleak that Alan, Scratch and I had even started talking about getting back into our old career as a sideline to try and get a much needed injection of cash. Not that you could really call it a career as such because we were pretty shit at the whole bank robbing business. And like somebody once said, the definition of insanity is doing the same thing over and over again and expecting different results.

But then something weird happened. Just a few hours after our most recent little chat about returning to a life of crime, in walks this woman and says, 'I need a coffin.'

OK, that's not particularly weird in itself, given that selling coffins is a big part of what we do, and apart from the one we'd used for yesterday's funeral, we hadn't sold a single one in weeks. No, the weird part came a little later, but bear with me if you will, and

I'll get to it soon.

I'm sitting behind the reception desk at the funeral parlour, sifting through the morning mail, and I look up to see this woman who's knocking six feet tall and slim as a catwalk model. She's wearing a well-faded denim jacket and she's got lightish brown hair with a tinge of red. I'm guessing she'd be about early forties and, as far as I could tell, no stranger to a healthy lifestyle. So when she says 'I need a coffin', I smile up at her and say, 'Not from where I'm sitting, you don't.'

Hand on heart, I've no idea why I said it and instantly wished my gob had a rewind button. I certainly hadn't meant to sound flirty – which is very probably the way it came across – and besides, it's not the sort of remark you'd normally expect from a funeral director when you were no doubt grieving over the loss of a loved one and all you were after was a bloody coffin.

'What?' she said.

I got to my feet, feeling the heat glowing in my cheeks. 'Er, sorry. I thought you were someone else.'

She arched an eyebrow at me like she knew full well I was bullshitting, then perched herself on one of the two seats on the opposite side of the reception desk. 'You do sell coffins, I presume?'

She waved an arm in the general direction of the dozen or so display coffins in the main body of the funeral parlour, and I sat myself back down again.

'Yes, of course,' I said, desperately trying to assume my well-practised sombre-but-friendly undertaker expression. 'May I ask who the deceased might be? A family member perhaps?'

'Deceased?' She asked the question as if it was as

inappropriate as my earlier comment.

'Uh-huh.'

'No. No deceased. There isn't one.'

'Excuse me?'

'Don't tell me there's some kind of law that I can't buy a coffin unless I've got a dead body to go in it.'

'Not at all. It's just a little... unusual, that's all, but as you can see, we have an excellent range of coffins on display and also a brochure with—'

'What's your cheapest?'

'*Obviously not a big fan of whoever it is she's planning on burying.*'

(That was the voice in my head, by the way, and not what I actually said. And to be clear, it's only ever the one voice. It's not as if I get all kinds of weird satanic voices ordering me to commit unspeakable acts or anything like that. I'm not crazy, if that's what you're thinking.)

We never actually had our cheapest coffin out on display – or the Skinflint Special as we liked to call it – because we didn't want to encourage the tightarses, so I opened a desk drawer to take out one of our glossy brochures. But when I passed it to her, she ignored it completely and simply stared at me with what could only be described as a knowing smile. Not just stared, but pointed at me as well with a long and scarily red fingernail.

'Don't I recognise you from somewhere?'

'I don't know. Do you?'

'Wait a second and let me think.'

With that, she closed her eyes and switched her pointing finger to rhythmically tapping it on the top of the desk.

While I waited in silence as instructed, I scoured

my brain cells for any memory that I may have come across *her* before but came up with a resounding blank. As it turned out, though, I could easily be forgiven for failing to recognise her.

'That's it!' she said as her pale green eyes popped open and she slapped her palm down onto the desktop. 'You were wearing a mask at the time and the rest of your face was covered with dust, but I'm sure it was you.'

'*What the fuck is she talking about*?' said the voice in my head.

She leaned forward towards me. 'It's all in the eyes.'

'Sorry,' I said, 'but I'm afraid you've lost me.'

'Oh surely you must remember. Must have been about eight or nine months ago. Bit more perhaps. You drilled a bloody great hole into my dungeon from the basement of the shop next door. How could you forget something like that?'

Dungeon? Bloody hell. It was her. Miss Whiplash or whatever she called herself. It was our last catastrophic attempt at bank robbery before it finally dawned on us that we weren't cut out for that sort of thing at all. Alan, Scratch and I had rented an empty shop with the intention of drilling into the vault of the bank next door except Alan had got the wrong sodding wall, and instead we ended up in a veritable Aladdin's cave of whips, chains and a shitload of other S&M paraphernalia. 'Who's been a naughty boy then?' is what she'd said to me when I'd poked my head through the hole and she'd damn near caught me with a crack of her whip.

'I see from the way you've suddenly turned a rather unattractive shade of pale that it's all coming back to

14

you now,' she said.

And with it, the soul-crushing recollection of failure and toe-curling embarrassment.

'Christ. Was that *you*?'

The woman gave a sly smirk. 'Hardly surprising you didn't recognise me. I was presumably wearing my work clothes at the time.'

'Work clothes?'

'Black leather mostly. Probably a black leather mask and black wig as well.'

I didn't remember the details, but it certainly explained why I hadn't made the connection with the woman sitting across the desk from me. I also couldn't have foreseen how this chance encounter might lead to such a potentially lucrative partnership.

3

'So what did she want the coffin for?' said Alan when he and Scratch had got back to the funeral parlour after an extended lunch break at the pub and I'd told them about Eleanor Fairclough's visit – or "The Mistress" to use her professional title.

'Some weird fantasy of one of her clients,' I said. 'Wants to pretend to be dead and then find himself in Hell with everything that entails.'

'Blimey, that's a weird one. Which one did she buy?'

'The Skinflint Special, I'm afraid.'

Alan shrugged. 'Oh well, better than nothing, I suppose.'

'A few quid's hardly gonna get us out of the shit, though, is it?' said Scratch.

'Course not,' I said. 'But there's a lot more to it than that.'

I went on to fill them in on the rest of the conversation I'd had with Eleanor and how she'd told me she was thoroughly sick of the whole S&M

dominatrix thing and was desperate to retire. Trouble was, she'd got bugger all savings, so what was she going to live off? And that was when she seemed to have this sudden flash of inspiration.

'So now that you're an undertaker, I suppose you've given up on the bank robbing lark,' she'd said.

I'd blustered for a bit but eventually found myself admitting that the business was on the point of going bust, and we'd been "considering our options".

'Excellent,' she'd said. 'You know, I think I might have an idea how we might be able to help each other out.'

'Idea?' said Scratch. 'What sort of idea?'

'One that could very possibly benefit the both of us.'

'Yeah, you kinda said that already. You wanna be a little more specific?'

I took a deep breath. I wasn't at all sure how Alan and Scratch might react, and I wasn't entirely convinced it was such a great plan myself. 'Blackmail.'

'*Blackmail*?' they chorused.

'Well, not just blackmail. It also involves a bank robbery.'

'Oh great,' said Alan. 'So that's two reasons we could get banged up for most of the rest of our lives.'

Scratch gave him one of his steely glares. 'Why don't you shut yer pie-hole for a minute and let the man explain?'

I cut in quickly before he and Alan kicked off on one of their all too frequent bickering matches. 'The thing is, a lot of Eleanor's clients are totally loaded, and there's a fair few that are in pretty top jobs. Company directors, lawyers, and even a judge and a couple of well known politicians. But what none of them know is that she's started secretly filming every session she has with them. Can you imagine what sort of damage she could do to Lord So-and-So or whoever if it ever got out that what they loved to do most of all in their spare time was crawl around on the floor dressed as a baby or being tied up and given a right good thrashing?'

'OK, I get it,' said Alan. 'She could easily blackmail any one of them – or more if she wanted – and make a tidy little fortune for herself, but how does that help us out and where does the bank robbery come in?'

'Because,' I said, pausing for dramatic effect, 'one of these clients happens to be the manager of a rather large bank.'

I sat back in my chair behind the reception desk and waited for this additional piece of information to sink in. Neither Alan nor Scratch were as thick as they sometimes seemed to appear, and both were actually very bright, but it took a few seconds longer than I expected.

Scratch was the first to clock what I was getting at. 'Hang on a sec. She's gonna blackmail this bloke to rob his own bank?'

'That kinda thing, but there's a bit more to it than that. What she's going to do is get him to hang around one day after the bank's closed, then let us in through a back door so we can spend most of the night totally uninterrupted while we rob whatever the fuck we like.'

Alan frowned and fingered his padded neck brace. Apparently, he'd set off his old neck injury again when he'd shouldered the coffin at yesterday's funeral, or somesuch bollocks. 'It's an interesting idea, but what I don't understand is why she doesn't just make her money with all the blackmailing and leave the bank robbery part out altogether. Sure, *we'd* get nothing out of it if she did, but she doesn't owe us any favours, does she?'

I rubbed my forefinger and thumb together in the internationally recognised gesture to represent cash. 'Money, Alan. She reckons that there's a hell of a lot more to be made from doing over the bank than blackmailing even a dozen or so of her clients. And besides, this way she'd only have to blackmail one of them, so she'd drastically reduce the chances of anyone refusing to pay and going straight to the cops.'

'So when's all this supposed to happen?' said Scratch.

'I told her I'd let her know after I'd run it by you two first and see whether you were up for it.'

'And who's to say it won't end up a complete bloody catastrophe like nearly all the other jobs we've pulled?' said Alan.

I was about to point out one of the main advantages of this particular job when Scratch saved me the bother.

'OK, for one thing, we won't have to spend hour upon hour drilling through a fucking wall and end up with bugger all to show for it.'

Alan bristled. 'Jesus, Scratch, are you ever going to let up with that?'

'Well, you were the one picked the wrong wall. Not me, not Max, but you, yer dozy twat.'

'Oh yeah? So who was it that—'

'*Here we go,*' said the voice in my head. '*This could go on for quite a while. May as well slope off*

19

and leave 'em to it.'

As very often, the voice was right, so I disappeared up to my apartment above the funeral parlour for a quick snooze and maybe a crafty Jameson.

4

My quick snooze must have turned into quite a long kip because by the time I woke up and went back down to the funeral parlour, Alan and Scratch had gone home – or very possibly back to the pub. But wherever they'd gone, they not only hadn't locked up after them, they hadn't even bothered to shut the damn door. It was the sort of thing Sanjeev would have done, although I couldn't blame him on this occasion because we'd told him to take the rest of the day off before I'd gone up to the apartment. What with the distinct lack of customers, there was bugger all left for him to do as there were only so many times he could polish the display coffins without taking them back to their original wood.

Sanjeev, incidentally, is our general assistant, who we'd kept on when we'd taken over the undertaker business from the late, unlamented Danny Bishop. It hadn't been an easy decision, given that he'd been with Danny and apparently about to help his boss murder us all on top of a Scottish hill before Scratch appeared with a rifle, killing Danny and seriously wounding Sanjeev himself. But soon after he'd got out of hospital – and literally on his knees with tears in his eyes – he'd pleaded with us to be allowed to keep his old job. He'd convinced us that Danny had a hold over him which meant he'd been forced to do all kinds of shit he didn't want to do, but he'd never have killed us if it had come to it, so eventually we'd relented. Scratch and Alan had been even more resistant than I was, but a big part of what made them change their minds was that they both knew Sanjeev makes a bloody good cup of tea.

I closed and locked the door to the funeral parlour, and then it occurred to me that Alice might not have left yet. She's our only other employee, and unlike with Sanjeev, it had been a no-brainer to keep her on as our mortuary assistant. In her mid twenties and with enough facial piercings to throw an airport metal detector into a hissy fit, she was surly to the point of downright insufferable and a veritable pain in the arse. She was, however, incredibly good at her job at prettifying cadavers, often making them look better in death than they had been in life.

I went to the top of the steps that led down into the basement mortuary and called out her name, but there was no response. This didn't mean she wasn't still down there as she often had her ear buds in and her iPod turned up to almost full volume.

'*You'd better make sure,*' said the voice in my head. '*You know the shit she'll give you in the morning if you've shut her in all night.*'

The mortuary was somewhere I avoided as much as possible as it was almost guaranteed to set off one of my osmophobia attacks. It's basically a morbid fear of smells, and I've been plagued with it for most of my life. It doesn't have to be what most people would describe as *bad* smells that spark an attack, though, and even a whiff of jasmine or a certain brand of perfume would bring on the headaches, the nausea, the trembling and all the other shit. The smell in the mortuary definitely qualified as bad, however, and the chemically stink of formaldehyde and chlorine hit me as soon as I started down the steps.

Due to the lack of business, the four stainless steel cadaver tables were empty, and there was no sign of Alice. If she had no work to do, she'd normally have been sitting on a high stool at one of the workbenches at the far end of the room and most probably smoking a cigarette. This was strictly forbidden anywhere on the premises, and especially in the mortuary, but Alice wasn't a great one for following rules and became scarily belligerent if you tried to enforce them.

Relieved that I didn't have to stay down amongst the stench for even a second longer, I was about to head back up to the shop floor when something struck me as strangely out of the ordinary. It was nothing I could put my finger on. Just a feeling that we probably all get now and again when something doesn't feel quite as it should be. The voice in my head told me it was simply my subconscious reacting to the overall creepiness of the place, and I didn't need much persuading to carry on up the steps, taking two at a time.

I took a deep breath of relatively fresh air as I got to the top and was already looking forward to a couple of beers and an evening of mindless telly watching when there was an insistent knocking on the door at the front of the funeral parlour. It was a bit late for customers unless it was some kind of emergency, or maybe it was Alan or Scratch who'd forgotten something when they'd left for home and hadn't got their keys.

I threaded my way between the display coffins, and as I got closer to the door, I could make out a couple of figures through the glass. Judging by their shapes, I was almost sure that neither of them were Alan or Scratch. Closer still, I could see that it was a man and a woman. The man had black wavy hair, a rather podgy face and the beginnings of a double chin. The woman, who was marginally taller, had long dark hair tucked behind her ears and a straight-cut fringe that almost covered her eyebrows.

I unlocked the door, and no sooner had I opened it than the man flashed an ID badge at me.

'Detective Chief Inspector Parkin and Detective Sergeant Hibbert. I wonder if we might have a word.'

It was a moment I'd dreaded ever since I'd first begun to dabble in what society considered to be criminal activities, and holy shit, now it had become a reality.

'Er, what about?' I asked, aware of the slight tremor in my voice.

'Oh, nothing much,' said the chief inspector with a patently sarcastic smirk. 'Only that we have reason to believe you have been illegally removing certain body parts from some of the deceased in your care and selling them to research organisations.'

My brain and stomach instantly went into spasm. 'You can't be serious.'

'Never more so, sir. Mind if we come in?'

I took a step back to let them pass, more as a kneejerk reaction than any pretence at hospitality, but a thought occurred to me while I was closing the door behind them. 'Wait a minute. This hasn't got something to do with Scratch or Alan, has it?'

'Who?' said the inspector.

'Their idea of a prank, was it?'

He fixed me with an icy stare. 'I can assure you that this is no prank, and in my book at least, the misappropriation of human body parts for profit is one of the most morally repugnant crimes imaginable.'

I could think of a few others that were rather more morally repugnant but decided not to mention them.

'So,' he said, 'perhaps you wouldn't mind if we took a little look around.'

I was close to a hundred per cent certain that they wouldn't find whatever it was they were looking for, but nor did I want a couple of cops poking about in stuff that didn't concern them. 'Don't you need a warrant for that?'

'Not since you invited us in, sir, no.'

I'd no idea if that was true or not, but the inspector was already striding through the display coffins with the sergeant hot on his heels and making for the basement steps.

I hurried to catch up with them, and down in the mortuary they headed straight for the far end of the room. Pulling back the stool that Alice usually sat on, the sergeant crouched down and pulled out what looked like a plastic coolbox from under the workbench. She lifted the lid and the inspector peered over her shoulder.

'Hello,' he said. 'What have we got here then?'

5

Alan's jaw dropped, but only as far as his neck brace would let it. 'They found a what?'

'A human fucking heart,' I said. 'Or that's what they told me it was anyway. Packed in ice in a coolbox.'

'Not still beating, was it?'

'Course it wasn't still beating.'

'So why would anyone want a heart that wasn't working any more. Not much point using it for a transplant.'

'Cops said stuff like that gets sold to research companies and medical schools. Hearts, kidneys, livers and not just things like that either. Arms, legs, you name it. Even whole bloody heads.'

'Jeez,' said Scratch. 'That's disgusting.'

We were sitting in a café round the corner from the funeral parlour soon after I'd got back from the police station, and I'd been explaining about everything that had happened the evening before. As soon as the cops had discovered the coolbox and its grisly contents, they'd whisked me off to their HQ and questioned me for getting on for three hours.

"Whose body did you take the heart from?"

"Did you have donor permission?"

"How many other body parts have you stolen?"

"Who do you sell them to?"

I had a pretty good idea of my rights, so I'd asked for a lawyer before they'd even sat me down in the windowless interview room. I didn't know any myself, so they'd provided me with a duty solicitor, who hadn't arrived until an hour and a half after the interrogation had started. Even then, she was next to bloody useless, looked bored out of her mind and barely opened her gob the whole time I was being grilled. I could have stuck with the "no comment" routine, of course, but decided that was what people normally said if they were actually guilty.

But it didn't matter how many times I'd told them I knew nothing about the coolbox or selling body parts, DCI Parkin and DS Hibbert hadn't let up for a minute. I might as well have been a mass murderer as far as they were concerned, and Parkin was going to push for the maximum possible sentence if I didn't confess.

Eventually, though, they'd seemed to run out of steam, or more probably wanted to get home for their tea, so they'd switched off the recorder and got the custody sergeant to have me processed for a night in the cells. Or "custody suite", as they called it. Maybe that was to make it sound less intimidating – more inviting even, like it was on a par with a presidential suite or honeymoon suite. Nothing could have been further from the truth, of course, and I wouldn't have thought many presidents or honeymoon couples were strip searched on arrival.

That's what happened to me, though, and once I was stark bollock naked and bent over as instructed, the two duty officers had had a good old gawp up my poo chute. Christ knows what they thought they were going to find up there. More body parts? Some poor bugger's kidneys perhaps? At a guess, I'd say they were either just doing it for kicks or simply wanted to add another level to my already rocketing sense of humiliation.

After they'd finished and I'd been allowed to get dressed again, I was photographed and fingerprinted before being shown to my overnight accommodation. Toilet in the corner, concrete floor, tiled walls, tiny window and a metal bench with a thin plastic-covered mattress and matching pillow. Much as I'd expected really, although – osmophobia alert – the heavy atmosphere of disinfectant had failed to entirely mask the stink of piss and stale sweat.

And another new smell hit me twenty minutes or so after I'd been banged up when one of the officers brought me a microwaved vegetable curry. But I had to eat quickly. The only cutlery I was given was a paper spoon, which, as the officer warned me, would soon start to go soggy if it had been in contact with the food for too long.

Not surprisingly, I didn't sleep a wink that night. The metal bed base and pathetically thin mattress aside, the voice in my head wouldn't give me a moment's peace. *What if this? What if that? What if the other?* And so on, and so on until I wanted to scream at it to shut the fuck up.

When a duty officer came to let me out following morning, I managed to resist giving him a massive hug, and a kiss was definitely out of the question. Perhaps surprisingly considering my previous criminal activities, this was the first time I'd spent a night in a police cell, and it was certainly an experience I'd never want to repeat. That, however, was not going to be my choice to make.

DCI Parkin was waiting for me in the reception area of the custody suite and looked a lot less smug than he had the night before.

'This isn't over, sunshine,' he'd said as the custody sergeant gave me back my belongings. 'Not by a bloody long chalk. But I'm releasing you for now while we carry out further investigations. This, I might add, includes designating your business premises as an active crime scene, so you'll be barred from re-entering until we've carried out a thorough search and no doubt come across further evidence of your depraved and disgusting activities.'

And this was why Scratch, Alan and I were now in a café instead of the funeral parlour and attempting to get our heads round what the hell was going on.

'What about Alice?' said Alan. 'After all, they found this coolbox under the workbench she usually sits at, and if anyone has the opportunity to chop bits out of a corpse, it's her.'

'I dunno,' I said. 'Alice may be many things, but I'd put money on it that she'd never stoop to anything like that. And in any case, I've got another theory I reckon's a lot more plausible.'

'Oh?'

'Well, I can't be certain because it was all a bit rushed, but as they were bundling me into the car to take me to the cop shop, I caught a glimpse of a couple of people watching from the opposite side of the road. As I say, I might have been mistaken, but they looked a lot like our pals Ray and Roy.'

'The Ackroyd twins?' said Alan through a mouthful of bacon sandwich.

'There's something else as well. Did either of you lock up when you left yesterday afternoon?'

'Course we did,' said Scratch with more than a hint of indignation. 'We always do if you're not around.'

'I know that, but the reason I ask is because when I came down from the apartment, the door wasn't only unlocked, it was partly open.'

Alan used his fingernail to remove a piece of bacon from between his teeth. 'So you think Ray and Roy broke in?'

'Then planted the coolbox down in the mortuary before tipping off the cops. I mean, they knew *exactly* where to find it. Went straight to it without the slightest pretence of having a nose round first.'

Scratch slammed his meaty fist down onto the tabletop. 'Fucking bastards. They've stitched us up good an' proper this time.'

'Me anyway,' I said, 'although I wouldn't be at all surprised if the cops didn't try to drag you two into this as accomplices as well. Maybe Sanjeev and Alice too.'

'Shit,' said Alan. 'So they're not only trying to get us banged up, they've got the business closed down while it's a bloody crime scene and they've got themselves a nice little monopoly. Not that we've got too many customers coming our way as it is, but it's probably their idea of belt and braces.'

'And from what this Parkin guy told me, it might be days before we can open up again, and maybe not at all if they can get this body parts charge to stick. And in the meantime, I can't even get into my apartment, so I'm officially homeless.'

'Sorry to hear that, Max. What's been happening?'

I turned and looked up at the tall figure of Eleanor Fairclough looming over us.

'Oh, hi, Eleanor. Quite a lot, and none of it good, I'm afraid.'

'Yeah, I guessed as much from all the police activity at the funeral parlour. One of them told me they thought I'd find you here.'

I introduced her to Alan and Scratch as I'd been the only one she'd seen when I'd poked my head through the wall of her S&M dungeon. Then I gave her a quick rundown of everything that had happened since I'd last seen her.

She sat down on the chair opposite me and next to Scratch, her eyes locked onto mine. 'Hopefully I don't have to ask if you really—'

'No you bloody don't,' I snapped. 'The odd robbery here and there is one thing, but cutting up dead bodies...?'

Eleanor held up her palms towards me as if in mock surrender. 'OK, OK. Keep yer hair on. Just wanted to check, that's all. If we're going to be business partners, I need to know the sort of people I'm getting into bed with... so to speak. And while I'm on the subject – of business, that is, and not who I'm getting into bed with – I've got some rather interesting news.'

6

Eleanor took a sip of her coffee and sat back in her chair with a self-satisfied grin. 'He took a bit of persuading, but it's all sorted.'

'"He" being this bank manager client of yours?' I said.

'Alastair Chisholm. Or Worthless Lowlife Scumbag, as he prefers to be called during our sessions. I won't go into details, but I had to go rather further than I normally would with his punishment. Seems I must have forgotten our safe word,' she added with a chuckle.

'Safe word?' said Alan.

'It's some word you both agree on before you get started. Then you can use it as a signal to tell the other person to stop what they're doing to you when it gets too painful,' said Scratch.

Alan raised an eyebrow. 'How'd you know that then?'

'Saw it on the telly once... or read it. Can't remember now.'

'You sure you haven't—'

'No, Alan, I bloody haven't, OK?'

Before their latest squabble could get out of hand, I asked Eleanor if she was positive the bank manager was completely on board.

'He totally freaked when I showed him all the photos and videos I'd got, although like I say, I had to use a little more "elbow grease" than usual, and he came round eventually. The thing that bothered him most was that the robbery would obviously be an inside job, and he'd be the number one suspect for letting you into the bank.'

'Not an unreasonable assumption,' I said. 'He'd hardly want to explain to the police exactly *why* he was being blackmailed.'

'No, so I told him he should tell the cops that the robbers' accomplices were holding his wife and kids hostage and were going to kill them if he didn't do as he was told.'

'Whoa there. Hold yer horses,' said Alan. 'We'd already be in the frame for robbery and blackmail. I really don't fancy having kidnapping added to the list of charges.'

'You wouldn't have to,' said Eleanor, 'because you wouldn't have to kidnap them at all.'

'I don't understand. It's a cast iron certainty that the cops would question the family to check out his story, so what happens when the wife says no they weren't held hostage and hubby was talking bollocks?'

'Well, naturally he couldn't tell her the real reason for the blackmail or he'd have to fess up about his pervy extramarital activities, which is the whole point of the blackmail in the first place. So he'd spin her some bullshit about losing heavily on the stock market

33

and was seriously in debt to some rather unscrupulous loan sharks. And if he didn't pay up soon, the consequences would be very unpleasant indeed.'

'So he tells her the robbers bribed him so he could pay off his debt,' I said, 'and he'd get her to play along with the hostage story because if the cops knew he'd simply taken a bribe, he'd definitely be facing a jail stretch.'

Eleanor opened her mouth to speak, but Scratch cut in with: 'The robbers being us, of course, which means we'd have to actually pay him this bribe with a chunk of our takings.'

'Not at all,' said Eleanor, repeating her self-satisfied grin. 'We won't have to pay him a single cent because when his wife asks where the money is, he tells her there's nothing left as he's already used it to clear his debt with the loan sharks. The bribe was precisely the same amount as what he owed. Not that his missus would have been too chuffed about him gambling away a small fortune on the stock market, but better that than admitting what he'd really been up to most Wednesday evenings for the past few months.'

I was impressed. Like Scratch, I'd been beginning to think we'd have to split the proceeds one more way instead of the fifty-fifty we'd already agreed with Eleanor. Maybe it wouldn't have mattered too much, but that all depended on the total haul we ended up with.

I asked Eleanor if Chisholm had given her a date yet.

'Saturday,' she said. 'After the bank closes at one.'

'What, *this* Saturday?'

'Why? Is that a problem? I mean, it's not as if you've got a shitload to do to prepare. No bloody great drills or anything like that this time. Just a few bags for the loot and some sort of disguises for the CCTV wouldn't be a bad idea.'

'Yeah, I know, but in case you've forgotten, I have this body parts thing hanging over me, so it's a fairly safe bet that the police will be keeping a pretty close eye on me at the moment. And who's to say they might dig up some other bits and pieces while they're doing the search? Jesus, come Saturday I might even be banged up awaiting trial.'

'But surely there won't be anything else for them to find,' said Scratch.

'I dunno, Scratch. I wouldn't put it past the Ackroyds to have planted some other shit as well as the coolbox.'

'May as well get hung for a sheep as a lamb, though,' said Alan.

'Thanks, mate, that's really helpful. But don't forget what I was saying before about it being more than likely that you and Scratch might get done for aiding and abetting as well.'

Alan's hand froze with the last of his bacon sandwich halfway between the plate and his open mouth. Clearly, he *had* forgotten that he was very probably as deep in the doo-doo as I was.

'Well, guys,' said Eleanor, draining the last of her coffee and getting to her feet. 'Speaking of doo-doo, I've got an appointment with a client I need to get ready for, so I'll have to love you and leave you. But you'll have to let me know asap if Saturday's a goer or not. Oh, and Max, if your apartment's still off limits by tonight, give me a shout. I've got a spare bed at my place if you need it.'

Was that a wink she gave me? No, probably my

imagination, but I thanked her and said I'd call her if it came to it. As she closed the café door behind her, though, I couldn't help wondering what she meant by her "place". Not the bloody S&M dungeon, surely.

7

With little else to do, Alan, Scratch and I hung around in the café for another hour or so until we decided a change of scene was called for. In reality, though, it wasn't so much a change of scene that Alan and Scratch were after but a change of liquid refreshment. And so it was that the three of us were now sitting at one of the corner tables of the not-too-bad White Hart pub, supping pints of bitter and mostly in silence.

There wasn't a lot more to say after we'd spent the rest of the time at the café after Eleanor had left going over and over the rights and wrongs of doing the robbery while I— *we* still had the body parts thing hanging over us. That there were plenty of "wrongs" and very few "rights" had been the almost inevitable conclusion, and if we were officially charged and arrested, the decision would be out of our hands anyway.

I also had to admit – but only to myself – that the night I'd spent in the police cell had been a bit of a wake-up call. Even if nothing came of the body parts charge – and I couldn't quite see how that was likely – what was going to happen if the bank job got cocked up somehow and we all got nicked? Not just a single night in a cell but bloody thousands of 'em. Was I getting cold feet? You bet your arse I was.

'*And there was me thinking you were flat broke,*' said the voice in my head. '*So you got a better plan for getting your mitts on some cash, have you?*'

Well, no, I hadn't, and therein lay the problem, of course.

I sat staring into the last half inch of beer in the bottom of my glass, my mind too tired to think any more, until Alan broke the silence.

'Your round, I believe, Scratch.'

From an abundance of past experience, such a simple remark from Alan would quite probably have sparked a snarky response from Scratch along the lines of Alan being a tightarse and it was actually *his* round. On this occasion, however, Scratch stood up and headed for the bar without a word or even so much as an acrimonious scowl.

'So then, Max,' said Alan. 'Are you gonna stay with Miss Whiplash tonight or what?'

I shifted my gaze from the bottom of my glass to the sly grin on Alan's face. 'Eleanor? She calls herself The Mistress apparently, and no, probably not.'

'Goes without saying you'd be more than welcome to crash at mine if you want.'

I thanked him for the offer, but there was no way on earth I'd take him up on it. I'd only ever been to his flat once and five minutes was about as much as I could stand. In the kitchen there was about a month's worth of dirty crockery, pots and pans piled up in the sink and on the draining board, and the contents of the rubbish bin had overflowed to cover a good part of the sticky linoleum floor. As for the lounge, there was barely anywhere to sit, given the amount of empty or partially empty takeaway cartons strewn over almost every available surface. I'd also made the horrific mistake of using the toilet while I was there, and without going into the gory details, it was this that finally convinced me to make my excuses and leave, nursing a head-poundingly severe attack of my osmophobia.

Scratch had a small terraced house but would never have anyone to stay because they might bring something in that would set off one of his allergies. There didn't appear to be a lot of logic to this, but Scratch was a law unto himself as far as his allergies were concerned.

And apart from Alan and Scratch, I didn't really have any friends, or at least any that were close enough to take me in for a night or so. There were a couple of people at the bank I'd used to manage, but they'd cut me dead ever since I'd been sacked for embezzlement. As for any of the neighbours where I used to live with my ex-wife Carla in leafy suburbia, they were mostly hedge fund managers or something "big in the city" and basically a bunch of total wankers that I wouldn't piss on if they were on fire.

I couldn't afford to splash out on even a cheap bed and breakfast, so Eleanor's was beginning to look like the only realistic possibility, short of a layer of cardboard and a sleeping bag on the street.

Scratch set the three pints of bitter down without spilling a drop. 'Guess who I've just seen.'

Alan clearly couldn't resist. 'The Pope? Bono's second cousin? Queen Victoria's ghost? That bloke off *Emmerdale* that—'

'Only Edgar bloody Ackroyd, that's who.'

'Wouldn't have thought this'd be his kind of boozer,' I said. 'One of those up-market bistro-type gastropubs more his style, I reckon. He on his own?'

'Some guy I didn't recognise, but seemed like they were pretty pally. I couldn't hear much of what they were saying, but I'm almost sure your name was mentioned.'

'Mine?'

Scratch nodded and took a slug of his pint. 'Not by Ackroyd, though. It was the other guy.'

Curiosity got the better of me, so I went to see for myself, taking my pint with me. The pub was L-shaped, and by standing at the bar I could look across the corner into the shorter leg of the L. There were only two customers, and they were sitting facing each other and sharing what must have been a particularly hilarious joke. One of them was unmistakably Edgar Ackroyd, and although the other man had his back to me, I had little doubt who he was.

I took a couple of steps sideways so I couldn't be seen and asked the woman behind the bar to send over a round of whatever the two of them were drinking. She started to object that this wasn't the sort of place where they did table service, but the two quid tip I promised her did the trick, and she even treated me to a flicker of a smile.

A few minutes later as she placed a gin and tonic in front of Ackroyd and a half pint of lager for the other guy, there was a brief inaudible exchange, and the bartender turned to point at me. I'd now made myself visible at the corner of the bar and watched Ackroyd's expression morph from convivial contentment to a grimace of contempt. The other man – Detective Chief Inspector Parkin – turned in his chair to face me, and I raised my glass in a toast while his own expression went through much the same transformation as Ackroyd's but tinged also with something between embarrassment and horror.

I sauntered over to their table. 'Afternoon, gents. Having a good time?'

DCI Parkin quickly recomposed his features into a supercilious smirk and tapped the rim of the glass of lager I'd bought him. 'Trying to bribe a police officer now, is it?'

'Not at all,' I said. 'Merely a gesture of goodwill, that's all.'

'Well, you know what you can do with your gesture of goodwill, don't you?'

'Now now, Craig,' Ackroyd intervened. 'Let's not be uncharitable.' He took a sip of his G and T. 'Thank you, Mr Dempsey. Cheers.'

'You're welcome,' I said, forcing a smile, then switched my attention back to Parkin. 'Any news on when you might finish your search of the funeral parlour and we can get back to work?'

I ignored Ackroyd's snort of derision and eyeballed the DCI.

'Couldn't possibly comment,' he said. 'Ongoing investigation and all that.'

'Yeah, right,' I said and turned to go and rejoin Alan and Scratch.

Parkin called out after me, 'Just make sure you don't leave town, as they say in the movies.'

8

Eleanor's place consisted of two storeys above her S&M dungeon and would have been described as "deceptively spacious" in any estate agent's blurb. The lower floor was open plan with a well-equipped kitchen, dining area and lounge, and upstairs was a bathroom and two bedrooms. She obviously had a leaning towards minimalism, but the décor and what little was on display demonstrated a clear eye for the tasteful.

When I'd turned up there shortly before midnight, she'd poured me a large whisky and asked me if I'd like a tour of her "workspace", as she called it. It was an offer I quickly and easily declined. I'd seen more than enough of her dungeon and its S&M paraphernalia when I'd first peered through the hole in the wall and had no desire for a more detailed inspection. Besides, and admittedly with little likelihood, I had a vague feeling that she might be tempted to give me a personal demonstration of some of the equipment.

Spending the night at Eleanor's had been very definitely a last resort. The only other options I could come up with were Carla or Scratch's Aunt Betty, but I'd dismissed the Carla idea the moment it had entered my head. She and her half-her-age boyfriend, Dimitri Spiropoulos, had an apartment above the Acropolis Restaurant, which he'd reluctantly inherited after the sudden and violent death of his uncle Nikos. Carla and I hadn't exactly been on the best of terms since the divorce, but then again, the same also applied to the last year or so of our marriage. I knew precisely what her response would be if I'd asked her if I could have a bed for the night, and I certainly wasn't about to beg. There was also the issue of the stink of fried food that would inevitably be drifting up from the restaurant below. A sure guarantee that it would have triggered one of my osmophobia attacks.

For similar reasons, Aunt Betty's narrowboat on the canal was also a non-starter. I had nothing against the woman herself. Quite the contrary, in fact. Well into her seventies, she was wildly eccentric and one of the kindest and most warm-hearted people I'd ever met. She'd even helped us out in the past by harbouring our defecting Russian spy, Oleg Radimov, so I had no doubt at all that she would have welcomed me with open arms. And despite the dilapidated state of the narrowboat's exterior, the interior was immaculately maintained and perfectly comfortable, but there was a serious downside. Aunt Betty smoked roll-ups almost incessantly, and wasn't averse to the odd spliff either, and combined with the thick fug of smoke, the stench of paraffin, engine oil and diesel was even more of a no-no for my osmophobia than at Carla's place.

'Better make this the last one, I guess,' said Eleanor

as she poured me my third single malt. 'I have to be up in the morning.'

We'd been chatting almost non-stop for nearly two hours since the first whisky, and I'd totally lost track of the time. In all honesty, though, it had been Eleanor who'd been doing most of the talking, which was fine by me. Without naming names, her descriptions of some of her clients' wackiest requests had been fascinating as well as downright stomach churning on some occasions. Whips and chains were involved fairly often, of course, but one of the strangest fetishes was the guy who came once a week to clean her house and actually paid *her* for the privilege. Quite a substantial little earner, and all she had to do was shout at him now and then that he'd missed a cobweb or hadn't polished the coffee table properly or whatever.

'Needless to say,' she said, 'he's one of my all time favourite clients.'

'He's not coming tomorrow, is he?' I asked, not wanting to be around when all that was going on.

Eleanor laughed. 'No, you're quite safe. He's not due till next Monday. I'll be down in my workspace most of tomorrow morning, so you can hang around as long as you like and let yourself out when you're ready.'

'That's great. Thanks. No job to go to, so I don't think I need to be going anywhere in a hurry.'

She threw back the last of her whisky and got up from her steel-framed designer armchair. I was sitting in an identical one almost opposite hers, and she took me by the hand and helped me to my feet.

'And so to bed,' she said with a curious smile that I struggled to interpret.

Did we? Didn't we? Look, I'm not one to kiss and tell, but what I will tell is that I got the shock of my life when Eleanor woke me the next morning. I'd been having some strange dream about being dressed in a gorilla costume and attempting to clean the inside of a toilet bowl with a toothbrush and Eleanor yelling at me to work faster.

Except I wasn't dressed as a gorilla, and she wasn't yelling at me. She was talking a little louder than normal, yes, but presumably that was to snap me out of my slumber and bring me back into the real world.

'Rise and shine, sleepyhead. Got a nice coffee for you.'

I began to slowly peel open my eyelids, but as soon as I was able to focus, my eyes popped, and I jackknifed into a sitting position.

'Jesus Christ!'

Eleanor was standing next to the bed and wearing much the same gear as when I'd first caught sight of her through the hole in her dungeon wall. Black leather almost from head to toe with straps and buckles at regular intervals and her forearms clad in long black gloves. A black eye mask perched on her forehead, a thick, black leather collar studded with viciously long spikes, glossy scarlet lips and a wig of gleaming black hair.

'Not sure about Jesus Christ,' she said, setting a mug of coffee down on the bedside table. 'I was aiming for more of a satanic look.'

'Oh, right. Yeah, I er—'

'My work gear, as you may have guessed by now.'

'Yeah, sure. You look…'

'Scary? Intimidating?'

'I was gonna say "stunning",' I said, but this didn't appear to be the response she was looking for, so I quickly added, 'But definitely scary and intimidating as well, yes.'

Her smile broadened, and she leaned forward and kissed me softly on the cheek. 'OK, I'm off. See you later?'

'Uh-huh.'

She was halfway to the bedroom door when she called back over her shoulder, 'And don't do anything I wouldn't do, eh?'

'Well, that's a pretty low bar if ever I heard one,' said the voice in my head, and I lay back on the pillow, determined to get some extra – and hopefully dreamless – sleep.

But at the exact same moment, my phone rang.

It wasn't a number I recognised, but I answered it anyway.

'Mr Dempsey?'

I didn't recognise the voice either. 'Yes?'

'DCI Parkin here. I need you to come into the station.'

9

'It was a what?' said Alan.

The funeral parlour was no longer a crime scene and Alan, Scratch and I were sitting facing each other across the reception desk inside the front door.

'A pig's heart,' I said.

Scratch sat back and frowned. 'The heart from a pig?'

'Isn't that what he just said?'

'But where'd the Ackroyds get a pig's heart from?'

'A pig?' The "duh" in Alan's tone was heavily implicit.

'I dunno,' I said. 'Maybe they've got a contact at an abattoir or a pig farm, but that's hardly the point, is it? What's important is there's no law about being in possession of a pig's heart, so the cops have got nothing on us.'

I'd been telling them about my summons to the police station and my little chat with DCI Parkin. The bastard had made me sweat before giving me the good news, though. From the moment he'd called me, I'd been expecting to be formally charged and banged up in a police cell again. But when I'd arrived, he'd had one of his uniformed minions shut me in an interview room where I'd stayed for over an hour before Parkin and DS Hibbert made their appearance.

He was carrying a buff-coloured folder that he slammed down onto the table in front of him before he and his sidekick took their seats opposite me. Hibbert's face was expressionless, but Parkin had murder in his eyes.

He glared at me for several seconds before he spoke. 'You a superstitious man, Dempsey?'

'Not particularly,' I said, although this wasn't entirely true. 'Why d'you ask?'

'Well, you must have been avoiding walking under ladders, black cats and all that other tosh because you're a very lucky man. A *very* lucky man.'

He flipped open the folder and turned a couple of pages, pausing briefly while he seemed to be reading, although I was pretty sure he already knew exactly the words he was looking for.

'It would appear that, after careful forensic examination, the heart found on your premises once belonged to a pig and not a human being.' He slowly closed the folder and eyeballed me once again. 'As I said, you're a very lucky man indeed.'

'I don't see what luck's got to do with it,' I said, suddenly beginning to relax but with more than a touch of anger rising from my gut. 'Whether the heart came from a human, a pig or a fucking wildebeest, I've no idea how the damn thing got there, as I've told you over and over again. It was bloody planted, that's what it was. Perhaps you should have a word with your mate Edgar Ackroyd if you really want to get to the truth.'

If Parkin had murder in his eyes before, that instantly switched to something like hanging, drawing and quartering. He hammered his fist down onto the table, which made even DS Hibbert flinch. 'Get the fuck out of my station! Right now before I change my mind.'

I didn't know quite how he was going to be able to change his mind now that he clearly hadn't got a scrap of a case against me, but I let it slide and headed for the door.

Parkin had one last parting shot before I got there. 'I'll be watching you, Dempsey. You mark my words. One step out of line and I'll have your bollocks for pinballs.'

'Interesting analogy,' said Scratch when I'd finished filling him and Alan in on the details. 'Or is it a metaphor?'

'Who gives a shit what it is,' said Alan. 'The point is we're in the clear, so does that mean that we're on for tomorrow after all?'

'The robbery?'

Alan sighed. 'Yes, the bloody robbery, Scratch. What else?'

To be honest, I hadn't given it a lot of thought since I'd convinced myself that I'd be banged up in a police cell come Saturday, but I supposed there wasn't much to hold us back now.

'I don't see why not,' I said, 'although I guess we need to take Parkin's threat about keeping an eye on me seriously.'

'Just you then?' said Scratch. 'Not me or Alan?'

'Apparently. Seems he's got it in for me personally for some reason.'

'So in that case, why don't you stay here under his

radar till the time comes while Alan and I do whatever we need to do to get ready?'

'Like what?' said Alan, always wary of being asked to do anything that didn't involve sitting on his arse.

Scratch shrugged. 'I dunno. I reckon we'll need some kind of disguises for the CCTV cameras and maybe a few tools to open any deposit boxes they might have.'

'Basically a shopping trip then.'

Alan sat back in his chair with the hint of a smile, probably relieved to hear that he wasn't being asked to do anything that smacked of any actual manual labour.

There was no way of knowing whether Parkin was serious about keeping an eye on me, but there was no point taking any chances.

'OK,' I said, 'let's do that then. I'll stay put while you two go on your shopping spree, and in the meantime, I'll get in touch with Eleanor and tell her we're on for tomorrow.'

The pair of them pushed back their chairs, but before Alan stood up, he fixed me with a sly grin. 'So how did it go?'

'How did what go?' I said.

'Well, you spent the night at her place, didn't you? I'm just curious to know if anything... happened.'

'None of your business, Alan. So why don't you piss off and do what you're supposed to be doing.'

'You know,' he said, 'I heard a joke once about a sadist and a masochist. The masochist said, "Beat me. Beat me", and the sadist paused for a moment and said, "No". Get it?'

Yes, I got it, but didn't find it particularly funny.

Once they'd left, I picked up my phone to call Eleanor.

10

To pass the time while I waited for Scratch and Alan to get back, I decided to do some tidying up. Well, not just to pass the time. It was something that desperately needed doing if we were to be able to start functioning as a funeral directors again. The cops had certainly been thorough in their search of the place but a lot less diligent when it came to clearing up after themselves. Every one of the display coffins had been opened, and their lids lay strewn across the floor along with the purple velvet cloths we used to cover the plinths the coffins rested on.

A quick glance down in the mortuary revealed a scene of utter chaos with overturned cadaver tables and a sea of broken equipment. It was almost as if the Pamplona bull run had taken a diversion through the whole basement. Still, this was Alice's domain, and she was fiercely opposed to anyone "messing with my shit", so I'd leave that part of the cleanup to her.

Besides, I had my own apartment to deal with to make it at least reasonably habitable again. If anything, it was even more of a disaster site than the mortuary. Every shelf, every cupboard and every drawer had been emptied onto the floor, and I had to pick my way carefully through the debris to reach the bedroom. It was in much the same state as the rest of the apartment with the addition that the mattress from the bed was propped against a wall and the cover so badly shredded that the springs showed through in several places. So they'd reckoned I'd hidden human body parts inside my mattress, had they? No, there was more to all of this than a straightforward search for evidence. It was vindictive, pure and simple, and it wasn't hard to figure out who'd ordered his troops to inflict the maximum amount of damage while they conducted their search.

'*Standing there staring at it isn't gonna get the job done, is it?*' said the voice in my head. '*You need to crack on if you want somewhere to kip tonight… Unless of course you fancy another night of passion with Miss Whiplash?*'

As very often, the voice was quite right – apart from the bit about the night of passion, obviously – so I rolled up my sleeves and set about sorting out the wreckage. I'd need to buy a new mattress, but that would have to wait. Instead, I focused on the living area and putting the bed settee back together. Oddly enough, the cops had stopped short of slashing the covers to shreds, so I'd have somewhere reasonably comfortable to sleep.

❖

It was about six in the evening when Alan and Scratch made their reappearance, and after three solid hours,

I'd scarcely made a dent in rehabilitating my apartment.

'Bloody hell,' said Alan. 'What a mess. You wanna get this lot cleared up if you want somewhere to sleep tonight.'

I ignored him and asked how they'd got on with their shopping trip.

Alan was carrying a large black canvas holdall, and there was the telltale clank of metal on metal as he dropped it onto the floor. 'There you go. Every tool that no self-respecting bank robber should be without.'

I turned to Scratch, who took out three masks from a small carrier bag and laid each one side by side on the coffee table, which was now the right way up. They were plastic, full-face and had a thin piece of elastic attached to keep them in place. All of them scarily realistic.

'Are you kidding?' said Alan.

'Why? What's wrong with them?'

'Boris Johnson, Donald Trump and Prince fucking Andrew? Every one of them a total bloody wanker.'

'So what? They're meant to be disguises, not fan club masks.'

Alan scowled and picked up the Prince Andrew mask. 'Well, I'm not wearing this one for a start. I'll have Johnson or Trump, but I'm not robbing a bank disguised as a bloody nonce.'

'Jesus, Alan,' I said, stepping in before another of their petty arguments got out of hand. 'I'll have the Prince Andrew one if it makes you any happier. And by the way, you'll need to lose that before we go in.'

He fingered the neck brace I was pointing at that he'd had on permanently for the last couple of days. 'Bugger off, Max. I'm still in a hell of a lot of pain, and without this thing, I'd—'

'It'll make you more identifiable when the cops check the CCTV footage.'

'But I thought part of the deal was that this bank manager bloke was gonna switch off all the cameras.'

'That's the plan, but there's no guarantee he'll actually do it. Why'd you think we're bothering with masks?'

Alan muttered something I didn't pick up and tossed the Prince Andrew mask back onto the coffee table.

At the same moment, my phone rang. It was Eleanor, so I went down to the funeral parlour to let her in. Fortunately, she'd ditched the leather gear and was back in her faded denim jacket, T-shirt and jeans. It was definitely a look I preferred.

'How's it going?' she asked as I led the way up the stairs.

'OK, I guess. Alan's got a bit of a strop on, though.'

'Getting antsy about tomorrow maybe?'

'Not particularly, I don't think. That's just the way he is sometimes.'

Back in the apartment, she exchanged brief greetings with Scratch and Alan, then nodded down at the three masks on the coffee table. 'Interesting choices.'

I shot Alan a warning glare before he could open his gob, and again he muttered something inaudible.

'I hope they're comfortable, though,' she went on, 'because you'll need to keep them on the whole time you're in the bank. You don't want Chisholm being able to identify you to the cops if anything goes wrong.'

'No, we don't,' said Scratch, apparently without any hint of sarcasm.

'Right then,' said Eleanor, clapping her hands together. 'I suppose you'll be needing a few more details about the job.'

True enough. Until now, all we knew was how she'd blackmailed her bank manager client and the stories he'd tell his wife and the cops so he wouldn't get done for aiding and abetting. She'd also told us that he'd be letting us into the bank after it closed at one o'clock on Saturday – tomorrow. What she hadn't said yet was exactly which bank we were meant to be robbing. And that's when she dropped the bombshell.

11

There was still a couple of hours left before the bank closed at one, so we cruised past it in my old VW Polo to give it a quick once-over. Not that I really needed to. I was more than familiar with the place I used to manage myself before I got caught with my fingers in the till. It had come as quite a shock when Eleanor had told us that this was the bank we'd be robbing, but she assured me she'd had no idea where I used to work, and it was a complete coincidence. As she'd put it, though, it could only be to our advantage as I'd at least know the layout of the place and what kind of systems were in use in terms of security and so on. This was probably true, except some of the security systems might well have been changed since my little criminal indiscretion. Alan had asked me if I knew the manager who was going to let us in, but I had no memory of anyone called Alastair Chisholm. Must have been brought in from outside after I was sacked.

'So what do we do now while we're waiting?' said Scratch from the passenger seat beside me.

'We could always find a caff and grab a bacon butty or something,' said Alan.

'I thought you'd already had breakfast.'

'So what? I need to keep my energy levels up.'

Scratch snorted. 'Oh yeah? For what exactly?'

'Er, maybe you'd forgotten, but we're supposed to be robbing a bank in the next couple of hours or so.'

'Hardly like a raid, though, is it? It's not like we're gonna be bursting in, then legging it afterwards as fast as our legs can carry us. The guy's gonna let us in, we rob what we want, then we casually saunter out with the loot and head for home.'

'We'll find a caff,' I said, cutting in as I so often did to prevent their bickering escalating into a full-scale row.

It wasn't as if they hated each other's guts or anything. Far from it. We'd all known each other for donkey's years and were the best of mates. It's just that Alan and Scratch had developed the squabbling and mutual pisstaking into a kind of hobby that had become almost an addiction. The only real pain of it was that I usually ended up having to play referee.

Anyway, from what I remembered, the only café that wasn't too far from the bank was a fairly run-down greasy spoon kind of place, which didn't please Scratch at all.

'Just going inside there is bound to set off one of my allergies. More than one probably, and I definitely wouldn't eat anything this shithole's got to offer.'

'You know,' said Alan, 'sometimes I reckon you make all this allergy stuff up, so you can get a bit of sympathy.'

'Oh yeah? Like that so-called terrible pain you get from your neck all the time.'

Alan visibly bristled. 'What do you mean, "so-called"? You've no idea what pain is till you've had an injury like mine.'

This time, I couldn't be arsed to play referee, so I left them to it and went into the café. I had more important things to think about like a bank robbery, for instance, and I have to admit I was getting pretty bloody jittery about the whole thing.

❖

We left the car about two hundred yards from the bank, not wanting it to be associated with the robbery in the inevitable CCTV sweep of the surrounding area. Also, if everything went to plan, we wouldn't need it to be nearby for a quick getaway.

I led the way past the front of the bank, glancing inside to check that it was empty of customers and staff, then turned left down an alleyway that ran down the side of the bank. We stopped, and I checked my watch. Almost one-thirty. Halfway along the wall was a heavy steel door that – in my time anyway – was used by all staff when they arrived for work and left at the end of the day. It was always possible that not everyone had gone yet, so we gave it another ten minutes to make sure. Another reason for hanging back was that I noticed the CCTV camera above the door was blinking red.

'I thought Chisholm was supposed to turn all the cameras off before we got here,' said Alan.

'Maybe he forgot,' said Scratch.

'Oh great. Well, that's a brilliant start, isn't it?'

'Good thing we've got the masks then.'

If we waited any longer, we'd start to attract

unwanted attention, so we'd just have to bite the bullet.

With Alan in his Boris Johnson mask – minus his neck brace – Scratch as Donald Trump and me as Prince Andrew, we slowly made our way along the alleyway and stopped in front of the steel door. The camera still hadn't been shut down, so we kept our heads down, and I stabbed a finger at the intercom button on the right of the door.

Several seconds passed without any response, so I tried again.

The intercom stuttered into life with plenty of hissing and crackling. 'Yes?'

'It's us,' I said.

'What?'

I leant closer to the intercom. 'It's *us.*'

'Us who?'

'Jesus, this isn't a knock-knock joke. We're friends of... The Mistress, or whatever it is you call her. Are you gonna let us in or what?'

There was a brief pause, and then: 'How do I know you're who you say you are? You could be anybody.'

'Oh really? So exactly how many people are you expecting to turn up wearing masks today?'

'I think the Prince Andrew one is in rather poor taste, by the way.'

I took a deep breath, attempting to stay calm but failed. 'Just open the fucking door, will you?'

Another pause. 'What's the password?'

'The what?'

'Password. The Mistress told me she'd give you a password.'

This was the first I'd heard of it. I turned to Scratch and Alan. 'She say anything to you about a password?'

They both shook their heads.

'Christ almighty. I'll have to call her or we'll be here all day.'

I took out my phone and walked a few paces away from the door.

Eleanor answered on the second ring. 'Max?'

'Prick says he needs a password.'

'Shit. Sorry. Didn't I tell you?'

'No, you didn't. So what is it?'

'OK, it's "If I told you you had a beautiful body, would you hold it against me?".'

It was my turn to pause. 'Run that by me again.'

She did.

'I'm not saying that. What if he takes me seriously?'

Eleanor chuckled. 'He's got a wife and two kids.'

'So did Oscar Wilde.'

'Sounds like you're being a tad homophobic, Max.'

It wasn't only the accusation that annoyed me, but the obvious amusement in Eleanor's tone. 'Absolutely not. It's just that we've got a job to do, and I don't want any... complications.'

'Well, if you don't give him the password, he's not going to let you in.'

'Yeah, thanks for nothing.'

I ended the call and went back to the door.

'You get the password then?' asked Scratch.

I ignored him and pressed the intercom button. 'You still there?'

'Yes. So what's the password?'

My mouth was almost touching the intercom, and I repeated the words that Eleanor had told me in little above a whisper, mainly so that Alan and Scratch couldn't hear me.

Apparently, nor did Chisholm. 'I didn't quite catch that. Could you speak a bit louder?'

'If I told you you had a beautiful body, would you hold it against me?'

Predictably enough, Scratch and Alan giggled like a pair of pre-pubescent schoolboys, but at least I could finally hear the sound of bolts being slid back and locks being unlocked before the heavy steel door swung slowly inwards.

Chisholm took a step back to let us through. Eleanor had said he was in his mid forties, but he looked much older with a neatly arranged comb-over and round rimless spectacles. His complexion, as the song goes, was a whiter shade of pale.

12

The public area of the bank was much as I remembered it, although it had been spruced up quite a bit since I'd been the manager. Presumably to make it more "customer friendly". It was roughly square and sparsely furnished with half a dozen comfortable chairs along one side for customers waiting to be attended to. These were new, as was the royal blue carpeting which covered the entire floor. On the opposite side were two desks with equally comfortable chairs for customers seeking mortgages, opening accounts or anything else that required specialist attention from a member of staff. Next to these, and tucked away in the corner was the manager's office, which looked as if it had seen a major upgrade since my day.

One thing that was noticeably different were the tellers' glass-fronted positions on the wall that was furthest from the main entrance. Whereas there used to be five, there were now only two. No doubt the result of even more people doing most of their banking transactions online nowadays, which also explained the diminishing number of high street banks.

Between the tellers' positions and the manager's office was a door that led down into the vault, and it was highly unlikely that this had been changed.

I glanced up at the ceiling and counted ten CCTV cameras, all of them with their little red lights blinking.

'You were supposed to turn all of these off,' I said to Chisholm, pointing up at the one directly above our heads.

'Ah yes. Sorry about that. I'll go and do it now,' he said and headed for the manager's office.

He scuttled rather than walked, his legs seemingly too short in proportion to the rest of his more or less average height. Or perhaps it was due to the considerable extra weight he was carrying, his belly marginally overhanging the waistband of his suit trousers. I couldn't help but picture him strapped naked to one of Eleanor's contraptions, but thankfully my imagination shut itself down before anything else happened that I really didn't want to witness.

A minute or two later, the lights on the CCTV cameras flicked off as one, and Chisholm scuttled back to us.

'Right, let's get to it,' I said, and we followed him to the vault door.

There was a keypad built into the handle, and Chisholm was about to punch in the code when he hesitated. 'You'll have to look away while I do this.'

'Why?'

He stared at me like *I* was the idiot. 'Security?'

'A few minutes ago you let us in to the bank so we could rob it, and now you're worried about security?'

'Even so.'

He was clearly determined to stand his ground, so Alan, Scratch and I turned our backs and listened to the bleeps as he tapped in the numbers, followed by a loud click.

'OK, you can look now,' said Chisholm and pushed open the door.

We let him go first down the concrete steps – now carpeted as they hadn't been when I was the manager.

'*Probably to impress the posh knobs when they come down to visit their deposit boxes,*' said the voice in my head. '*Makes it look less like they're going down into some place like Eleanor's S&M dungeon.*'

There was a tiled area at the bottom of the steps, at the far end of which was the steel door to the vault. It was about six feet by six feet square and, if memory served, was two feet or so thick. Something else I remembered was that there were two combination dials set far enough apart that one person couldn't operate them simultaneously.

'You do realise that you'll have to give us the combination so we can get in,' I said to Chisholm.

This obviously hadn't occurred to the security-minded bank manager until now.

'Ah yes,' he said, and then added as an afterthought, 'I can always change it after you've gone.'

'*How in God's name did an idiot like him ever get to be the manager of a bank?*' said the voice. '*Does he really expect that we'll be coming back again or that he'll even be in a job after this?*'

The idiot in question stepped forward and placed his right hand lightly on the combination dial on the left and gestured to the dial on the right. 'You take that one, and I'll call out the numbers as we go, but we have to turn the dials at precisely the same time or it won't work.'

I was well aware of this already, but I wasn't going to let on that I'd done this hundreds of times in the past, albeit legally. Knowing that I used to manage the bank would be one way the cops would be able to identify me later if Chisholm did the dirty on us.

'Twenty-seven,' he began, and after another five digits announced that, 'OK, we're done.'

Then he took hold of the wheel in the centre of the door and turned it before heaving the door open as far as it would go. In front of us was a steel-barred gate that he unlocked with a simple key from a bunch he took from his jacket pocket.

He ushered us inside, but we hung back.

'After you,' I said, not totally trusting that he wouldn't shut us all in and call the police.

'As you wish,' he said and entered the vault with Scratch, Alan and I close behind.

The vault was divided into two sections. The section on our right was the area where the cash was kept and was separated off by a wall and a steel-barred gate like the one we'd just come through. The section we were standing in was for the deposit boxes, which lined the two other walls of the vault from floor to ceiling. In the centre were a large table and two chairs for the benefit of customers who wanted to attend to their deposit box, adding or removing items or simply checking out its contents.

'Better get on with it then,' said Alan, eyeing the array of deposit boxes and taking a cordless electric drill from the canvas bag of tools he'd dropped by his feet. 'We just gonna pick ones at random?'

'May as well,' I said, but then a couple of thoughts occurred to me at the same time. Each box had two locks, the box's owner having the key to one while the bank had a master key for the other. I turned to Chisholm. 'You got the bank's key for the boxes?'

He nodded and obligingly sifted through the bunch of keys from his pocket. This was going to save us a lot of time if Alan only had to drill out one of the locks instead of both, and as Chisholm handed him the master key, I asked my second question.

'I presume you have a list of who all the boxes belong to?'

Based on personal experience, I knew that he would have, but he paused momentarily before replying. 'In my office, yes.'

'Good,' I said. 'I'll come with you then, but before we go, you can unlock the gate to the cash vault.'

13

When Chisholm and I came back down into the vault, Alan had opened about a dozen of the deposit boxes, and there was already a decent pile of money and jewellery on the table in the middle. Scratch was in the cash section, busily stuffing banknotes into the canvas holdalls we'd brought with us.

Chisholm had printed out the list of who owned which deposit box – although strictly speaking they're only rented – and I was working my way through it to see if any names stood out. Mainly looking for any that I recognised, such as celebrities or very rich people whose boxes might be worth checking out. So far, I'd marked three that were definitely worth some close attention, but then I came across a name that was all too familiar.

'Well, there's a coincidence,' I said aloud and then shouted to Alan to make myself heard over the noise of his drill. 'Leave that one for now, Alan. Give two-six-four a go.'

Alan stopped drilling. 'Why? Whose is it?'

'I'll tell you when you've opened it. But it could turn out to be rather interesting.'

He moved about six feet to his right, scanning the numbers on the deposit boxes as he went. 'Two-six-four, you say.'

'Yeah.'

Having used the master key on one of the locks, he fired up the drill and set about the second.

A couple of minutes later, he pulled the box out and placed it on the table next to the pile of cash and jewellery. 'What's so special about this one then?'

'Let's find out, shall we?'

I slowly raised the lid of the metal deposit box, which, like most of the others, was about three inches high by six inches wide and a foot long. There was a large brown envelope, and on top of this were four necklaces and half a dozen bracelets. Even to my untrained eye, they looked as if they must have been worth a fair old bit, and after all, if they weren't, why bother keeping them in a bank deposit box?

Next to the jewellery there was a small black velvet bag tied at the neck. I weighed it in my hand before loosening the draw string and gently emptying the contents onto the envelope.

'Fuck me,' said Alan, peering over my shoulder. 'Are those what I think they are?'

I took a deep breath to compose myself. 'Not that I'm an expert or anything, but yes, I'm pretty sure I know what a bunch of diamonds looks like.'

Alan whistled through his teeth. 'So go on then. Who do they belong to?'

I thrust the list in front of him and pointed at the row beginning with "264".

'Jesus wept,' he said. 'You gotta be kidding.'

'Oh yeah?' I said with a gleeful grin. 'So how many Edgar Ackroyds do you know?'

'Well, if all this gear really is his, I think we may have just struck gold – or diamonds anyway. What else have we got?'

I carefully tipped the diamonds back into their velvet bag and put it to one side along with the necklaces and bracelets. The large envelope contained nothing more interesting than what appeared to be a copy of Ackroyd's last will and testament, but as I was flicking through the pages, Alan gave me a nudge.

'Hello. What's this then?' he said.

I switched my attention back to the deposit box and its last remaining item. A mini cassette tape. I picked it up and turned it over. There was nothing written on either side to indicate what was recorded on it.

'I've not seen one of these for years,' I said. 'I wonder what's so important that he's got it stashed away like this.'

But finding out would have to wait. Apart from the fact that we had nothing with us to play the tape on, we still had plenty of work to do, so I helped Alan with more of the deposit boxes. There were a handful of other names on the list that caught my eye, including some well-known multi-millionaires and a couple of politicians – so we concentrated on those first.

As Alan removed each box, I took it from him and, making sure I kept all of Ackroyd's stuff separate from the rapidly growing pile, sorted through the contents for anything of value. I wasn't at all disappointed, although I'd rather hoped that there'd be something dodgy in the box of a certain Member of Parliament that I particularly despised, but it wasn't to be. Of course, the wads of five hundred euro banknotes could very possibly have been a bribe from some lobbyist or other, but I was hardly in a position to prove it.

Perhaps not surprisingly, some of the boxes I opened were complete duds with little more inside than legal documents, innocent family photos or a collection of trinkets and other bits and pieces that were clearly highly treasured by their owners but would have been of zero interest to any fence. There was also the occasional oddity, such as the TV star – and no, I'm not going to name him – whose apparently most prized possessions included an impressive range of women's underwear and a set of false teeth. Go figure, as they say.

So engrossed was I in my work that it took several seconds before I became fully aware of the sounds coming from the floor above. Given the thickness of the ceiling, the sounds were faint, and I couldn't make out what was causing them, but they were there, nevertheless, and became even clearer when Alan took a brief pause from his drilling.

I rounded on Chisholm, who was sitting slumped in the corner with his head in his hands in much the same way as he'd been since we'd come back down from his office.

'What the fuck is that?'

With an irritating lack of urgency, he lifted his head from his hands. 'What's what?'

I pointed upwards. 'Is somebody else here?'

'Oh, that'll be the cleaners,' he said as if it was the most natural thing in the world.

Well, maybe it was to him, but not when you're in the middle of a bank robbery.

'They come in every day after the bank closes,' he added. 'Got the passcode to the side door so they can let themselves in.'

'Jesus Christ, that's all we need.' I told Alan to stop drilling and pointed up at the ceiling again. 'Seems like we have company.'

Alan screwed up his face as he listened. 'Bloody hell. Not the cops, is it?'

'Cleaners apparently,' I said and turned back to Chisholm. 'How long'll they be here for?'

He shrugged. 'Two hours usually. Sometimes more. I don't really know. I'm hardly ever here when they come.'

Getting him to go and tell them to clear off for the day wasn't an option. It'd look way too suspicious, and who knew if one of them might decide to call the police?

'And what about down here? They clean this as well?'

'Not the vault itself, of course, but I think they vacuum the steps and give the tiles a bit of a mop at the bottom.'

'So if the vault door's open, they'll be able to see us.'

'I suppose so, yes.'

'*You know what the answer is then, don't you?*' said the voice in my head.

I did, and I was glad I only suffered from osmophobia and not claustrophobia. As far as I was aware, nor did Scratch or Alan, but if Chisholm wasn't keen on confined spaces, that was tough shit. He'd just have to lump it.

14

Three sodding hours. That's how long we'd been cooped up in the vault until we could be sure that the cleaners had buggered off. The masks hadn't done much to improve our mood either. They'd never been comfortable, but the heat they'd been generating was almost unbearable. We couldn't even take them off for a bit of a breather in case Chisholm went back on the deal later and gave our descriptions to the cops.

As it turned out, he really did suffer from claustrophobia, so we'd spent a lot of the time trying to calm him down, and on two occasions had to physically restrain him from using the emergency handle on the inside of the vault door to make his escape. And yes, we'd made bloody certain that there was one before we'd shut ourselves in.

Other than stopping Chisholm from totally freaking out, there wasn't much we could do except sit and wait. Scratch had already finished loading his holdalls with cash, and we'd decided it was too risky for Alan to carry on drilling the deposit boxes. It was unlikely that the noise could be heard through the thickness of the vault walls and door, but why take any chances? We had more than enough loot from the boxes to fill our other two canvas holdalls, so once we'd opened the vault door, we reckoned we might as well call it a day.

After that, it had simply been a case of bidding farewell to Chisholm, reminding him of what he was going to tell the cops, and taking a leisurely stroll to where we'd left the car. We'd already asked him if there were any dye packs amongst the cash we'd nicked, and he'd assured us there weren't, but it was still a big relief when we briefly opened the holdalls to find that none of the notes were covered in indelible dye.

It was about seven in the evening by the time we got back to the funeral parlour, and the first thing we did was head up to my apartment and crack open the single malt.

'Here's to a job well done,' said Scratch and knocked back his whisky in one quick gulp.

'Let's just hope that Chisholm doesn't lose his nerve and blab his mouth off to the cops,' said Alan, who was once again sporting his beloved neck brace.

Scratch poured himself another whisky. 'Trust you to find the cloud in every silver lining.'

'Just sayin', that's all.'

But Alan was right. Based on how Chisholm had been when we'd shut ourselves in the vault, there was no way of knowing whether he'd have the bottle to keep his cool under police interrogation. Of course, this would have meant admitting to the real reason he'd been blackmailed, and that depended on how worried he was about his wife finding out what he'd been up to most Wednesday evenings at Eleanor's dungeon. It was by no means a cast iron certainty that we were in the clear quite yet, and if he really did spill the beans, we'd be right royally screwed.

In the meantime, though, we had to assume that everything would go according to plan and get on with the next part of the operation. Naturally enough, this involved dealing with all the gear we'd robbed, so if the cops did come calling, there'd be nothing for them to find. We'd already dropped most of it off at a nearby lockup Eleanor had rented – under a false name – where we could stash it until we'd sorted out a fence for all the jewellery. She'd told us she had a contact who'd take it off our hands for a fair price but hadn't yet given us any details.

I say we dropped "most of it" off at the lockup because we'd kept back a hefty amount of the cash to cover any unforeseen expenses, which might or not include having to leave the country in a bit of a hurry. We couldn't just leave it lying around, and the small safe in the storeroom-cum-office behind the funeral parlour's reception desk would be the first place the cops would look, so we'd had a much better idea where to keep it. That was going to take more than a few minutes, though, and it could wait till we'd had a couple more drinks and got our adrenalin levels back down to something like normal.

Then there was the question of Edgar Ackroyd's little pile of belongings that I'd laid out on the coffee table in front of me.

'Either of you got anything we can play this on?' I said, picking up the mini cassette tape, which, for the time being at least, was of far more interest than even the bag of diamonds.

They both shook their heads.

'Big Jim might have something,' said Scratch, 'but he won't be open again till Monday.'

Big Jim had a pawnbroker's shop round the corner from the funeral parlour, and Scratch was right. He had a massive amount of stuff that was either pawned or unwanted, so if anyone had a mini cassette player, it would be him. In fact, he'd very probably have a dozen or more and in every make and colour. I could hardly contain my curiosity, but that took a very fast back seat when there was a heavy knock on the apartment door.

Alan, Scratch and I shot a quick glance at each other, all of us wide-eyed in terror, and then instantly switched our focus to the door.

'Cops?' Alan mouthed silently.

'Dunno,' I whispered, 'but they must've broken in downstairs, so why would they knock?'

Even so, my stomach was doing cartwheels as I stood up and made my way towards the door – on tiptoe for some reason – but before I got there, it swung open and there stood Eleanor with a beaming smile plastered over her unmade-up face. I'd completely forgotten I'd given her a key to the main door of the funeral parlour so I wouldn't have to keep going down to let her in every time she came round.

'Hello, guys. I thought I'd drop by and— Christ, you all OK? Looks like you're about to shit yourselves.' The smile broadened as the penny dropped. 'Oh, I get it. You thought I was the Old Bill, didn't you?'

'Not really, no,' I lied. 'We're all just a bit on edge at the moment, as I'm sure you can imagine.'

'Sure, yeah. So how'd it go? I've been dying to

75

know, and I would have come sooner except I had a client.'

She closed the door behind her and perched herself on the edge of the settee next to Alan and Scratch.

'Fine,' I said. 'You wanna drink?'

She arched an eyebrow at me, which was more than enough to convey that this was a particularly stupid question.

'Please tell me this isn't all of it,' she said as she pointed at the small number of items on the coffee table.

'Course not,' I said, handing her a whisky. 'You might find that wee bag interesting, though.'

She picked up the velvet bag of diamonds and undid the draw string, then nodded her approval as she peered inside before tipping the contents onto her palm. 'Hmm. Nice ice. Let's hope they're the real thing.'

'Don't see why they wouldn't be. I mean, who'd wanna keep fake diamonds in a bank deposit box?'

Eleanor took a sip of her whisky. 'True enough.'

Scratch, Alan and I then spent the next half hour or so filling her in on everything that had happened at the bank.

'And no cops yet,' she said, 'so hopefully Chisholm's been sticking to his side of the deal. For now at any rate.'

'Which reminds me,' I said. 'We've got another job we need to do a bit sharpish. You any good with a needle and cotton?'

Eleanor gave me what I guessed must have been one of her dominatrix looks. 'Bit sexist.'

'Not at all. It's only that Alan and I are crap at it, and Scratch has got fingers like Havana cigars.'

Her expression softened but not by much. 'We'll see, shall we?'

'*Ooh, you've done it now,*' said the voice in my head. '*If you ask me, I'd say you'll be in for a right good spanking later on.*'

15

It hadn't taken too long to open up the blue satin lining of one of the display coffins, stuff in the cash and Ackroyd's diamonds, then sew it back up again. It was an idea I'd got from our defecting Russian spy, Oleg Radimov, when he'd pretended to use the same method to hide a thumb drive from MI5. Anyway, as it happened, Eleanor was far more adept with a needle and cotton than the rest of us, although this probably had less to do with her being a woman than the fact that Alan, Scratch and I were all a lot more pissed than she was and could barely even focus.

When we'd finished, Eleanor headed for home, exhausted from a particularly demanding session with a client earlier that evening, while the rest of us had a couple more nightcaps back in my apartment. We'd all crashed out eventually, and it was almost lunchtime on Sunday when we began to regain consciousness along with some seriously unpleasant hangovers. Scarcely able to function as sentient human beings, we'd therefore spent the rest of the day lounging around, watching crap TV, occasionally dozing and drinking vast amounts of black coffee.

By the middle of the evening, Scratch and Alan had just about recovered sufficiently to make it back to their own places, and I'd climbed under my duvet, grateful that there'd still been no sign of the police.

Come Monday morning, my faculties had returned to something approaching normal, and my brain cells had realigned themselves sufficiently to enable a degree of rational thought. The first thing that occurred to me was that I was desperate to pay Big Jim a visit so I could get something to play Ackroyd's tape on, but the second thing made me realise that there was another more pressing matter to attend to.

Alan, Scratch and I had an appointment with Eleanor to go to the lockup for a meeting with her fence contact, so he could give us at least a rough idea what our haul was worth and how much of it he could shift. I glanced at the clock on my bedside table, which told me I was already running late, so I grabbed a quick shower, threw on some clothes and raced off in the Polo. Well, "raced off" is a bit of an exaggeration really, but these things are relative, I suppose. The top speed of my battered and ancient VW was about fifty miles an hour, and that was downhill with a following wind.

Anyway, the others were already there – minus the fence – when I turned down a narrow side street and parked up. There were a dozen or so rusting garage doors built into some old railway arches, and Eleanor, Scratch and Alan were hovering about halfway along the row.

'Good of you to join us,' said Alan, making a show of checking his watch.

I ignored him. 'I take it the fence hasn't turned up yet then?'

But no sooner were the words out of my mouth than a top-of-the range Audi appeared at the end of the street and came to a halt behind my Polo. There was a pause of almost a minute before a thick-set man in an expensive camel-hair overcoat stepped out of the car and came sauntering towards us.

'Not short of a few bob, is he?' said Scratch. 'Must be pretty good at his job, I guess.'

Alan snorted. 'Either that or he's a ripoff merchant that fleeces everybody he does business with.'

From what little I knew, I assumed that this probably applied to most people involved in his line of work, but I didn't say so as the guy was now within earshot.

'Let's see the goodies then, shall we?' he said without so much as a "hello" or especially a "sorry to keep you waiting".

Clearly a man in a hurry, his whole demeanour proclaimed in no uncertain terms that he wasn't someone to be messed with and fools were most definitely not to be suffered lightly. Curiously, though, and for a man of his size, the effect was somewhat diminished by the almost shrill pitch of his voice, accompanied by a tendency to lisping.

After Eleanor had unlocked and opened the garage door, we unzipped each of the canvas holdalls and stood watching while he rooted around inside them. Every so often, he'd take out a necklace or a bracelet and give it a thorough examination with one of those little eyeglasses that jewellers use. On the odd occasion, he'd let out the slightest of grunts, but it was impossible to tell whether they were grunts of approval or disdain. Otherwise, he said not a single word the whole time he was inspecting the loot, and half an hour after he'd arrived, he replaced the eyeglass in his overcoat pocket and spoke directly to Eleanor.

'I'll be in touch.'

What? Was that it? "I'll be in touch"? Unable to hide my disappointment, I asked him if he couldn't at least give us an approximate idea of how much we'd get.

In response, he fixed me with a pair of red-rimmed brown eyes and sneered. 'I'll. Be. In. Touch,' he repeated, emphasising each word in turn.

With that, he went back to his Audi, reversed back onto the main road and sped off with the screeching sound of rubber on tarmac.

'What a wanker,' said Alan, and I have to say I couldn't disagree. 'Why couldn't he give us a price right here and now?'

'He probably needs to find buyers first and find out what they're willing to pay,' said Eleanor.

'Must have a photographic memory then. He didn't make a note of any of the stuff he looked at. You sure we can trust him?'

'He's the only fence I know, but if you've got other contacts, go ahead and get a second opinion if you want.'

The heavy sarcasm in Eleanor's tone was all it took to dissuade Alan from making any further remarks on the subject, and instead he suggested we find somewhere we could get some lunch. For once, though, both he and Scratch were determined we should avoid anywhere that served alcohol.

16

I parked up back at the funeral parlour and took Ackroyd's mini cassette tape from my pocket and held it out to Alan.

'D'you mind taking this round to Big Jim's and seeing if he's got anything to play this on?'

'Why me? Why don't you go?'

He was still in a mood about the disappointing result of our meeting with the fence.

'Because I'm desperate for a piss, Alan. That's why.'

'Oh well, in that case we don't want you wetting your pants, do we?' he said and snatched the tape out of my hand.

We all got out of the car, and as Alan slouched off to Big Jim's, Scratch and I went into the funeral parlour. But no sooner had we stepped through the door than Sanjeev came rushing up to us, his arms thrashing at the air and babbling like he was speaking in tongues.

'You wanna calm down, mate?' I said. 'I can't

understand a word you're on about.'

He took a few deep breaths and began again, the words tumbling out of his mouth with scarcely a beat between them. 'There was nothing I could do. I'm sorry, guys, but they came bursting in and threatened to beat the shit out of me if I didn't do what they told me. The coffin was one thing, but when they forced me to go down into the mortuary and I realised what they were after, that's when I totally freaked out.'

The poor guy was close to tears by now, and for the first time I noticed he had a cut lip and dried blood beneath his nose.

I put a hand on his shoulder, having now totally forgotten about my urgent need for a pee. 'Sanjeev, I still don't know what you're talking about. Who's "they" for starters?'

'The twins. Ray and Roy Ackroyd.'

Well, that made some kind of sense, but as for the rest of what he'd said, I was none the wiser. 'OK, why don't you have a sit down and tell us exactly what happened. Slowly this time, yeah?'

Sanjeev sniffed back the tears and slumped down onto one of the customer chairs at the reception desk. After a few more deep breaths, he began at the beginning.

He'd been alone in the parlour when the Ackroyd twins showed up, carrying baseball bats and demanding to know when our next funeral was. As it happened, and despite the almost complete absence of customers lately, we had one due in two days' time.

'They had a good laugh about that for some reason,' Sanjeev went on. 'But then they said they wanted to see the body – the one whose funeral we're doing the day after tomorrow – and when I told them that it was out of the question, one of them punched me in the face. Ray or Roy. I'm not sure which. Anyway, I didn't have much choice, but on the way to the mortuary steps, Roy or Ray pointed at one of the display coffins and said, "This'll do, I s'pose", and they picked it up and carried it down into the mortuary.

'"Show us the stiff then," one of them said, and he jabbed me in the chest with his baseball bat when I hesitated. Like I say, though, I didn't have any choice, so I opened the door to the storage cabinet that Mr Billings was in and slid out the body. They had a quick peek under the shroud and asked me again if the funeral was the day after tomorrow. I told them it was, and they lifted the body into the coffin, put the lid on and Roy or Ray said, "Tell Dempsey that if he wants the stiff and the coffin back before the funeral, he'll have to cough up a grand or he'll have a very pissed off family on his hands". Then they punched me in the face again and carried the coffin back up the steps.'

'Fucking bastards,' I said. 'You all right now, Sanjeev?'

He fingered the cut on his lip. 'Yeah, I'll survive. More in shock than anything else really.'

'They're right, though. Billings's family are gonna go apeshit if we have to tell them we've lost the body, not to mention our reputation goin' right down the toilet.'

'More than likely that was their main reason for doing it, especially if they thought we couldn't pay up,' said Scratch.

'Yeah well, what they don't know is that we're fairly flush right now, and it wouldn't be a problem paying them the grand they're after, but somehow I don't feel like giving them the satisfaction.'

'No point calling the cops. From what we saw in the pub the other day, Parkin and old man Ackroyd are pretty pally. Maybe we don't have any option.'

Scratch was probably right, and I was beginning to wonder if we might just have to swallow our pride and hand over the cash when another potentially disastrous thought popped into my head. Surely that would be far too much of a coincidence, though.

I turned to Sanjeev, my already high blood pressure cranking up another notch. 'As a matter of interest, which coffin was it they nicked?'

He scratched his head while he considered the question. 'Er, the Windermere, I think.'

'The deluxe or the standard?'

'Deluxe maybe?'

'Blue satin lining?'

'That's right. I saw it when they were putting the body in.'

'Holy shit,' said Scratch as we both raced through the display coffins to the far end of the parlour to find an empty plinth where the Windermere Deluxe should have been.

'That wasn't the one we were going to use for the funeral, was it?' said Sanjeev, coming up behind us.

'No,' I said, 'and that's the least of our worries.'

We hadn't yet told Sanjeev anything at all about the robbery, although we'd have to at some point. Now was not the time, though, and I needed a quiet word with Scratch.

'Tell you what, Sanjeev. As you say, you've had quite a shock, so why not grab yourself a cuppa? Scratch and I could do with one too if you wouldn't mind, although perhaps you could make mine a

85

coffee.'

'Sure. No problem.'

As he made his way to the storeroom-cum-office at the front of the parlour, I turned to Scratch. 'I suppose the only good thing about this – and the *only* good thing – is that it's highly unlikely the Ackroyds will know what's hidden in the coffin. Sounds like they just picked it at random, and I can't see why they'd have any reason to search it.'

'Hopefully not, but it's a bit ironic, isn't it? All they want from us is a thousand quid when they've no idea they're sitting on a hell of a lot more than that plus a bunch of diamonds that happens to belong to them in the first place.'

I started to consider that a grand would be a small price to pay for what we'd get in return. There also the no less important matter of honouring our obligations to the Billings family, but my train of thought was interrupted by Alan striding towards us and shouting, 'Hey guys. Look what I got.'

He was triumphantly brandishing what appeared to be a mini cassette recorder, but listening to Ackroyd's tape was no longer quite so high on my list of priorities.

17

After Scratch and I had told Alan quite how far we'd been plunged into the shit by the Ackroyd twins, we spent the best part of an hour arguing about how to resolve the situation and were still no closer to a consensus.

Scratch was firmly of the opinion that our only option was to bung them the thousand quid and be done with it. 'It's a piss in the ocean compared to what we've got stashed in that coffin. And don't forget the Billings funeral the day after tomorrow. What are we supposed to say to the family? "Look, we're really sorry, but we appear to have mislaid Mr Billings's body"? Jesus. Can you imagine? Not only would they sue the arse of us, but they'd almost certainly make a formal complaint, so we'd lose our licence and get closed down for good.'

He was quite right about honouring our commitment to the Billings family, of course, so handing over a grand was a small price to pay for that reason alone. But losing our licence wasn't really the issue. With the stash we had in the coffin and the rest of the gear in the lockup, we'd surely have more than enough to be able to jack in this undertaker business altogether. On the other hand, I was still having difficulty accepting that the Ackroyds had screwed us once again and we were just going to take it lying down without so much as a whimper.

Alan was of a similar view. 'Fuck 'em, I say. Never mind losing our licence. I've had it up to here with letting them get away with this kinda bullshit. It's about time we hit back. They want a thousand quid, they can bloody whistle for it.'

'Oh yeah?' said Scratch. 'Fighting talk like that's all well and good, but if you've got a better idea, I'm sure we'd love to hear it.'

'Look, all I'm sayin' is—'

But whether Alan really did have a better idea, we weren't about to find out because at that moment Eleanor came breezing into the funeral parlour with a cheery, 'So how are my favourite bank robbers then?'

'Not so good,' I said.

A faint frown creased her forehead. 'No, I can tell by the somewhat frosty atmosphere. You wanna tell me about it?'

So, for the second time in an hour, we repeated the whole sorry tale of the Ackroyds' latest little scheme.

'Shit, that's a bummer,' she said. 'What's the plan then? Pay up or what?'

I gave her a brief summary of where we were up to so far in our deliberations, and she fell silent for several seconds while she appeared to be considering her own point of view.

'You know what?' she said at last. 'I reckon two can play at that game.'

'Meaning?'

'We steal it all back again. The coffin, the loot, the body. The whole kit and caboodle.'

This wasn't an option that had been given a second or even first thought during our earlier discussion, so it took Scratch, Alan and I a few moments to digest what Eleanor was suggesting.

It was Scratch who was apparently quickest on the uptake. 'Are you out of your fucking mind?'

'My therapist doesn't seem to think so. And in any case, what's the big deal? If you can carry off a bank robbery like you did, doing over an undertaker's should be a walk in the park.'

'Yeah, the difference being we had an insider for the bank job. With the Ackroyds' place, we'd be going in blind.'

'Not totally, though,' I said, beginning to warm to Eleanor's idea. 'For a start, we know that they don't live on the premises, so as long as we leave it till well after they close for the day, there'll be nobody to catch us out.'

Scratch wasn't convinced. 'Burglar alarms? CCTV cameras? What about those, eh?'

'Cameras won't be a problem even if they've got them,' said Alan, seemingly veering towards my side of the fence. 'We just use the same masks we had for the bank.'

'Oh right. So then the cops can link us with that too because you know damn well that we got caught on camera before twatface Chisholm turned the sodding things off.'

'Fuck's sake, Scratch. We use different bloody masks, OK?'

'And the burglar alarm?'

'We don't have one, so who's to say they have? I doubt many undertakers do, come to that. I mean, what do they expect anybody's gonna nick?'

'A coffin stuffed with diamonds and a shitload of cash perhaps?'

Alan was right about the CCTV side of things, but I didn't necessarily buy his theory on undertakers in general having such a cavalier disregard for security measures. Just because we didn't have an alarm ourselves could hardly be taken as the norm.

'How about going in to check the place out first and see what they've actually got?' said Eleanor, who'd been listening patiently to Scratch and Alan's latest round of bickering.

'Perfect,' said Scratch, 'although you seem to be forgetting one rather important flaw in that plan. The Ackroyds know exactly who we all are, so it's not as if any of us can simply stroll into the gaff and—'

'They don't know me, though, do they?'

'What?'

Eleanor sat back in her chair with a kind of Mona Lisa smile. 'I'd need to figure out a plausible reason for being there, of course, but maybe I could use the same one as before. You know, about wanting to buy a coffin for a client with a particularly weird fetish. Or better still, I'm looking for an undertaker to take care of my recently deceased mother, but I've been hearing all sorts of rumours about body snatchers and stolen body parts, and I want to make sure nothing like that's going to happen to my dear old mum.'

All of a sudden a tear began to trickle down her cheek, and her voice switched into posh mode. 'You see, Mr Ackroyd, I was so desperately fond of Mama, that I'd never forgive myself if anything so terrible were to befall her before she is finally laid to rest.'

She choked back a few more tears. 'Consequently, I would need your categorical reassurance that these premises have the necessary security measures to prevent any intruder gaining access to my poor beloved mother and committing such unspeakable acts as I mentioned earlier.'

Instantly, the tears dried up, and her voice dropped in pitch to a low baritone. 'Most certainly, Mrs Woodley-Smyth. I completely understand your concerns, and perhaps you might wish to inspect our security arrangements for yourself.'

The silence that followed was eventually cut short when Alan slowly clapped his hands together.

'Blimey,' he said. 'That was quite some performance.'

Eleanor's Mona Lisa smile had been replaced by a beaming grin. 'In my line of business, acting is a big part of the job, so I've had plenty of practice.'

I was equally as impressed as Alan, and even Scratch nodded his approval but with an almost inevitable caveat.

'I guess that might work,' he said, 'but how do we get round the burglar alarm if they *have* got one.'

'Let's cross that bridge when we get to it, shall we?' I said, although in all honesty I hadn't got the faintest idea how we'd disable an alarm system if Eleanor found out that the Ackroyds really did have one.

18

We were all set. Eleanor – or Mrs Woodley-Smyth – had paid her visit to Edgar Ackroyd and Sons the following morning and reported back to us around lunchtime. Everything had gone much as she'd planned, and Edgar Ackroyd had fallen over himself to show her his entire security setup, and apparently with no little pride. Almost every area was covered by a CCTV camera, and there was indeed a fairly sophisticated burglar alarm.

'I think maybe he fancied me,' Eleanor had said, which was perfectly understandable given the lengths she'd gone to with the expertly applied makeup, hairdo and low-cut blouse, 'because nothing was too much trouble. In fact, when I asked him how the alarm worked, he not only explained that it was linked to every door and window in the building, he even switched it on and opened a window to demonstrate how efficient it was. But here's the best bit. When he punched in the numbers on the keypad to reset the alarm, the dozy twat didn't bother to ask me to turn away while he did it.'

'So you got the code?' Alan had asked.

Eleanor had shot him a look that was very obviously a non-verbal "duh" and added, 'I also asked him where my mother would be kept until the funeral, and he took me down into the mortuary, which is where I spotted our rather valuable coffin.'

And that was that. Scratch had finally run out of objections and I had to admit I was a lot happier than I had been that the job was even possible. It still didn't stop me having a serious case of the jitters, though, and especially when I checked my watch and realised there was less than an hour to go before it all kicked off at midnight. It was a pity that Eleanor hadn't been able to join us since she had first-hand knowledge of the layout of the Ackroyds' place, but she had a full schedule of clients that night, and anyway she'd left us with a fairly detailed sketch before she'd wished us luck and headed off.

Alan, Scratch and I were all hanging around the reception desk at our own funeral parlour, each of us silently lost in our own private thoughts. It reminded me of one of those war movies where a bunch of paratroopers are sitting along the sides of a massive cargo plane, waiting to be dropped behind enemy lines, most of them with heads bowed and not a single word passing between them.

As far as I could recall from at least one of those movies, Alan, Scratch and I were similarly dressed in black from head to toe but without any face-paint. Instead, we'd opted for black balaclavas with holes only for the mouth and eyes. Scratch had been right about the plastic masks we'd worn for the bank job. Not only were they utterly ridiculous and highly uncomfortable, but they could also provide the cops with a link between the bank robbery and what we were about to do at Edgar Ackroyd and Sons.

I glanced at my watch for the umpteenth time. The minutes were ticking by much faster than I would have liked, although there was something to be said for getting the thing over and done with as soon as possible.

'How long?' said Scratch, breaking the silence and presumably having noticed me checking the time.

For some reason, I looked at my watch again, even though it was only seconds later. 'Ten to.'

'May as well start getting our shit together then, I s'pose.'

Ackroyds' wasn't too far away and would have been a reasonably short walk, but the three of us carrying a coffin through the streets in the early hours would definitely have raised a few eyebrows, so we took the hearse instead. After all, what could be more natural than a hearse parked outside a funeral director's whatever the time of day or night?

We took a jemmy with us to force the door open, but in the absence of a key, we had no idea if that would set off the alarm even if we then dashed inside and entered the code on the keypad to disable it. It was hardly a question Eleanor could have asked Ackroyd, so we'd just have to risk it and be ready to scarper if it all went horribly wrong.

As it turned out, though, we didn't have to jemmy the door at all. It was already slightly ajar.

'What the fuck?' said Scratch. 'Maybe Ackroyd or the twins are still inside.'

'Doubt it,' I said. 'There's no lights showing anywhere.'

'What if they've had a power cut?'

This seemed unlikely since pretty much every other building in the street had lights on, although there was always the possibility that the Ackroyds' electricity had tripped and they'd gone in to fix it.

'So what do we do?' said Alan.

'*Jeez, don't tell me you're gonna bottle it before you've even started,*' said the voice in my head.

I was sorely tempted to do precisely that, but that would mean we'd have to admit defeat and pay the Ackroyds the grand they were demanding. Was I prepared to give them the satisfaction? Was I bollocks.

'We go in,' I said with feigned confidence. 'As long as we take it slow and don't make any noise, it should be OK.'

'*Should be*?' Alan repeated. 'What if there really is somebody in there, which, by the way, would appear to be very bloody likely from where I'm standing?'

'Well, in that case, we run like hell. We're all wearing balaclavas, so nobody's gonna recognise us.'

'Oh yeah? And what if they clobber us before we can get away?'

'I don't know, Alan. We clobber 'em back then. You've got the jemmy with you, haven't you?'

He glanced down at the jemmy he was holding firmly with both hands. 'Not gonna do a lot of good if they've got guns, is it?'

'Guns?'

'It's the fucking Ackroyds we're dealing with here. For all we know, they might have a whole sodding armoury.'

Even though Alan may well have been right, it wasn't something I wanted to contemplate, but if we didn't make our move now, it was never going to happen.

I gently eased the door fully open with the side of my foot and stepped halfway inside, straining to listen for any sign of movement.

'You hear anything?' Scratch whispered.

I shook my head and motioned to both of them to follow me as I took a couple more paces and switched on my head torch. We'd gone for the ones that had a red light function as well as the white so as to be rather less obvious to any passerby who might have a look in through the front window, and it cast a weirdly satanic glow as I scanned the area around me.

As Eleanor had told us, the layout of the Ackroyds' funeral parlour was very similar to our own with the exception that everything was quite a bit bigger and "much fancier-looking" as she'd put it. It was hard to tell if she was right about the fancier part in the red beam of my head torch, although there were certainly far more coffins on display than *we* had room for.

I turned my head and was relieved to find that Scratch and Alan had followed me inside instead of loitering around in the doorway ready to leg it if anything went pear-shaped. I'd have been amazed if they hadn't been behind me, of course – as well as mightily pissed off – because we'd always looked after each other in all the years we'd been mates, whatever the circumstances.

I pointed to the far end of the display area to where we knew the steps were that led down to the mortuary and again gestured to them to follow me.

Our rubber soles made barely a sound as we crept slowly forward, but even at that pace, I couldn't help myself from tripping over something that I hadn't spotted with my head torch. And the only reason I didn't end up sprawling flat on the floor is that I managed to grab hold of the nearest display coffin, which almost toppled off its plinth but was just about heavy enough to support my weight.

My heart pounding from the shock and already wondering if the noise might have alerted anyone who happened to be inside the building, I hauled myself upright. But before I could see for myself what it was that I'd tripped over, Scratch got there first.

'Jesus Christ. It's a fucking body.'

19

It's not at all out of the ordinary to find a dead body in a funeral parlour, of course, but rarely one that's lying face down on the floor in a pool of blood. In the red beams from our head torches, the blood looked even brighter than normal. It was also fairly fresh, which I knew because I must have stepped in it before I tripped and left a couple of neat crimson footprints where I'd stumbled to keep myself upright.

'So who the hell is it?' said Alan, crouching to examine what little was visible of the man's face.

Given Scratch's phobia about anything to do with death and dying – unusual for an undertaker – he kept his distance but still felt able to offer an opinion. 'Hard to tell exactly, but from what I can see, I reckon it's old man Ackroyd.'

'Murdered by the look of it.'

'You think?'

There was a broken ceramic cremation urn not far from the victim's head, although it was unlikely to have been the murder weapon as most of the blood seemed to have come from underneath the torso. I'm no detective, but my guess would be that whoever'd killed him had whacked him on the back of the head to knock him out – or at least stun him – and then stabbed or shot him when he turned to face his attacker. But if the intention had been to kill him from the start, why bother hitting him with the cremation urn first? Why not just do him in from behind and have done with it?

'*Yeah, perhaps the answers to questions like that aren't your biggest concern right now,*' said the voice in my head. '*In fact, I'd go so far as to say that you should forget trying to figure this shit out altogether and get the hell on with what you actually came here to do.*'

I passed this advice on to Scratch and Alan, who'd now moved on to debating why anyone would want to murder Ackroyd and who might have done it.

'The quicker we grab the coffin and get the fuck out of here, the better,' I added.

'You kidding?' said Alan. 'This isn't about the coffin any more, Max. This is a bloody murder scene. I say we cut our losses and leave the damn thing where it is. Piss off out of it before anybody shows up and then pay the Ackroyds their money tomorrow. That way, we don't get done for murder and still be massively in profit as well as being able to go ahead with Billings's funeral.'

'Pay the Ackroyds?' Scratch repeated. 'This place is gonna be swarming with cops by then, and you seriously think the twins are gonna give a rat's arse about a thousand quid when their dad's just been croaked?'

For once, Alan didn't have a snarky comeback, but

no way was he going to admit that Scratch was right.

'Fuck it,' he said after a few seconds' silence. 'Let's get on with it then. We've wasted enough time already.'

'I'll stay up here and keep watch,' said Scratch, who'd always refused to go down into the mortuary even at our own place.

Alan knew perfectly well about Scratch's phobia but couldn't resist a dig anyway. 'What, in case Ackroyd miraculously rises from the dead? Make sure you get it on video if he does. I'd love to see that.'

There was always a chance that Ackroyd's killer might still be in the building, and unless they'd been hiding somewhere amongst the display coffins, the only other possibility was down in the mortuary. The same thought had obviously occurred to Alan as he was more than happy to let me go first and positively insisted on it. I took the steps as silently as I could, pausing after every third or fourth one to listen out for any sound that might indicate an unwelcome presence. The flight of steps butted up against a wall on the left, but the right side was open, giving me a good view of most of the mortuary, which, like everywhere else here, was considerably bigger than our own. As far as I could tell from the red beam of my head torch, it was also far better equipped, and the only thing that was exactly the same was the familiar stink of formaldehyde and chlorine.

Finally reaching the bottom of the steps, I swung the beam in every direction without detecting any sign of life, but I couldn't be entirely certain that somebody wasn't lurking in the shadows, ready to leap out at us at any moment.

'You still got the jemmy?' I whispered to Alan.

By way of an answer, he held it out in front of me, then shone his torch at a coffin on one of the cadaver tables near the far end of the mortuary. 'Ours, I think.'

We headed towards it, constantly swinging our torch beams this way and that as we went.

'Definitely ours,' I said, and having no desire to stay any longer than we had to, grabbed hold of the head end.

Alan took the foot end, but as we lifted the coffin, it was immediately obvious that something wasn't quite right.

'This feel a bit light to you?' said Alan, and I couldn't disagree.

We set the coffin back down onto the cadaver table and slowly lifted the lid.

'Oh, bollocks,' I said, shining my torch into the empty space where the deceased Mr Billings should have been.

Alan did the same. 'So where is he then?'

'Christ knows, unless they had the uncharacteristic decency to put him in one of their cold storage cabinets till we paid them their money.'

We both looked over at the far wall where there was a bank of twenty cabinets, four high by five wide, and it was anyone's guess which one Mr Billings might be in.

'You start that end, and me at this end,' I said to Alan and pulled out the top drawer on the right of the row.

'Any idea what he looks like?' Alan asked.

'No. Never saw the body myself. Just look for the tag with his name on.'

'Tag?'

'Alice tags all of ours. It'll be on one of his toes.'

101

Fortunately, all of the bodies had their feet at the front of the cabinets, so all I had to do was open the drawer by no more than a few inches, quickly lift the cover and glance at their toe tags before sliding the drawer back in again.

The Ackroyds clearly had a lot more clients than we did, but five cabinets later, I struck lucky. 'Gotcha.'

20

Safely back at our own funeral parlour, we carried the coffin down into the mortuary and laid it on a cadaver table. Once again, Scratch refused to join us, so Alan and I lifted Mr Billings out of the coffin and slid him into a storage cabinet.

That's when I noticed that Alan was wearing his neck brace. 'Please tell me you didn't have that on when we were at the Ackroyds'.'

'Yeah. So what?'

'Jesus, Alan. That's why I made certain you weren't wearing it when we did over the bank, and this time all the CCTV cameras were working. You might as well have had your name and address printed on it.'

'Come off it, Max. It was pretty dark in there, and *you* didn't spot it till now, did you? And even if it does show up on the CCTV, I can't be the only bloke on the planet with a neck brace.'

'No, I'm sure you're not, but I don't suppose the cops'll be knocking on *their* doors any time soon and giving them a grilling about a recent local murder.'

'What would they do that for? It's got nothing to do with us.'

Alan was a hell of a lot brighter than he sometimes appeared, but there was the odd occasion when I had to point out the glaringly bloody obvious. 'I know it's got nothing to do with us, but the police aren't necessarily going to see it that way, are they? Who'd you think their prime suspects are gonna be? They know damn well about our feud with the Ackroyds – especially that Parkin wanker – so they'll reckon we had plenty of motive to do the old man in. And what about the twins? You think they're gonna hesitate for even a nanosecond before they put *us* in the frame?'

There was a lengthy pause while Alan took all this in, somewhat ironically stroking his neck brace as he did so.

'Wait a minute, though,' he said at last. 'If you're going to start pointing the finger at me for dropping us in it, what about the footprints you left all over the place?'

This was something I couldn't deny. After I'd stepped in the pool of blood beside Ackroyd's body, I'd left a trail of perfect footprints, which I'd only realised when Alan and I were on our way back up the steps from the mortuary. There'd been little point wasting time by trying to wipe them off as the forensics people were bound to have found traces anyway.

'Yeah, OK, Alan,' I said. 'That was *my* fuckup, I admit, but unlike you, at least I can cover my tracks. Quite literally, as it happens.'

'Oh really? And how's that then?'

'I just dump the boots somewhere. Burn them even.

Simple as that. Maybe even hide them in Mr Billings's coffin when he goes for cremation.'

'What if his feet aren't the same size as yours?'

'I'm not talking about him *wearing* them. I mean I'll stick them under his body somewhere that the family won't see them.'

'Alright, but the funeral's not till tomorrow. What if the cops come snooping around before that?'

So, Alan had finally cottoned on to the idea that we'd be prime suspects for Ackroyd's murder, but he wasn't going to acknowledge the fact that I'd been right. Instead, he'd gone for the best line of defence being attack. The police linking us with the murder had nothing to do with his neck brace. It was all down to my bloody footprints.

'Fine,' I said. 'I'll go and burn the sodding boots as soon as we get back upstairs. And I'm even going to do that before I knock back a few much-needed and very large drinks.'

'Good plan,' said Alan, but as we were about to replace the lid on Mr Billings's now empty coffin, we both simultaneously spotted something that freaked the hell out of us. Burning my boots and sinking a few whiskies were going to have to wait.

❖

'What do you mean "it's gone"?' said Scratch when Alan and I had raced up from the mortuary to tell him the bad – no, *catastrophic* news.

'All of it. The whole bloody lot,' I said. 'Every bit of cash and all the fucking diamonds. We only realised when we noticed the stitching of the lining had been undone, and when we searched inside...

nothing.'

'You sure you got the right coffin?'

'Yes, Scratch. We got the right coffin.'

'So how come you didn't spot it before when we were still at the Ackroyds'?'

'Hang on. What's with the "you"?' said Alan.

'Well, if you recall, I was up top when you and Max were down in the mortuary, and I only saw the coffin when you brought it up. I never saw inside it, did I?'

'Fuck's sake, Scratch. We were in a hurry, right? And what with the crap lighting, we—'

'Look, I don't think any of that matters right now, does it?' I interrupted. 'We've just lost a shitload of our gear and haven't got the faintest idea who's got it and how we get it back again.'

'What about the Ackroyd twins?' said Scratch. 'Must be them surely.'

It was a possibility, of course, but I had my doubts. 'I dunno. They couldn't have known the loot was in the coffin when they nicked it, and it was pretty well hidden, so I can't see they came across it by chance.'

'Also,' said Alan, 'it can't be a coincidence that our stuff must've been taken at round about the same time Edgar Ackroyd was murdered, and why would they kill their old man to get at it? They're all as crooked as each other, so the stash would all have been divvied out between them. No, if you ask me, Ackroyd probably got in the way of whoever it was came after the cash and the diamonds, so they did him in.'

Scratch grunted. 'Nice one, Sherlock. So, all we have to do now is find the killer and we've got our gear back.'

'Yeah, well, if you try using your brain for once

instead of taking the piss, you might wanna ask yourself who knew where to find it in the first place. This was no random robbery, my friend. This was all planned in advance.'

Jesus. Alan was right. And besides the three of us, that left only one possible candidate.

21

It was already the early hours of the morning, so I waited till about eight before I phoned her. Or tried to anyway. Every one of a dozen calls went straight to Eleanor's voicemail, and having left several messages, I still hadn't heard back from her. And why hadn't she called *me* to find out how we'd got on at the Ackroyds'?

'*Face it, Max*,' said the voice in my head. '*She's stitched you up good and proper. Knew what time you were planning to go and get the coffin, so went there first and took the stash all for herself. Must've done old man Ackroyd in while she was at it too.*'

That was certainly how it was beginning to look, but I hardly dared believe it. We were friends, weren't we? Well, more than just friends really, or had even that been part of her scheme all along?

I tried phoning her a couple more times on my way round to her place but with the same result, and ringing her doorbell got no response. As a last resort, I went down the front steps to the separate entrance to her basement dungeon and hammered on the metal door. By now, I couldn't give a toss whether she had a client with her or not. All I cared about was finding out the truth. But I wasn't going to get it just yet. The basement door remained firmly closed, and with my ear pressed up against it, I thought I at least might hear the sounds of a session in full sado-masochistic flow. No, not even so much as a whimper.

'*Told you so,*' said the voice. '*Done a runner, hasn't she?*'

I turned to make my way back up to street level, my head a cacophony of competing emotions. An almost overwhelming sadness at how Eleanor had betrayed me but mixed with a heavy dose of blind fury. There was also the anger at myself for having been so easily conned, and then of course there was the no small matter of the cash and diamonds she'd got away with. The only consolation at all was that this was merely a fraction of the total haul we'd got from the bank robbery, and the vast majority was still safely tucked away in the lockup.

'*Er, you sure about that? I mean, in case it had slipped your mind, it was her who rented the lockup, so she's got a key to it.*'

Fuck!

❖

Apparently, it was my day for people not answering my calls. The moment I realised that we needed to get to the lockup sharpish in the hope we'd get there before Eleanor had a chance to clear it out, I phoned both Alan and Scratch, but neither of them picked up.

But when I got back to the funeral parlour, I knew why straight away.

Parked outside was a police car, and a couple of uniformed cops were guarding the door. One of them held up a hand to stop me as I approached.

'Sorry, sir. You can't go in, I'm afraid.'

I was about to explain who I was when I heard a familiar and unwelcome voice from a few feet inside the doorway.

'Ah, Mr Dempsey. Delighted you could join us. Let him in then, Constable. Let him in.'

The uniform lowered his hand and let me through.

'DCI Parkin,' I said, faking a smile. 'What a pleasant surprise. You mind telling me what's going on?'

He stroked his chin as if he was having trouble knowing how to answer. 'Well now, let me see. How about we start with the little matter of breaking and entering and work our way up to the murder after that, shall we? That sound all right to you?'

'Murder? What the fuck are you talking about?'

'All in good time, Mr Dempsey. All in good time. For now, though, perhaps you'd like to join your chums and DS Hibbert for a bit of a chat.'

I'd already spotted Scratch and Alan, who were perched on the edge of the reception desk with Sanjeev hovering nearby. The detective sergeant was standing with notebook and pen in hand, presumably waiting for Parkin's further instructions.

'Now then. Where were we, DS Hibbert?'

'Er, I believe you were saying we should wait for Mr Dempsey before we got going, sir.'

'Indeed I was. Indeed I was. So, now that we're all present and correct – or should I make that "incorrect"

– let's kick off with one or two questions, eh?'

The irritating bastard was clearly enjoying himself, which wasn't good news for us at all.

'If I may continue with the footballing analogy and get the ball rolling,' he went on, 'why don't we begin with an easy one? You want to tell me where you all were last night?'

'*Last* night?' said Alan.

'Yes.'

'Oh, I don't know really. I'm not sure we do actually.'

'What?'

'Well, you asked if we *wanted* to tell you where we were last night, and I'm not sure we do. Isn't that right, guys?'

Alan glanced briefly at Scratch and me, and we both nodded.

Parkin visibly bristled, his fists clenching and unclenching at his side. 'Now, you listen to me, you lot. You answer my questions or I'll have you down the nick as fast as you can say Jack fucking Robinson.'

'Jack fucking Robinson,' Scratch repeated and scanned the immediate area. 'Still here, though, aren't we?'

Out of the corner of my eye, I could see that DS Hibbert was scribbling away in her notebook, and the hint of a smile flashed across her face.

'In any case,' Scratch added, 'we don't have to go anywhere unless you arrest us. And I don't think any of us are all that keen to go voluntarily.'

'All right, have it your own way, smartarse,' said Parkin, the veins in his temples throbbing wildly and his cheeks an alarming shade of crimson. 'You're all under arrest.'

'On what charge?'

'What?'

'You can't just arrest us for no reason. You have to have—'

'Obstructing a police officer in the execution of their duty,' Parkin blurted.

The detective sergeant coughed ostentatiously, and Parkin glared at her. 'What is it, Hibbert?'

'Might I have a quick word, sir?' she said, and with a petulant scowl her superior followed her as she walked away from the reception desk.

'I reckon she's telling him that refusing to answer his questions isn't actually an offence,' said Scratch as the two detectives went into a whispered huddle.

'Oh yeah?' said Alan. 'Since when did you become such an expert on the law?'

Scratch shrugged. 'Saw something like it on the telly once. Mind you, it might have been an American cop show, but I'd guess the same applies here as well. Seems as though they haven't got any real evidence that we were even at the Ackroyds' last night, never mind committing a murder, so Parkin's grasping at straws.'

Parkin cleared his throat as he and Hibbert rejoined the group. 'Very well then. I'll let you off with a warning on this occasion, but what I will need is every item of footwear the three of you possess. Also, and for the second time in a week, I shall be conducting a thorough search of these premises.'

'You'll be needing a warrant then,' I said, 'but please do try not to be quite so ham-fisted about it this time, will you?'

The chief inspector ignored my remark other than

112

to make a strange sound that was somewhere between a sigh and a grunt. 'Come along, Hibbert. We're leaving.'

But as he turned towards the door, he suddenly stopped and pointed at Alan's neck brace. 'Bit of a problem, have we, eh? Not too painful, I hope.'

'On and off, yeah. Old injury from my weightlifting days.'

'How very interesting,' Parkin said, his mood appearing to lighten slightly. 'Remind me to have a proper look at that CCTV footage when we get back to the station, would you, Hibbert? There might have been something I missed when I gave it a quick run-through earlier.'

22

What with everything that had been going on since we'd discovered our coffin stash had gone missing, we'd almost forgotten about Mr Billings's funeral that afternoon until Sanjeev reminded us. He'd just come up from the mortuary to tell us that everything was ready, although Alice was still seething about how little time she'd been given to prepare and dress the body.

Understandably, Sanjeev also wanted to know why we were being accused of Edgar Ackroyd's murder, which he was totally unaware of before DCI Parkin's visit.

So far, we'd kept him in the dark about all the stuff we'd been up to, but it now seemed only fair to let him in on our various secrets. These included the bank robbery and how we'd hidden some of the cash and diamonds in the lining of one of the display coffins.

'Oh God,' he said. 'I thought the only reason the Ackroyd twins had taken the coffin and Mr Billings's body was for the ransom money and to generally piss us off.'

'Yes,' I said. 'That *was* why they did it because they'd no idea about the cash and the diamonds.'

And while Alan, Scratch and I got changed into our undertaker outfits, we went on to explain how we'd gone to the Ackroyds' last night and found the old man had been murdered.

'And the cops think it was you that did it,' said Sanjeev.

'Not exactly a big surprise,' I said. 'We're fairly obvious suspects, and Parkin's got a very big axe to grind as far as we're concerned.'

Sanjeev carried on asking questions as we loaded Mr Billings into the back of the hearse with my boots carefully hidden under his body. Fortunately, his family hadn't chosen the Windermere Deluxe, so we didn't have to waste time repairing the lining before we set off. And time was of the essence since we had to make an urgent detour on the way to the bereaved family's home.

❖

Even though we'd half been expecting it, the sight of the broken padlock lying on the ground in front of the lockup still came as a gut-wrenching shock. None of us spoke a word while Scratch slowly pulled open the metal door.

'Fucking bitch,' said Alan as we all stared into the totally empty space. 'Bloody all of it. Gone.'

He kicked the doorframe hard and let out a yelp of pain.

'Hang on, Alan,' I said. 'We can't be certain it was Eleanor.'

'Oh, can't we? So why else wouldn't she be answering her phone and vanish into thin air? Bit of a coincidence that, don't you think?'

'All I'm saying is that—'

'Course we all know why *you'd* stick up for her, don't we? And I use the term advisedly.'

'All I'm saying—' I repeated but still didn't get any further before Alan interrupted again.

'She knew exactly what time we were gonna break into the Ackroyds', so she decided to get there first, and not only that, but don't forget she also had a key to this place.'

He jabbed a finger at my chest, his eyes filled with rage as if all of this was my fault, but it was Scratch who came to the rescue.

'Actually, that's quite interesting now you come to mention it.'

'What is?' Alan snarled, switching to this new victim to vent his fury on.

'Like you just said. If Eleanor had a key, why'd she have to force the lock?'

It was a fair point, and it left Alan floundering.

'Christ, I don't know,' he snapped. 'Maybe she lost the bloody thing, or maybe it was to throw us off the scent. Make it look as if somebody else had done it.'

I could tell by the way his voice began to tail off by the end of his outburst that he was already beginning to lose faith in his own argument.

To be perfectly honest, though, and despite my attempt to cast doubt on Eleanor's guilt, I wasn't at all convinced that he was wrong. But if it wasn't her, then who else could it have been? Who else knew about the loot we'd stashed in the lining of the coffin and the exact time we were going to try and get it back? And

116

what about the lockup? Sure, there was an outside chance that Alan was right and she'd faked a break-in to cover her tracks, but why bother when she knew she'd be our only suspect for nicking the other stuff? Or was that why she'd suddenly disappeared off the face of the Earth?

No, the only possible explanation was that she'd fucked us over and very probably had it all planned out right from the start. Setting us up with the bank robbery had just been the beginning.

'*Hold your horses, though*,' said the voice in my head. '*What about Eleanor's fence? He knew what was in the lockup, so maybe he decided he'd come back and grab the lot without having to pay you a single cent.*'

I certainly wouldn't have put it past the devious little shit, but Eleanor was the only one who knew how to contact him, so without her, we had no way of getting hold of him. We didn't even have a name. All he was to us was "Eleanor's fence".

'*Perhaps they're in on it together*,' said the voice. '*She got the cash and the diamonds from the Ackroyds', and he cleared out the lockup. A nice little earner split between the two of them.*'

A nice little earner that we'd done all the work for and now we had piss all to show for it. Alan was definitely right about one thing. Eleanor really was a fucking bitch.

23

It was a big relief to get Mr Billings's funeral over and done with – as well as the successful incineration of my incriminating boots – especially as it had seemed for a while that we might not have a body at all. So that was one crisis narrowly averted, but we still had plenty more to deal with.

When we got back to the funeral parlour and changed out of our undertaker outfits, Scratch and Alan headed straight for the pub. I wasn't in the mood myself so decided to have a quiet night in instead. Well, that was the plan anyway.

Sanjeev had already gone home for the day, so I locked up and went upstairs to my apartment.

'Jesus,' I said as soon as I walked through the door. 'What the hell are you doing here?'

Eleanor was sitting on the edge of the settee and smiled weakly. 'You gave me a key, remember?'

'That's not what I meant. I've been trying to get hold of you all day. Thought you'd done a runner.'

'I kind of have in a way. Not from you, though.

118

From the cops.'

'What?'

'Chisholm. Ratted me out, didn't he?'

'Chisholm?'

'The bank manager.'

'Yes, I know who Chisholm is, but what's he been saying?'

'Told the police everything about the robbery apparently and how I'd blackmailed him into letting you guys into the bank.'

'When was this?'

'Some time late last night. I've got a… "friend" in the local force, and he tipped me off so I could get away before the police came calling.'

'But the robbery was what? Five days ago? I've been checking the news every day since then, and from everything I've heard, it seems he's been sticking to his story about the robbers' accomplices threatening to kill his family if he didn't do what he was told. I even caught a piece on the telly where the police were asking for the public's help because they'd got zero leads so far.'

Eleanor spread her palms wide. 'Max, I've no more idea than you have why he's fessed up after all this time. I can only assume that the cops didn't believe him and ground him down in the end. Or maybe his wife found out he was lying about taking a bribe so he could pay off a debt and told the police she and the kids hadn't been held hostage at all.'

When we'd got back from the funeral, I'd intended to have a rare night off from the booze, but I hadn't been expecting to be ambushed by Eleanor with more bad news, so I reached for the Jameson's.

'Don't I get one?' said Eleanor as I poured myself a

generous measure and replaced the cap on the bottle.

I ignored her. After everything that had happened, I wasn't feeling particularly well disposed towards her, and there were plenty of questions I needed answering before I could even begin to trust her again.

Eleanor sighed, seemingly reading my mind. 'I'm the only one Chisholm's been able to finger if that's what you're worried about. He doesn't know who you and the others are as long as you kept your masks on the whole time, so he can't give the cops any descriptions, can he?'

'No, he can't. But there's a lot more to it than that. For starters, why didn't you let me know the police were onto you, and why haven't you been answering my calls?'

'Yeah, I'm sorry about that, but I ditched my phone soon after I went on the run. Didn't want them using that to track me down or checking out my list of contacts if they did catch up with me. A list which includes you, by the way.'

This made some kind of sense, although there was still the matter of the empty lockup and who nicked our gear from the Ackroyds' and murdered the old man. I decided to leave the lockup business till later, but when I told her what had happened at the Ackroyds', she denied all knowledge of the murder and the missing loot.

'But apart from me, Alan and Scratch,' I said, 'you were the only one who knew what we'd stashed in the coffin and when we were going to get it back.'

Eleanor got seriously pissy then. Either that or she was faking it. 'I hope you're not accusing me of—'

'So where were you last night?'

'Christ, Max, you're beginning to sound like a cop.

I told you I was going to be with clients most of the night, which was why I couldn't come with you when you went to the Ackroyds'.'

'Oh yeah?'

'Yes, and if you want me to prove it, I can't. Even if I told you who they were, you really think any of my clients are going to admit what they were up to and give me an alibi?'

'But if it wasn't you, then who the hell was it?'

'How should I know? All I can tell you is that it definitely *wasn't* me, so you'll just have to take it on trust.'

'Well, that's the part I'm struggling with to be honest. But even if I believed you about that, what about the lockup?'

'What about it?'

'It's fucking empty is what it is.'

The look of horror on Eleanor's face was either feigned or genuine, but it was certainly convincing. 'You're joking.'

'Quite the opposite. We went there earlier and it had been broken into.'

'Oh, and you reckon that was me as well, do you?'

'Like with the Ackroyds', how many people knew what was in there?'

'Wait a minute. You say it was broken into. So why would I do that when I've got a bloody key to the place?'

'I dunno. Throw the suspicion onto somebody else maybe?'

'Like who?'

'Your fence guy. And speaking of which, why haven't we heard back from him about a price? Or perhaps you have, and you're keeping it quiet because you're both in on it together.'

'Fuck's sake, Max. You really don't think much of me, do you?'

'Right now? No, I don't, I'm afraid.'

Eleanor slumped back on the settee, her head tilted backwards and her hands covering her face.

I poured myself another Jameson's and waited till she sat forward again and uncovered her face.

'Think about it,' she said. 'If I'd done all this shit you're accusing me of, why would I come to you of all people?'

'So why did you?'

'Because the police are after me, and I need somewhere to lay low for a while.'

'*Here*?' I said, pointing at the floor as if I needed to make sure I hadn't misunderstood her.

'It was the first place I thought of, considering our, you know... relationship, but that was before I had the slightest inkling you were going to spout all this bollocks about me ripping you off.'

I didn't need more than a couple of seconds to make my decision. 'Sorry, Eleanor. Ain't gonna happen.'

'OK,' she said, getting up from the settee and fixing me with her pale green eyes, 'I totally understand where you're coming from, and I'd be the same if it was the other way round, but there's another way of looking at it. What if you kicked me out and the cops *did* pick me up? They're gonna want to know who was responsible for the actual bank robbery and not just who it was that set it up, and I'm the only one who can positively identify you.'

'Huh! Now I get it. You're becoming quite the expert at this blackmail business, aren't you?'

'Jeez, Max, I'm fully aware that you don't think too highly of me at the moment, but giving you guys up is obviously the very last thing I'd do.'

'Oh well, I'm glad to hear you'd leave that little snippet of information till last.'

'That's not what I mean, and you know it,' she said, then suddenly changed tack. 'All right, try this on for size. You let me crash here for a day or so, and I'll help you get hold of this fence. I'd swear on my life that he's got all the gear from the lockup, and I very much doubt you'd be able to find him without me.'

'*She's got a point there,*' said the voice in my head as I drained my glass of whiskey. '*You haven't got a scooby where to even start looking for this tosser, and if she does manage to bring home the bacon, that'll at least go some way to proving her innocence. OK, maybe not necessarily for the Ackroyds' thing, but it's also not a bad idea to keep a close eye on her to see what she gets up to. How's that saying go? "Keep your friends close, but your enemies closer"*?'

Generally, the voice wasn't too far off the mark when it came to giving advice, but I still took my time before making up my mind.

'All right, fine,' I said eventually. 'You can stay here tonight, but I'll have to see what Scratch and Alan have to say about it in the morning.'

Eleanor's face lit up and she quickly came towards me with her arms spread wide like she was about to give me a hug.

I held my palm out towards her to warn her off. 'The settee pulls out to make a bed, so you'll be comfortable enough on that.'

Her smile flickered, then died completely like a dodgy light bulb.

'*Oh, and one more thing*,' said the voice when I went into the bathroom to fetch some bedding from the airing cupboard. '*Don't forget to lock your door when you go to bed.*'

24

I didn't seriously think that Eleanor would murder me in my bed during the night, but I locked the door anyway. Even then, I'd hardly slept, mulling over everything she'd said and trying to figure out whether any of it was true or all of it was a load of bullshit.

I still hadn't come to any kind of conclusion when there was a knock on the bedroom door next morning.

'You awake, Max? I've got you a coffee.'

'Hang on a sec,' I said as I scrambled out from under the duvet and crossed the floor in three strides.

'I see you locked the door then,' Eleanor said after she'd obviously heard me fumbling with the key and I was standing in the open doorway.

'Oh that,' I muttered. 'Old habit, I guess.'

If the hint of a smile was anything to go by, she clearly didn't believe me, but what did I care?

'Here,' she said and handed me a steaming mug of coffee. 'No milk, no sugar. Is that right?'

I took it from her but didn't answer. Christ, she was acting like she hadn't a care in the world – as if last night's conversation had never even happened. All she was wearing was a loose-fitting white T-shirt and knickers, which struck me as being way too casual as well, given the circumstances. Mind you, I was dressed much the same, but at least I had the excuse of having only just leapt out of bed, and I hastily grabbed a pair of jeans.

'Is it OK if I make some toast or something?' she called out over her shoulder as she headed for the kitchen. 'I'm bloody starving.'

'Be my guest,' I said, struggling to do up the fly buttons on my jeans. Why couldn't they put zips on these things in this day and age?

I could already smell the toast when I stepped out into the living room, noticing at the same time that she hadn't bothered to fold the bed back into a settee and the bedding was in a right tangled mess.

'You want some?' she asked.

'Eh?'

'Toast. You want some?'

'Please.'

'I've got a couple of pieces almost ready. What d'you want on them?'

'There's butter and marmalade in the fridge.'

'*You do realise you're coming across like a grumpy teenager, don't you?*' said the voice in my head.

Well, yes, I did, but I also felt morally justified. If Eleanor had betrayed me and the others, as I still suspected she had, I wasn't exactly going to be all sweetness and light towards her until proven otherwise. She, on the other hand, was behaving like we'd merely had some minor marital tiff and was making a show of putting it behind her.

Bloody hell, is that her humming to herself now? I

swear to God, if she actually breaks into song, I'm gonna totally freak.

'Here you go,' she said, handing me a plate of toast, neatly spread with butter and marmalade.

I mumbled a barely audible 'Thanks' and perched myself on the edge of the bed settee, but before I'd even taken a bite, there was a knock on the apartment door.

'You want me to get that?' Eleanor said chirpily from over in the kitchen area.

'No!' I snapped, and stomped past her to see who it was.

'Fuck me,' I said when I opened the door and came face to face with my ex-wife.

'Nice offer,' said Carla, 'but I think those days are well and truly over, don't you?'

When we were married, she used to take a lot of pride in her appearance, which didn't come cheap in terms of designer clothes and frequent visits to the hairdresser, but evidently that was a thing of the past. Her blonde shoulder-length hair looked like it had been washed in cooking fat, and the complete absence of makeup aged her well beyond her mid forties. I knew for a fact that she would never have gone within a mile of any charity shop, but the state of her cream trouser suit now suggested otherwise.

'So, you going to invite me in or not?' she said, but before I could answer, she brushed past me, wheeling a very large plastic suitcase behind her.

Three paces into the flat, she stopped dead in her tracks as she took in the sight of the unmade bed settee and then the rather scantily clad Eleanor.

'Oh dear. Seems I've interrupted something.'

'It's not what you think,' I said, ready for her

reaction but sensing the heat rush to my cheeks.

'None of my business, Simon,' she said, having always insisted on using my real name.

I'd never told Eleanor about my change of name, but she didn't seem particularly fazed by the Simon thing. I'd explain it to her later, though.

In the meantime, Carla was examining Eleanor with undisguised contempt. 'Aren't you going to introduce me then?'

'Er, yes, sure. This is Eleanor, an... associate of mine, and this is Carla, my ex-wife.'

Carla turned to me with a raised eyebrow. 'Bit of a heavy emphasis on the "ex" part there, wouldn't you say? Not that I mind in the slightest, of course. Divorcing you was the best thing I ever did. Don't know why I waited so long really. Any chance of a coffee? I'm gasping.'

Interesting twist on reality, since it was me that had divorced her on the grounds that she'd already been having an affair with Dimitri – a half-her-age toyboy – when she'd pissed off to live with him in the flat above his Acropolis Restaurant.

'So, you're Simon's "associate" are you?' she said, switching her attention back to Eleanor.

'That's right, yes.'

'And how exactly do you... "associate"?'

It was Eleanor's turn to blush. Something I'd never seen her do before. 'We're business partners.'

'Oh really? You're an undertaker as well then, are you?'

'Kind of, yeah.'

'Kind of?'

To prevent Carla's interrogation going any further, I eyeballed her and cut in with: 'D'you mind telling me how you got in? I'm sure I locked up last night.'

'What's-his-name let me in. Sanjeev, is it? Quite the early bird, isn't he?'

'OK,' I said. 'Here's another question. You want to tell me what it is you're doing here?'

Carla sighed heavily and plonked herself down onto an armchair. 'Rather a long story, I'm afraid, but to cut to the chase, I've left the dozy little twat.'

'Dimitri?'

'Who the fuck else do you think?'

Until that moment, Carla had been... well, not quite talking posh but definitely putting on airs. Presumably for Eleanor's benefit. Now the genuine article was beginning to make an appearance.

'Oh, that's a shame,' I said, stifling a smirk and not in the least surprised that Carla had finally had enough. Not only of Dimitri himself, who wasn't by any means the sharpest knife in the drawer, but also having to slave away in the restaurant kitchen morning, noon and night with minimal financial reward. It certainly wasn't the sort of lifestyle she'd always aspired to.

'What about the kids?' I asked. 'Brad and Emma.'

Carla tutted. 'I'm surprised you even remember their names.'

'That's bollocks and you know it. I see both of them at least a couple of times a week.'

This was true, and I got on with both of them far better since the divorce than I ever did when we all lived under the same roof. It probably also helped that they were at last showing signs of shedding their curled lip, teenage angst phases.

'They're staying with my sister for the time being.'

'Melanie?'

'Oh, full marks to you. You remember her name as well, eh?'

I may have been slow on the uptake, but it was at that moment that the awful truth started to dawn on me. Perhaps I'd been in denial, although the big plastic suitcase should have set off my inner alarm bells as soon as I'd spotted it.

'Do I take it you're not staying with her as well?' I said, aware of the faint tremor in my voice.

Carla exhaled slowly. 'Um, how shall I put it? Let's just say that Melanie and I had a rather unfortunate falling out.'

Oh fuck, here it comes.

'So I was wondering,' she went on, her tone softening dramatically all of a sudden, 'if I might doss down here for a while.'

25

God knows how I was going to cope with both Eleanor and Carla staying in my apartment but, for now, there wasn't much I could do about it. If we were to stand any chance of retrieving our stash from the lockup, we'd certainly need Eleanor's help in tracking down the fence, and as for Carla, she wasn't the sort of woman you could really say no to. Anyway, I was already late for work – even though there probably wasn't any – so I left them to it and went downstairs to the funeral parlour.

'You must be joking,' said Scratch with a bit of a chuckle when I'd finished filling him and Alan in on the latest news. 'Eleanor and Carla together in your apartment? That'll be fun.'

'Yeah, I'm not sure that's the main issue here,' said Alan. 'What about Miss Whiplash? I don't know if I can believe a word she says. OK, I can just about go along with it being the fence that cleared out the lockup, but who took the gear from the coffin if it wasn't her?'

I agreed that this was still a total mystery, but pointed out that this was only a fraction of what we'd robbed from the bank, and the priority had to be using any means possible to retrieve the stuff from the lockup.

Alan started to question how this was going to happen if Eleanor was bullshitting us, but I cut him short by reminding him that DCI Parkin might be turning up at any minute with his precious search warrant. And more importantly, he'd probably have checked out the CCTV footage from the Ackroyds' by now and be particularly keen to talk to the suspect with the neck brace.

'Fair point,' said Alan. 'Guess I'd better make myself scarce then.'

'Might not be a bad idea to lose that while you're at it,' said Scratch, nodding at the offending item round Alan's neck. 'Bit less conspicuous if they do find you perhaps?'

Alan muttered something about the terrible pain without it, but wrenched it off anyway and headed for the door. But before he'd even touched the handle, he froze.

'Oh, shit,' he said, looking through the glass. 'Bastards are here already.'

Over his shoulder, I could see a police car pulling up outside and DCI Parkin and DS Hibbert stepping out of an unmarked car in front of it.

'All right,' I said. 'Change of plan. Get yourself up to the apartment and hide in a wardrobe or something. We'll try and sneak you out later.'

'Bugger that,' Alan scowled. 'I'm not going up there with Carla and Miss Whiplash. I'll find somewhere down in the mortuary.'

So saying, he hurried through the display coffins, and seconds after he'd disappeared down the steps, the door to the funeral parlour flew open and there stood DCI Parkin brandishing a piece of paper and grinning his face off.

'Morning, gents,' he said. 'Look what I got.'

'A "peace for our time" agreement signed by Herr Hitler himself?' said Scratch.

'No, funny guy, it's a warrant to search every inch of these here premises and quite possibly make a godawful mess in the process.'

DS Hibbert and two uniformed officers had followed him in, and he gave them their instructions, which included bringing him every boot and shoe they could find so they could be compared against the bloody footprints from the Ackroyds' murder scene.

'And while we're on the subject,' he said, turning back to me and Scratch, 'where's Neck Brace?'

'Who?'

'Don't piss me about. You know perfectly well who I'm talking about.'

'Oh,' I said. 'You mean our friend and colleague who sometimes has occasion to wear a surgical support for his upper vertebrae due to an injury he sustained during his younger days as a weightlifter.'

'If you say so. Where is he?'

'Dead, I'm afraid.'

'Dead? Since yesterday?'

'Sadly, yes. Tragic accident involving an industrial lawn mower.'

Parkin thought for a moment as if he was trying to figure out whether I was talking bollocks or not.

'So,' he said with a hint of triumph in his tone, having apparently come to what, to me, was a pretty obvious conclusion, 'if he really is dead, you'll be able to show me his body, won't you? You are undertakers, after all, so I would assume it must be down in your mortuary.'

I shook my head with a sombre, undertakerish expression. 'Terribly sorry, Chief Inspector, but that won't be possible unfortunately.'

'Why the hell not?'

'He's been cremated, you see. I can show you his ashes if you like. His "cremains", to use the official terminology.'

'Cremated? Already?'

'Yes, he was very religious.'

'What the fuck's that got to do with anything?'

'The Church of the Latter Day Adventist Buddhas is very strict about these things. Any member of their flock who dies must be buried or cremated as quickly as possible after their demise or risk eternal damnation.'

I had no illusions that Parkin was really going to swallow any of this, but I was buying Alan a little more time to hide. I was also having fun winding him up until Scratch failed to suppress a snigger at my latest nonsense.

'Oh, very bleedin' funny,' said the DCI, visibly shaking with fury. 'Think I was born yesterday, do you? Well, let me tell you this. Now that I've studied the CCTV footage from the murder scene in more detail, it is crystal clear that one of those who entered the Ackroyds' funeral parlour that night was indeed wearing a neck brace and, mark my words, I shall move heaven and earth till I collar the little bastard and he gets what's coming to him. And while I'm at it, you two will be laughing on the other sides of your faces when you're rotting in some hellhole of a jail because I'd lay a pound to a penny that you were the other two men who were with him.'

By the time he got to the end of his rant, his volume had risen by several decibels, but despite his crimson-faced rage, I still felt the need to ask what I believed to be a rather pertinent question.

'This CCTV footage you mentioned. Did it show the actual murder being committed?'

'Eh?'

It was a question that had clearly taken him off guard, so I repeated it, and he muttered something inaudible in response while looking down at his feet.

'Sorry,' I said. 'I didn't quite catch that.'

Parkin's eyes instantly shot upwards and locked onto mine. 'No, it didn't. Cameras everywhere, and that was the one blind spot in the whole bloody place. Now sod off out of my way. Some of us have got work to do.'

He was almost shouting again, and when he'd finished, he stomped off to join his subordinates, who were systematically inspecting the insides of every coffin we had on display.

26

DS Hibbert and the two uniforms still hadn't finished searching all the display coffins, and after barking more orders at them, Parkin headed for the steps that led down to the mortuary.

'Shit,' I said to Scratch. 'I'd better go with him while you keep an eye on the rest of them, OK?'

I hurried to catch up with Parkin, and I was right behind him when we reached the bottom of the steps. Apart from having had to clear up all the mess the cops had left after their last search, there was nothing for Alice to do now, so she was sitting in her usual position on a high stool at one of the workbenches at the far end of the room. Also as usual, she was smoking a cigarette and tapping her fingers on the surface of the workbench, presumably in time to whatever she was listening to through her ear buds. Fortunately, so far anyway, there was no sign of Alan.

'Who the fuck are you?' she said as Parkin moved further into the mortuary, his eyes scanning the area like a roving searchlight.

'Detective Chief Inspector Parkin,' he answered with scarcely a glance in her direction.

'What?' Alice snapped and removed one of her ear buds, which then emitted a very loud but rather tinnier version of Meatloaf's *Bat Out of Hell*.

Parkin repeated himself, and Alice slid off her stool, standing with her hands on her hips with the glare of the overhead fluorescent strip-lights glinting off the larger of her many facial piercings. From her body language alone, it was perfectly clear – as I knew all too well – that she didn't take kindly to uninvited visitors in what she considered to be her own personal domain.

'I don't care if you're the chief bloody constable,' she snarled. 'Nobody comes down here without my say-so. Got it?'

For the first time, Parkin looked directly at her with an obnoxiously smarmy grin. 'Allowed to smoke down here, are you?'

Alice took a long drag on her cigarette and exhaled the smoke slowly through her teeth. 'Why? You gonna nick me for it, are yer?'

'Strictly speaking, and as far as I'm aware, it's not against the law in a place like this. And besides, I've got rather more important matters to investigate right at the moment.'

'Oh, have you? Well, in that case, I suggest you go back into whichever shithole you happened to crawl out of and investigate that instead.'

Parkin's grin had evaporated entirely, which was all too evident when he spun round to face me. 'Don't you have any control over your staff?'

It wasn't something I was willing to discuss – and definitely not in Alice's presence – so instead I told her that the detective had a warrant to search the place and there wasn't much we could do to prevent him.

'What's he looking for then?' Alice asked me while Parkin began randomly opening cupboards and peering inside. An odd place to start, but maybe he thought they might be big enough for a body to fit inside.

'I dunno,' I said. 'Got a bee in his bonnet about some crime we're supposed to have committed.'

'No "supposed" about it. I *know*,' said Parkin, groaning slightly as he stood upright after examining one of the floor-level cupboards. 'What's in those?'

He was pointing at the bank of twelve storage cabinets on the opposite wall.

Alice stubbed out her cigarette in an already overflowing ashtray on the workbench. 'Christ, call yourself a detective? This is a bloody mortuary, so what do you think is in them?'

But before Parkin could even get close to the storage cabinets, Alice was there, blocking his path.

'Not on my watch, you don't.'

'I'm only going to ask you once, sweetheart. Get the hell out of my way.'

'Call me sweetheart again, and you're gonna regret it.'

Parkin snorted. 'Oh really? Fancy doing time for assaulting a police officer, do you… sweetheart?'

I could see Alice clenching her fists, and before she could actually throw a punch, which I was sure she was perfectly likely to do, I cut in with: 'You'd better let him look, Alice. He's not going to find anything anyway.'

I knew this wasn't the case, of course, since the only place Alan could be hiding down here was inside one of the cabinets, but short of letting Alice batter a cop, we didn't have much of a choice.

With one of her trademark scowls, Alice took two slow steps to the side, but as Parkin reached for the handle of the top right-hand cabinet, I had a flash of inspiration.

'Before you open that,' I said, 'there's something you might want to consider.'

I must have sounded convincing because Parkin's hand froze in mid air, so I launched into a largely nonsensical lecture about the cabinets being kept at a specific temperature and how the rapid decomposition of a corpse would occur if it was exposed to the outside air even for a couple of seconds. I threw in some other equally absurd details to keep going as long as I could, even though I knew I was only temporarily postponing the moment when Parkin opened one of the cabinets and discovered Alan alive and well, albeit a little chilly.

'That's just a load of bollocks,' he said predictably when I had nothing left in the bullshit tank. 'And to be honest, I don't really give a toss whether it's true or not.'

With that, he pulled open the cabinet door and found nobody inside, either alive or dead. Of course, I knew full well that all the cabinets were empty apart from the one that Alan must have been hiding in, so it was almost like a weird version of Russian Roulette before Parkin struck lucky. One down, eleven to go.

'Business not doing too well, I see,' he said when he closed the door to the fifth vacant cabinet.

He was about to open the sixth when the sound of someone rapidly descending the mortuary steps and the sudden appearance of DS Hibbert interrupted him.

'We need to stop,' she said, breathing heavily.

Parkin turned towards her with fire in his eyes. 'Stop? What the hell are you talking about?'

'It's the bloody search warrant,' said Hibbert and thrust the sheet of paper at him. 'It's not legally valid.'

'Who says?'

'The woman upstairs in the apartment.'

'What woman?'

'Dempsey's wife.'

'Ex wife actually,' I muttered.

'Insisted on reading the warrant before she'd let me in,' Hibbert continued. 'Said the name on the warrant is Max Dempsey, but his real name is Simon Golightly. Also, it specifies that we're only entitled to search his *business premises*, so his personal apartment is off limits.'

Parkin snatched the warrant from her and studied it closely for several seconds as if he couldn't believe what he was reading. 'Jesus wept. What an almighty fuckup. Is this true about your name?'

The question was obviously directed at me, so I told him that, yes, Simon Golightly was the name on my birth certificate but I'd never bothered to change it officially.

'So what do we do, sir?' said Hibbert. 'Get another warrant and come back?'

'Not a lot of point, is there? By the time that's been granted, this lot will have got rid of all the sodding evidence, won't they?' As he spoke, Parkin used both hands to screw the warrant into a tight ball and hurled it over his shoulder, then stormed off towards the mortuary steps, but determined to have the last word. 'And don't think you've heard the last of this, Dempsey, or whatever your name is. I'll have you

140

behind bars if it's the last thing I do.'

Hibbert followed him meekly up the steps, and as soon as I was sure they'd gone, I asked Alice which of the cabinets Alan was in.

'That one,' she said and pointed to the very cabinet Parkin had been about to open before his DS had arrived on the scene.

'Shit,' I said. 'That was a close one then.'

I pulled open the cabinet door to find Alan hugging his arms around himself and shivering violently.

'Get me the fuck out of here,' he said through chattering teeth. 'Another couple of minutes and I'd have been dead from hypothermia.'

'Well, you couldn't be in a better place then, could you?' said Alice, sauntering back to her stool and lighting another cigarette.

27

Once I'd helped Alan back up from the mortuary and he'd begun to thaw out with the aid of a blanket and a mug of tea, I legged it up to the apartment. Scratch was hovering outside the open doorway. Naturally enough, he was eager to know what had happened with Alan, so I told him how close Parkin had been to finding him before Hibbert arrived.

'Yeah, we've got Carla to thank for that,' he said. 'Wouldn't let the cop in till she'd read the search warrant line by line, and by God did she rip into her when she spotted the mistakes. She's quite a force to be reckoned with when she gets going, your ex.'

'I think we knew that already,' I said. 'So, what's been happening between her and Eleanor?'

'It was quite odd really. They started off mostly ignoring each other, although Carla was doing quite a lot of muttering when she put the sofa bed back together and did some general tidying up. Eleanor had kept out of sight while Carla was mouthing off at the cop, of course, but she'd heard every word. And after the cop had gone, she told Carla how impressed she was with the way she'd handled the situation, and that's when things began to thaw between them.'

'Oh?'

'Well, you could see how chuffed Carla was at being complimented like that, and a few minutes later the pair of 'em were chatting away like they were the best of mates.'

'Chatting about what?'

'I didn't catch all of it, but I think it was mostly about you, Max. There was quite a lot of laughing as well.'

Yeah, I bet there was, and Carla would have jumped at the chance to tell Eleanor about all my faults and fuckups from when we were married – especially as she obviously thought we were having some kind of relationship.

'And just so you know,' said Scratch. 'Carla's been giving me the third degree about why the cops wanted to search the place, but I said she'd have to ask you.'

'Oh right. Cheers, mate.'

'Sorry, Max. I didn't know what I was supposed to tell her.'

'Me neither, but I'll have to come up with something, I s'pose.'

Scratch stepped aside, and the first thing I noticed when I entered the apartment was a sickly-sweet aroma of gone-off raspberries or some other fruit. My osmophobia had already taken quite a battering down in the mortuary with its all-pervading stink of formaldehyde and chlorine, and this was hardly any better. But I instantly understood the source of the peculiar fruity smell when Carla sucked on one of those e-cigarette things and exhaled an enormous

143

cloud of smoke – or vapour to be strictly accurate, I guess.

'Jesus, Carla. When did you start with that shit?' I said, trying not to breathe in any more than necessary.

'Never mind about this,' she said. 'You want to tell me what the hell is going on around here?'

'Not really, no.'

In the few seconds I'd had to think up some plausibly innocent explanation, simple evasion was as far as I'd got.

'What do you mean, "not really"?'

'Exactly that. It's actually none of your business, and if you want to stay here, you might want to keep your nose out of what doesn't concern you.'

Carla's jaw dropped open. Speechless. Amazing what a little assertiveness could achieve. I should have tried it years ago when we were still married.

'My house, my rules,' I added while I seemed to be on a roll. 'And if you want to use that vape thing, you'll have to go outside or stick your head out the window.'

She mumbled some words I didn't quite catch. Something about this being a flat and not a house, I think, but otherwise there was silence. She was clearly fuming inside, although probably realised there wouldn't be any room at the inn if she fought back.

Throughout this brief encounter, I'd kept half an eye on Eleanor, who was standing over in the kitchen area and unable to resist the occasional smirk.

'We need to talk,' I said to her. 'Downstairs with the others.'

I must have unintentionally been in assertive mode still because she raised an eyebrow at me like she didn't appreciate my tone.

'Good to meet you,' she said as she passed Carla on her way to join me in the doorway.

'You too,' said Carla and gave Eleanor a friendly pat on the arm.

❖

Scratch, Eleanor and I went down to the funeral parlour to find Alan sitting in the chair behind the reception desk, having shed his blanket and no longer shivering.

'It appears we have Carla to thank for saving your arse,' I told him.

'Blimey, that must be a first,' he said, then switched his attention to Eleanor. 'Max seems to think we can trust you, although the jury's still out as far as I'm concerned.'

Eleanor shrugged. 'Up to you, of course, but I don't know how you're going to get back the gear from the lockup without my help.'

'From this fence of yours, you mean.'

'Apart from us four, he's the only one who knew about it.'

'Right, so we just call him up and ask for it back, do we?'

'Very funny, but we can't even do that, I'm afraid. Like I was telling Max, I had to ditch my phone with all my contact numbers on it, including his.'

'And you didn't write his number down anywhere?'

'No, I didn't. How stupid of me,' Eleanor said with blatant sarcasm.

'All right. No need to get pissy. Some people do still write stuff down even these days, you know.'

Maybe Scratch had decided to play peacemaker, but

whatever the reason, he stepped in with a perfectly valid question. 'We all saw his car, didn't we, so does anybody happen to remember the registration number?'

The ensuing silence and general shaking of heads were evidence enough that none of us did, which wasn't all that surprising really.

'Oh well,' Scratch went on. 'Bit of a long shot, but thought it was worth mentioning anyway. All I remember is that it was a top-of-the-range Audi. Silver, I think.'

'That's brilliant,' said Alan. 'Can't be too many of those around, I reckon.'

Scratch flicked him the finger, then turned to Eleanor. 'OK. So you don't have the guy's phone number, we don't know the reg of his motor, but you were saying you were the only one who could help us track him down. How's that gonna work then?'

'Because I know which boozer he drinks in as that's where I met him when I first made contact, and from what I could tell, he's pretty much a regular there.'

Finally, we had an inkling of a lead, and we all waited expectantly for the next crucial piece of information.

'That's all you get for now, guys,' Eleanor said with a wry smile. 'If I tell you where the pub is, who's to say you wouldn't just cut me out of the loop altogether? Trust – or rather, lack of it – goes both ways as I expect you'll agree. Either we all go together and I show you where it is or we don't go at all.'

Alan, Scratch and I exchanged glances, but it was patently obvious that we didn't have any other option.

'Fine,' I said. 'Let's get to it then, shall we?'

The others were straight out onto the street, and I was about to follow when Sanjeev popped out from the storeroom-cum-office behind the reception desk.

'Hey, Max,' he said. 'Look what I got.'

He was waving the mini cassette player that I'd all but forgotten about, given everything else that had been flung at us over the past few days.

Sanjeev's eyes were brimming with an excitement that I'd very rarely seen in him before. 'I found it next to the kettle just now when I was making a brew and thought I'd give it a listen. I'd never come across a gizmo like this, so it took me a minute to figure out how to work it, but when I did… Holy crap, you really need to hear what's on here. It'll blow your friggin' mind.'

I hesitated momentarily in the doorway, caught between satisfying my curiosity as to what it was that Sanjeev had found quite so mind-blowing on the tape and the urgent necessity of recovering the vast bulk of our haul from the bank robbery. Maybe the fence had sold all of it on already, but if not, we couldn't afford to waste any more time catching up with the bastard.

'Sorry, Sanjeev,' I said. 'We're in a bit of a hurry right now. We'll listen to it when we get back, OK?'

Poor bloke. Judging by the sudden extinguishing of the light in his eyes, this was not OK at all, but I couldn't hang around a second longer to offer him the explanation he no doubt deserved. I'd make it up to him later somehow.

28

When Scratch, Alan, Eleanor and I piled into the VW Polo, I turned the key in the ignition, expecting the usual backfire, but all I got instead was an ominous click.

'Sounds like the battery's dead,' said Scratch, unhelpfully.

'The man's a genius,' said Alan, who was sitting beside him on the back seat. 'We'll just have to take the hearse then.'

'Yeah, 'cos there wouldn't be room for us all in the Lamborghini, would there?'

As soon as we started the short walk from the Polo to the hearse, Alan and Scratch both shouted 'Shotgun!' at the same time, knowing that the bench seat in the front of the hearse was only big enough for three. Unaware of this fact, Eleanor would therefore have to suffer the indignity and discomfort of half crouching and half lying in the back where a coffin would normally be. She tried to argue that she wouldn't be able to give directions from that position, but Alan and Scratch were having none of it and even put on a spurt to make sure they got to the hearse first.

'Such gentlemen,' Eleanor said as I opened the rear hatch and helped her inside.

'Or to put it another way,' Alan said, 'we wouldn't want to appear sexist by giving up our seats for a woman.'

Despite her objections, Eleanor had little trouble directing us to the fence's favourite watering hole, which was less than half an hour from the funeral parlour, and I parked up on the opposite side of the road.

Scratch began to open the passenger door.

'Where do you think you're going?' I said.

'Er… pub?'

'No, I don't think we should go in mob-handed. Maybe just Eleanor and I to start with.'

'Oh, why's that then?'

'Because if he is in there, he might decide to do a runner when he spots us, so you and Alan can grab him if he does.'

This was true, although I also knew that once Scratch and Alan were inside a pub, it was next to impossible to drag them out again.

'Don't worry,' I said as I stepped out of the hearse. 'We'll bring you out a couple of fizzy pops and some crisps if you promise to be good.'

'No crisps for me,' said Scratch. 'Probably set off one of my allergies. Not sure about the fizzy pop either, to be honest.'

'You do realise he's not actually being serious,' said Alan. 'But bugger the fizzy pop. Mine's a pint of bitter.'

The interior of The Rose and Crown was pleasantly

traditional with dark wood panelling, beamed ceiling and subtle lighting that contributed to the warm and cozy atmosphere. There was no piped music, and the only sound came from the gentle hubbub of voices, interspersed here and there with the clinking of cutlery and occasional burst of laughter. For an early weekday afternoon there was no shortage of customers, but the pub was far from overcrowded.

Eleanor and I stood in the doorway for a few seconds, surveying the scene before making our way to the bar. As yet there was no sign of the fence.

'I never thought to ask,' I said. 'Do you even know the guy's name?'

'Greg. Or that's what he told me anyway.'

There was no-one else waiting to be served at the bar, so we ordered a half pint of bitter for me and a gin and tonic for Eleanor.

'Any chance Greg's been in today?' I casually asked the middle-aged barman as he added ice to the G and T.

'Which one?' he said. 'We've got about three who drink in here.'

'Er, sort of thick set, bit of a high voice, maybe a camel-hair coat?'

The barman shook his head. 'Doesn't ring any bells, no.'

'You mean you don't know him or he hasn't been in yet?'

'I mean I don't know him, so how would I know if he'd been in or not? Twelve pounds eighty-two, please.'

The barman was getting distinctly ratty with all the questions, and I decided I'd be pushing my luck to ask any more, so I paid up, and Eleanor and I strolled over to a vacant table at the far end of the pub. We sat side by side on a padded wooden settle with our backs to the wall so we had an uninterrupted view of the main entrance without being immediately spotted ourselves.

'So this is where you met him to set up the deal, yeah?' I said.

Eleanor took a sip of her drink. 'It's where he suggested when I called him. Didn't want to do anything over the phone.'

'Fair enough. You never know who might be listening in these days. But what gave you the impression he might be a regular here. Perhaps it was just a one-off.'

'Dunno. Bar staff were different then, but they seemed to know him quite well, and he had a quick chat with a couple of the other punters who were here at the time.'

'Reasonable assumption, I s'pose. Question is, though, even if he is a regular, how often does he put in an appearance? I mean, we can't exactly hang around for days till he shows up.'

'Your guess is as good as mine, Max, but I've no idea how else we're gonna track him down.'

'*And then what*?' said the voice in my head. '*You find the bloke and he's going to hand over the gear, just like that, is he? Or if he's sold it already, a shitload of cash perhaps.*'

Sometimes I wished the voice wouldn't be quite so negative, but there was no denying it. The likelihood of a successful outcome was slim at best. If we'd still had the loot we'd hidden in the coffin, that would have meant we'd got at least *some* reward for our efforts, but even that had vanished. If Eleanor didn't have it – and I wasn't at all convinced that she didn't – then who the hell did? Then there was the small matter that she was on the run from the cops and would very probably rat the rest of us out to save her own skin if she got caught. And, oh yes, Edgar Ackroyd's murder. Parkin had made it crystal clear that he wasn't going to let up until he'd pinned that on me and the guys and wasn't averse to bending a few rules to make it happen.

'Same again?' said Eleanor, bringing my doom and gloom thoughts to an abrupt, but definitely temporary, end.

'Nah, better not,' I said. 'Scratch and Alan will only moan if they think we're in here having a jolly.'

I finished the rest of my beer and got to my feet.

'What about their crisps or whatever you said we'd bring them?'

'It was a joke,' I said, realising too late that she was taking the piss.

Back at the hearse, Scratch rubbed his hands together in gleeful anticipation of sinking a pint or two in the pub. 'Our turn then. Come on, Alan.'

But his enthusiasm was to be short-lived when I told him I didn't think that would be such a good idea. 'The thing is, like I said before, if he does show up and he recognises any one of us in the pub, he'll more than likely scarper the moment he claps eyes on us.'

'You and Eleanor went in, so what's the difference?'

'We just needed to check if he was already in there.'

'Took you long enough,' said Alan.

He was right, and I couldn't help but feel a tinge of guilt that we'd stayed in the pub longer than we'd needed to.

'We spent most of the time asking around if anyone had seen him lately,' I lied. 'And since nobody had, I reckon it'll be better if we sit tight and keep a lookout from here.'

'Oh, you do, do you?' said Alan. 'So who put you in charge then?'

'Course I'm not in charge, and you can take a vote on it if you want, but don't forget this'll probably be the only chance we have of finding the guy. We lose him now, and we can kiss goodbye to getting our stuff back.'

Instead of a show of hands, there was a subdued silence until the voice in my head came to the rescue.

'*If you're gonna stake out the pub for hours on end, you may as well do it in shifts, two at a time. There's bound to be another boozer not far away that Scratch and Alan can go to while you and Eleanor take the first stint.*'

The mood in the hearse lifted instantly when I passed on this suggestion to the others, and Scratch and Alan were out on the pavement before I could say, 'You've got two hours, and please try not to get too ratarsed. We'll give you a shout if our man turns up in the meantime.'

'Just you and me then,' said Eleanor as they disappeared round a corner.

'So it seems,' I said, not entirely sure how to interpret the faint smile that crept across her face.

29

By about four-thirty in the afternoon, several of the customers had left the pub, but there'd only been half a dozen new arrivals, and none of them were the fence – or Greg, if that really was his name. We'd been attracting a fair bit of attention from passers-by, as a hearse often would, and it had occurred to me that some may have thought we were parked opposite the pub so we could be first on the scene if someone happened to drop dead. I was probably being irrationally paranoid, but I'd driven the hearse a little further down the street and pulled up outside a mini-market, from where we still had an uninterrupted view of the pub. We'd still attracted a similar amount of attention, although perhaps we appeared a tad less ghoulish on the basis that people were more likely to drop dead in a boozer than in a mini-market. The voice in my head had told me that statistically this was almost certainly bollocks, but I'd done it anyway.

Scratch and Alan had been gone for almost an hour by now, and Eleanor and I had hardly spoken, or more accurately, she'd tried to start up a conversation as soon as the others had left, but I'd been steadfastly monosyllabic in my responses and she'd all but given up. I'd had more than an inkling that she was keen to rekindle what had barely amounted to a "relationship" in the first place, and there was no way I was going to play ball. Why would I? As far as I was concerned, there was still no reason to believe that she hadn't stitched us up, and until she'd helped us get our gear back from the fence, she was guilty until proven innocent.

The silence was eventually broken when my phone rang. It was Scratch.

'You'll never guess.'

'What?' I said, in no mood for any nonsense, which is how I read the somewhat chirpy tone in his voice.

'He's here, Max. He's bloody here.'

'Who is?'

'Who d'you think? Only the fence, that's who.'

'You're kidding. In the same pub where you are, you mean?'

'Absolutely. Didn't recognise him at first. Looks quite different from when we met him at the lockup.'

'In what way?'

'A bit kinda shabby, I s'pose. Certainly compared to how togged up he was in his fancy coat an' that. Reckon he's not had a shave in a few days either.'

I sat forward in the driver's seat. 'You're positive it's him, though, yeah?'

'Hundred per cent. It's him all right.'

'And he hasn't spotted you?'

'Soon as he came in, we moved out of sight into this sort of alcove place.'

'But you can still see *him*, right?'

'Enough, yes. He's sat at the bar with his back to us.'

'OK,' I said. 'Maybe you should slip out before he turns round. We can keep an eye on the place from outside and... I dunno... follow him when he comes out.'

I heard Scratch quietly passing this on to Alan, who muttered something about finishing his pint first.

'Never mind your pint. Get the fuck out of there now,' I almost yelled down the phone. 'What's the name of the pub?'

'Golden Lion. Just round the corner from where you are.'

'Fine. We'll be with you in a couple of minutes.'

I hung up and turned to Eleanor, who'd obviously heard most of the conversation.

'How was I to know he didn't always use the same pub?' she said in answer to my unasked question, but presumably clocking the accusing look on my face.

'We'll walk,' I said after a moment's pause while I continued to eyeball her, then opened the door of the hearse.

I was in a hurry, and Eleanor had to pick up her pace to keep up.

'You really think I'd lie to you about which pub I met him in?' she said. 'What would be the point of that? I need to get hold of the guy just as much as you do if I'm going to get my share.'

She was right, of course, although I wasn't feeling magnanimous enough to tell her so and carried on walking without a word.

When we rounded the corner, there was no sign of Scratch or Alan, but I could see a pub thirty or so yards ahead on our left. We crossed to the other side of the street and passed it with only the briefest of glances to check it was the right one.

A few steps further on, I was about to call Scratch and Alan to find out where the hell they were when there was a knocking sound immediately to our right. I turned to see Scratch's beaming face inches from the inside of a large plate-glass window, to the top of which was inscribed the name of the Fresh 'n' Fruity Coffee Shop in big swirly letters. He beckoned to us, and we went in through the already open door.

Scratch and Alan were sitting on high stools at a shelf arrangement that ran the length of the inside of the window. The aroma of freshly brewed coffee was almost overwhelming, but in a good way that was unlikely to set off one of my osmophobia attacks, although I'd no idea where the "fruity" part came in. And judging by the tasteful décor, smart furnishings and identical aprons the staff were wearing, the café itself was one of those up-market places where the baristas – as they'd no doubt be called – made arty designs in the froth at the top of your coffee.

'We thought we'd be a lot less conspicuous watching the pub from in here than hanging around on the pavement,' said Scratch.

'Good thinking,' I said. 'You managed to get out without him seeing you, did you?'

'Uh-huh.'

'On his own or with anyone else?'

'On his own, and like I was telling you, we almost didn't recognise him at first. Looked like a right scruffbag compared to how he was the other day.'

'*That's weird*,' said the voice in my head. '*Maybe he's on his uppers 'cos he hasn't sold any of the gear yet.*'

157

It was a possibility and meant that we stood a decent chance of getting it back. On the other hand, though, there'd been a shitload of cash in the lockup as well as the other stuff, so what had happened to that?

'What do we do now then?' said Alan without raising his gaze from the laminated menu card he was studying with what appeared to be mounting irritation.

'We wait till he leaves the pub, then follow him, I guess. See where that leads us.'

Alan jabbed a finger at the menu card. 'You checked out the prices on 'ere? And what in God's name is a mele cotte egg and avocado tostada when it's at 'ome?'

'Oh dear, Alan,' said Scratch with blatantly mock sincerity. 'No bacon or sausage butties then? What *ever* will you do?'

'What I'll do, my friend,' said Alan, finally looking up from the menu, 'is take the biggest bleedin' mele cotte whatsit they've got and shove it right where the sun don't shine if you don't shut your pie-hole. Got it?'

'*Jesus,*' said the voice. '*Let's hope this stakeout doesn't go on too long because these two are gonna drive me totally crazy.*'

I couldn't have agreed more.

30

Despite the mostly silent boredom of sitting in the café window and staring at the pub across the road for almost two hours, Scratch was quite a happy bunny. Given the up-market nature of the place, every item on the menu was clearly marked with any ingredient that could be potentially allergenic, so he was in his element and had ploughed his way through three different dishes. Alan, however, had been considerably less impressed and had found little on the menu to tickle his tastebuds and eventually settled for the tomato soup. But since this had been made with fresh tomatoes and not out of a tin, he'd pushed the bowl away after three mouthfuls and declared it inedible because it had "bits in it". Eleanor and I had just stuck with the coffee and were already onto our third cup, which definitely helped to keep me awake.

'Tell you what,' said Alan, breaking yet another lengthy silence. 'Why don't I nip back to the other pub so I can get something proper to eat and you can call me if anything happens?'

'And neck a pint or two while you're at it, I suppose,' said Scratch, being unusually judgemental on the subject of alcohol consumption.

'Come with me if you want. It doesn't need all four of us here to keep an eye out.'

'I'm fine where I am, thanks.'

'What's up with you? No room for beer after all that posh grub you've shoved down your throat?'

Not for the first time, I decided to intervene before things got out of hand between them, and I also genuinely thought it made more sense for us all to stick together. 'Might be best if we all stay put for now. The guy could come out any minute, and we need to be ready to get after him sharpish.'

Surprisingly, Alan seemed to accept this with reasonably good grace, and all I got in response was a faint scowl and a barely audible grunt.

Now that it was early evening, there were plenty more customers going into the pub than coming out, so it should have been simple enough to spot Eleanor's fence if he was one of the latter. It was also highly likely he'd be pretty pissed if he'd spent the past couple of hours swilling booze, which should certainly slow him down and make it easier for us to keep tabs on him wherever he was planning to go.

'You didn't happen to notice what he was drinking, did you?' I asked without taking my eyes off the pub door.

'Dunno,' said Alan. 'Lager maybe?'

'Not shorts or anything like that?'

'Not that I could see. Why?'

'Just that the more pissed he is, the better it'll be for us.'

Alan nodded his understanding, but then another

160

less positive thought occurred to me. 'Pub hasn't got a back exit, has it?'

Scratch and Alan looked at each other, both frowning slightly as if they were trying to remember.

'I think there might have been a back door, yes,' said Scratch, 'but it probably only went out onto a back garden.'

'Shit,' I said. 'Even if it is only a garden at the back, what's to stop him going that way and climbing over a wall or whatever?'

Scratch's frown returned but deeper this time. 'And why would he do that when he hasn't got a scooby that we're after him?'

It was a fair point, and perhaps I was worrying unnecessarily, although I still wasn't satisfied. 'All right, but even if he doesn't have to climb over a wall, maybe there's a gate onto a lane or something and he usually leaves that way. One of us ought to go and check.'

'How do we do that without going through the pub and run the risk of him seeing us? If he does, then he's bound to leg it.'

'I don't know, Scratch. There must be some kind of side road somewhere along here that'll take you round the back.'

I stood up, ready to go and suss it out for myself when Eleanor took hold of my arm.

'Looks like there's your answer,' she said, and I followed her gaze to see Greg the Fence stepping gingerly out of the pub and briefly grabbing hold of the doorframe to steady himself.

As I'd hoped, he was totally trollied, and Scratch was right. Scruffily dressed and unshaven, he was almost unrecognisable from the man in the expensive

161

camel-hair overcoat we'd met at the lockup.

'What's the plan then?' said Alan and immediately answered his own question. 'Perhaps we should do like they do in the movies so we overlap and take turns to follow him so he doesn't realise he's being tailed.'

Scratch snorted. 'God, Alan, you see the state of him? I doubt he knows whether it's Thursday or Christmas, never mind if he's being followed.'

'How about this?' I said. 'Unless he's a complete idiot, I wouldn't have thought he'd be driving anywhere in that state, but in case he does, at least one of us should stay with the hearse, and whoever's following him on foot can give them a call. My guess is he's not going far, though, so it probably won't be necessary.'

'OK,' said Alan. 'Who's doing what then?'

'He's Eleanor's contact, so I'd suggest she and I go after him and you and Scratch stick with the hearse.'

'And you two get all the fun again, eh?'

'I dunno about "fun", but we can swap if that'll make you happy.'

'Nah, you're alright. I'll stay and keep buggerlugs company, although you'd better make sure you give us a bell if anything interesting happens.'

'Course we will,' I said, and we all left the café, Scratch and Alan heading back to the hearse and Eleanor and I setting off after Greg the Fence.

He hadn't got more than twenty yards up the road, mainly because he was zigzagging along the pavement like a demented crab and clearly unable to walk in a straight line.

'It could take all bloody night at this rate,' said Eleanor.

'It takes what it takes,' I said, aware that this had come out rather more snappy than I'd intended.

As it turned out, what it did take was a little under half an hour, which would only have been about fifteen minutes if the guy had been sober. He finally staggered to a halt next to a fairly nondescript two-up-two-down terraced house towards the far end of a side street and made several attempts to unlatch the low wooden gate that opened onto a small but neatly kept front yard. Once he'd succeeded, he almost fell as he lurched up the short brickwork path to the front door and appeared to be frantically searching for his key in both of his trouser pockets. Eventually giving up on the search, he hammered his fist against the door repeatedly until it began to swing inwards.

Eleanor and I carried on walking slowly past, then turned right at the end of the road and stopped.

'Now what?' she said.

'I reckon we give it a few minutes to let Greg collapse in a heap somewhere, then pay him a visit.'

'All right, but let's just hope he'll be conscious enough to tell us what we need to know.'

I was about to answer when an image that I'd only peripherally registered a few seconds ago popped into my head.

'By the way,' I said. 'Did you happen to notice the small white van parked outside his house?'

Eleanor shook her head. 'Don't think so. Why?'

'The one with the words "Greg Murray - Fencing Specialist - No Job Too Small" printed on the side?'

She didn't respond, but even in the dim light from the streetlamp, I could tell that her face had become decidedly pale.

31

The woman who opened the door to us was presumably the same one that had let Greg the Fence into the house a few minutes earlier. She was a little on the short side and somewhere around the eighty-year-old mark. Her medium length, slightly curly hair was almost white, and a pair of thick-rimmed spectacles hung from her neck on a thin silver chain, resting on what would once have been called an "ample bosom". The lines on her face were of a kind that suggested she was one of those rare people that wore an almost permanent smile.

She was smiling now as she said, 'Hello. Can I help you?' with the slightest trace of a Scots accent.

'Hello,' I said, mirroring her smile. 'Sorry to bother you, but we're friends of Greg's, and we were wondering if we could have a quick chat with him.'

Having seen the van parked outside, I was feeling rather more confident that this really was his name. Besides, I'd decided against referring to him as "your son", even though this was probably a reasonable assumption, and I didn't want to cause offence if I'd got it wrong.

'Oh, I see,' said the woman, a faint frown almost succeeding in replacing the smile altogether. 'I'm afraid the poor lamb's a wee bit under the weather at the moment, so I'm not sure he's quite up to receiving visitors just now. But I'd be happy to pass on a message if you like.'

'That's very kind of you, Ms...?' I let the rest of the sentence hang with a question mark.

'Murray. Mrs Murray. I'm Greg's mum.'

'Yes, of course. He talks about you all the time. The thing is, Mrs Murray, we—'

'It's Sylvia. Since you're friends of Greggie's, you may as well call me Sylvia.'

'Right. Well, the thing is, Sylvia, we were in the pub with Greg before, and when he left he seemed a little "under the weather", as you say, and we wanted to check and make sure he was OK and that he got home safely.'

The smile returned. 'That's ever so thoughtful of you, dearie, but he'll be absolutely fine after a good night's sleep.'

'Not in bed already, is he?'

'No, no. Having a wee rest in the living room is all. Then he'll be wanting his cocoa, I expect. Never goes to bed without it.'

'*Hardened criminal that he is*,' said the voice in my head.

'Of course,' I said, desperately trying to think up a plausible reason why this ageing but very pleasant gatekeeper might let us in to the inner sanctum when Eleanor came to the rescue.

'I know this is an awful imposition,' she said, 'but I

165

wonder if I might trouble you for a glass of water. I've been feeling rather poorly myself lately, you see, because I…'

Neither Mrs Murray nor I got to hear why she'd been poorly because all of a sudden her eyes rolled back in her head and she grabbed hold of my arm as if to stop herself from falling.

'Oh gosh,' said Mrs M, her frown returning with a vengeance. 'You'd best come indoors and have a wee sit before you collapse in a faint, dearie. Come on. In you come.'

She stepped to the side, and I "escorted" Eleanor into the hallway, Mrs M giving me a sly wink as we passed.

'*You do realise the woman thinks Eleanor's up the duff,*' said the voice. '*And not only that, but she's got you down as the daddy.*'

Even if that's what she believed – which I somehow doubted – this could only be to our advantage, so we might as well play along.

'First on the right,' Greg's mum called out as she closed the front door. 'Make yourselves at home.'

The lemony scent of wood polish in the hallway was stronger still in the living room, but not unpleasantly so, and probably helped to mask the stink of booze and whatever else might be emanating from the semi-comatose Greg. He was lying sprawled on a two-seater settee beneath the window with one leg dangling over the side, his eyelids flickering as if he was fighting to stay awake and breathing heavily, almost to the point of snoring.

'For goodness' sake, sit yourself down before you fall down,' Mrs Murray said to Eleanor, breezing into the room and motioning her to an armchair on the left of an unlit open fireplace.

Eleanor slumped down into the chair with a more than passable impression of someone who was indeed about to fall down, and Mrs M scurried off to the kitchen to fetch her a glass of water.

'Now all we have to do is find out if he's in any fit state to answer a few questions,' I said, and gave Greg's dangling leg a gentle prod with my foot.

This was met with a moan and an unintelligible mumble, so I prodded harder – much harder, in fact, and only stopping short of a full-on kick in the shin. I was in no mood for the softly-softly approach, and it certainly did the trick. He didn't exactly sit bolt upright from the shock, but he stirred himself sufficiently to raise his head, and his red-rimmed eyes popped open like he'd been woken from a bad dream. Or one of them did anyway. The other was almost completely closed from a dark purplish swelling both above and below it, and there was a similarly heavy bruise close to his cheekbone as well as a cut lip. The wounds all looked quite recent, and I guessed he'd either been in a fight or, just as likely, sustained them stumbling about after a previous drinking binge.

'Wha de fug?' he slurred, glaring at me with his one good eye when he was finally able to focus.

'Remember me?' I said, taking care not to get too close to the anticipated evil stench from his mouth.

With superhuman effort he managed to prop himself up onto an elbow, and the glare became a squint as he studied my face for several seconds.

'Nah. Fug off,' he said at last and flopped back down again on the settee.

'I do hope you're not being rude to our guests, Greggie,' said Mrs M, appearing in the doorway with

167

the promised glass of water.

Eleanor thanked her and drained the glass in three gulps.

'My, my, you *were* thirsty, weren't you. Would you like some more?'

'No, you're fine, thanks,' said Eleanor, bravely forcing a weak smile. 'But if it's not too much bother, what I'd really like is a nice hot cup of tea.'

'Not a bother at all, dearie. Nice hot cup of tea coming right up. Good and sweet too. That'll get you back on your feet in no time or my name's not Sylvia Murray. And how about your friend? Nice hot cup of tea for you too? Or perhaps you'd prefer cocoa?'

The question was obviously directed at me, so I said tea would be great, even though I don't really like tea at all and I hated the very smell of cocoa. It was a small sacrifice to make, however, since I'd assumed that Eleanor's request for tea was purely designed to get Mrs M out of the way while we interrogated Greg, and I was simply following her lead.

But before I could begin the interrogation, Eleanor had leapt up from the armchair, miraculously recovering from her fainting spell, and laid a hand on my shoulder.

'It might be best if you keep his mum busy in the kitchen as long as possible while I talk to him on my own,' she said.

I was gagging to hear what had happened to our gear from the lockup, but I couldn't argue with her logic, so I did the decent thing and went off in search of the kitchen, stopping off briefly in the hallway to give Scratch and Alan a quick call. If I didn't update them soon, they'd be having a right old moan at me for not keeping them in the loop.

32

'It'll be proper stewed if I leave it any longer,' Greg's mum had said when I'd insisted that Eleanor and I both liked our tea incredibly strong.

This was a complete lie, of course, but I'd had to keep her out of the living room as long as possible to give Eleanor enough time to get what we needed to know out of her son. To be fair to Mrs M, though, the tea had been brewing for almost a quarter of an hour by then and was no doubt totally undrinkable. "Builders' tea" is what she'd called it, which is an expression I'd always thought rather builderist, and I was pretty sure that even the hardiest hod carrier would have poured it straight down the sink.

It hadn't been at all easy to keep her talking for quite that long either, but once I'd got her on to the price of food in the shops and the rising cost of gas and electricity, she was away. And fascinating as it was to hear how much a loaf of bread and several other items were in the 1960s, I was mightily relieved when Eleanor appeared in the kitchen doorway, said it was late and that we really ought to be heading home.

'But you haven't had your tea yet, dearie,' said Mrs M, 'although I expect it'll be well past its best by now anyway.'

'Yes, I'm sorry,' Eleanor said with a beaming smile, 'but I'm feeling so much better now. Right as rain, in fact, and we need to get back to relieve the babysitter before ten thirty or we'll have to pay her overtime.'

'Oh, you have children already, do you?'

'*Already*?' the voice in my head repeated. '*I told you she thought Eleanor had a bun in the oven.*'

'That's right,' Eleanor went on. 'Samson and Delilah. Twins.'

'*Samson and Delilah? Is she fucking serious*?'

'Ooh, how lovely,' cooed Mrs M, and before we got any further down the road to Fantasy Land, I decided to nip it in the bud.

'As you were saying, darling,' I said, pointedly tapping my watch. 'We really must be making tracks, I'm afraid.'

Mrs Murray walked us along the hallway, pausing only to put her head round the door of the living room and ask Greg if he wanted to say cheerio to his pals. Apparently he didn't, but his mother must have heard a word or two she didn't approve of, although the slight frown quickly gave way to her semi-permanent smile.

'Sorry about that,' she said as she opened the front door for us. 'He does tend to get a wee bit grumpy when he's feeling under the weather.' But before Eleanor or I could respond, she nodded across the road to where our hearse was parked directly opposite. 'Oh dear. Never a good sign that, is it? I dare say that'll be for old Mr Larkin at Number Eleven. Poor chap must be not far off a hundred by now, and he's not been right for a good twelve months or more from what I've been told. Still, not my turn for a wee while yet, I hope.'

She visibly brightened again with the last remark, wished us all the best with the new baby and said we'd be more than welcome to drop by any time we liked. In return, we thanked her for her hospitality and said we might well be taking her up on her invitation in the not too distant future, depending on how things turned out.

Then, as I closed the front yard gate behind us, I realised she was watching us from the open doorway and waving goodbye, so I took Eleanor by the arm and led her along the pavement away from the hearse.

As before, we turned right at the end of the street and stopped.

'And by the way,' I said while we waited for Alan and Scratch. 'Samson and Delilah?'

Eleanor shrugged. 'First names that came into my head.'

'But why feed her the whole twins stuff at all?'

Another shrug. 'Thought it would make us more sort of… authentic, I guess. Particularly after I'd faked the being pregnant and fainting act to get us into the house. And in case you've forgotten already, playacting is what I do for a living a lot of the time.'

'Which you'll be going back to do in your dungeon again if we don't get our hands on the gear from the lockup. So what did our Greggie say?'

She opened her mouth to speak, but at the same moment the hearse drew up alongside us and she made a grab for the passenger door.

'Shotgun!' she shouted, and since Scratch was

driving and Alan was in the middle of the front bench seat, this left me with no option but to climb into the back.

'So what's the story then?' said Alan, but even though I was as keen as he and Scratch were to hear Eleanor's answer, I wasn't going to be able to concentrate properly whilst rolling about in the back of the hearse.

'Pub,' I said.

There wasn't so much as a murmur of dissent, and ten minutes later the four of us marched into a boozer that normally I'd have given a very wide berth to. Too modernised, too garish and too loud. However, Scratch and Alan were champing at the bit to find out what had gone on at Greg the Fence's house, so personal preferences were hardly a priority. I'd already filled them in on the basics on the way to the pub but pointed out that I was as much in the dark as they were about what Greg had told Eleanor.

Once we'd got our drinks in at the bar, we sat down at an empty table that was as far away as possible from any of the other clientele, and Eleanor took a deep breath before she began.

'Well, I have to tell you it's not great news,' she said. 'It took me a while, but Greg eventually owned up to robbing the lockup.'

'Bloody knew it,' said Alan. 'So what's he done with all the stuff?'

Eleanor shot him a narrow-eyed glare. 'If you could shut your gob for two seconds, I'll tell you, OK?'

Alan held up his palms in mock surrender and sat back in his chair.

Now that she had the floor, Eleanor took a sip of her drink and carried on. 'Apparently, Greg managed to find someone who was willing to take the whole lot off his hands for a reasonably decent price. This would of course have been good news for us since all we'd have to do is get the cash off Greg and we'd be done and dusted. The only teeny-tiny problem is that he doesn't actually have it because the buyer hasn't paid up yet, even though he's sitting pretty on every last scrap of the loot from the lockup. That includes all the cash that was in there, which the buyer told him would need to be laundered.'

'Wait a minute,' I said, believing I could pipe up now without being on the receiving end of one of her withering looks. 'You're saying that he handed everything over before he got any of the money for it? Why the hell would he do that?'

'I suspect the beating he got from two of the buyer's goons must have been fairly persuasive.'

'Fuck's sake. And what do you mean by "hasn't paid up *yet*"? Is that gonna happen or not?'

Eleanor pursed her lips and slowly shook her head. 'Somehow I doubt it.'

'Jesus wept,' said Scratch. 'So we're totally screwed then, aren't we?'

'Not necessarily,' said Alan, surprisingly calm in the circumstances. 'Surely all we've got to do is have a quiet word with this buyer and get what's owing to us.'

'Unfortunately, I don't think that's going to be quite so straightforward,' said Eleanor.

'Oh? Why not?'

'You ever hear of somebody by the name of Mitchell Clayton? 'Cos he's the buyer.'

Christ on a bike. Scratch was right. Totally fucking screwed was precisely what we were.

173

33

Scratch was the only one of us who'd never heard of Mitchell Clayton, but Alan, Eleanor and I all knew him, if only by reputation. And knowing him only by reputation was about as close as I ever wanted to get. Officially, he was an extremely wealthy businessman with a variety of highly successful enterprises to his name, especially in property development and the hospitality industry. Unofficially, the guy was evil to the core, and his rapid rise to wealth and power had left many a dead body in its wake.

Unlike many crime bosses who'd worked their way up from impoverished childhoods, he'd had a privileged, upper middle-class upbringing, educated at Eton and gained a first class degree in economics and management from Oxford University. From then on, he'd risen rapidly through the ranks at one of the top investment banks in the UK, making a small personal fortune, which he'd substantially added to through a series of insider trading deals. However, one such deal brought him to the attention of the Financial Services

Authority, and after a lengthy investigation and trial, Clayton was eventually convicted and sentenced to three years in prison.

At Oxford, he'd learned about economics and management. In prison, he learned a new trade from some of the biggest villains in the criminal underworld. They'd also given him the names of several useful contacts on the outside, and he'd wasted little time in tracking them down when he'd been released. Now, ten years later, he'd built a thriving criminal empire, specialising mainly in drug trafficking, gunrunning and some general racketeering. The police were well aware of his activities but, try as they might, they'd never quite managed to make anything stick. This was partly due to the network of "friendly" cops he'd developed over the years, but also the fact that any witnesses or informants had a habit of mysteriously disappearing before they could give evidence against him.

Another crucial reason why Clayton had escaped conviction for so long was that he'd always made sure he never got his hands dirty himself. He had more than enough foot soldiers in his employ to create a chain of command that made it next to impossible to trace the original order back to him, whether it be drug deals, illegal arms transactions or even murder itself.

And how did I know all this extra detail on top of my general awareness that Mitchell Clayton was a complete and utter bastard? – Eleanor's own contact in the local police force.

Once we knew who it was that had got all our gear from the lockup, she'd got straight on to him to find out everything she could about the guy. Coincidentally, her tame copper had been part of a team that had tried to nail Clayton for a particularly nasty spate of murders a couple of years back, so he knew a lot. All useful stuff, but the cop had ended his information dump with a dire warning along the lines of: 'If you want my advice, I'd stay well clear of Mitchell Clayton unless you want to wind up dead or missing a limb or two.'

'Well, that's that then,' said Alan when Eleanor had finished passing on the scarily bad news. 'All that effort and bugger all to show for it. Thanks a bunch, Eleanor.'

'Oh yeah? So all this is my fault, is it?'

'You're the one who brought in Greg, the so-called fence. You see that van parked outside his house? "Greg Murray - Fencing Specialist - No Job Too Small"? I very much doubt he'd be quite so blatant advertising his criminal activities, so I'm guessing he'd be great if you wanted a nice little picket fence round your garden but not so hot at selling stolen jewellery or whatever.'

'OK, it was a simple misunderstanding, all right? I asked around and his was the only name that came up. Fucker never told *me* he didn't do the kind of fencing I was talking about. Probably just kept schtum because he saw a way of making a bit of extra money on the side.'

Alan snorted. 'A simple misunderstanding, eh? Oh well, that's all fine and dandy then, isn't it?'

'And don't forget he fooled you lot as well with his fancy car and flashy overcoat when he came to the lockup.'

'How were we to know he'd stolen 'em? That's what you said he told you, isn't it? To look the part?'

'Listen, we can argue the toss all you like, but

here's something else you shouldn't forget. If it wasn't for me, there'd never have been a bank job in the first place.'

Although I kept it to myself, I couldn't disagree with Alan. Eleanor had messed up big time, but rowing about it wasn't getting us anywhere. We were back where we'd started. Flat broke and not a clue what to do about it.

'*Not even back where you started,*' said the voice in my head, '*because at least when you were skint before, you didn't have the cops after you for Edgar Ackroyd's murder.*'

As if I needed reminding.

❖

The row between Alan and Eleanor had all but fizzled out by the time the pub closed a few minutes later, and we all climbed into the hearse and headed back to the funeral parlour in almost total silence. We still had the issue of keeping them both out of sight of the cops, although oddly enough, Eleanor hadn't seemed to have been particularly cautious in that respect. I'd have expected there would have been a fairly major police hunt for her right now, but she'd shown minimal concern about being seen in public when we'd gone into the café or the boozer. It wasn't as if it was just her head on the line either. Like she'd said herself, if she got nicked, there was always the possibility that she'd end up taking me, Alan and Scratch down with her.

'You'd better stay at my place again,' I said to her as we pulled up outside the funeral parlour. 'At least till we find somewhere better for you to hide out.'

By "somewhere better" I also meant anywhere that didn't involve having to share my flat with both her *and* Carla at the same time.

'What about me then?' said Alan. 'I can't go back to mine. Parkin's almost certainly got it under surveillance as it is. And no, I'm not gonna hole up in that bloody mortuary again, so you can forget that for a start.'

'What about my Aunt Betty's boat on the canal?' said Scratch, 'It's where we took Oleg when we needed somewhere for him to lie low, remember?'

'Yeah, course I remember. And look how well that turned out.'

Scratch stroked his chin. 'Hmm, what's that expression about beggars and choosers?'

Despite Alan's misgivings, he was forced to concede that it was probably the only practical option he had, so he and Scratch set off for the canal while Eleanor and I went into the funeral parlour and climbed the stairs up to my apartment.

Halfway there, I had a sudden fleeting hope that maybe Carla and Dimitri had reconciled and she'd buggered off back to their not-so-love-nest at the Acropolis Restaurant.

But no such luck.

And not only was Carla still in residence, I also had to wonder why Ray and Roy Ackroyd were sitting on the floor with their backs against the far wall of the flat and why they were gagged with their hands and feet tied together.

34

I was rooted to the spot in the doorway of the flat, my mouth hanging open, unable to form any words.

Carla was lounging on the settee with a glass of red wine in her hand and seemingly oblivious that there was anything out of the ordinary.

'What?' she said, her tone similarly implying that the presence of two bound and gagged men in the apartment was nothing out of the ordinary.

'Them,' I said, finally recovering the power of speech and pointing at the Ackroyd twins. 'I mean, what the hell?'

'Bastards broke in and attacked me, didn't they? God knows what they were after, but I didn't wait to find out.'

With the hand that wasn't holding the wine glass, she picked up a large heavy frying pan from the seat beside her and swung it casually to and fro.

'You hit them with *that*?'

'Course I did. Well, I throat-punched one of them first and kicked the other one in the bollocks. *Then* I

179

whacked them with the frying pan till they were both spark out.'

'Throat-punched?'

'Er, I think the clue's in the name. It's when you punch someone in the throat. Remarkably effective too if you want to incapacitate somebody in a hurry.' She took a sip of her wine and must have noticed my look of disbelief. 'Some arsehole tried to mug me in the street a few weeks ago, so since then I've been checking out the internet for some self defence techniques.'

'Good job she didn't know how to do that sort of shit when you were married,' said the voice in my head. *'You'd have been dead long ago.'*

Carla eyeballed Eleanor, who was hovering at my shoulder in the doorway. 'Hey there, Eleanor. How you doing?

'I'm all right, ta. Not been having as much fun as you by the sound of it, though.'

I took a few steps towards the twins to get a closer look. As I may have mentioned before, they were in their early forties and a million miles from being identical but they did share one particular physical characteristic. They were both extraordinarily ugly, albeit in their own individual ways. Ray had incredibly large ears set almost at right-angles to his face, which looked like open car doors when viewed from behind. He had an absurdly high forehead and a small patch of close-cropped hair perched like a saucer on the top of his head, and one of his eyes was half closed like he was permanently winking.

On the other hand, Roy had only the one ear, although it was a relatively normal size and shape compared to his brother's, and a neck that was so thick it was as wide as his head. His chin was almost non-existent, and what there was of it was mostly concealed by a heavily protruding lower lip, which tended to emphasise his perpetually gormless expression. Clearly unconscious, if he'd had a chin I would have said it was resting on his chest, but the gap was far too great to make that possible.

Ray, however, was not only conscious but wriggling like crazy to try and free himself from his bonds and glaring up at me as he yelled incomprehensibly through the gag that had been stuffed in his mouth.

I hesitated for a moment, then reached down and removed what I was fairly sure was one of my socks.

He waggled his jaws from side to side and up and down, presumably to ease the stiffness, then spat on the floor beside him. 'Fucking bitch.'

This was obviously directed at Carla, who simply raised her glass to him as if in a toast and blew him a kiss.

'She your wife, is she?'

This one was for me, of course.

'Ex,' I said.

'Good bloody riddance then, I'd say. She's a bleedin' maniac.'

I couldn't really disagree, but I certainly wasn't going to discuss it in front of Carla. Instead, I opted for: 'You want to tell me exactly what you're doing here?'

Apparently he didn't. 'Could've damn near killed the pair of us.'

I decided against rubbing it in about one woman and two muscular men with a history of convictions for GBH and repeated my original question.

Ray spat on the floor again. 'Lookin' for you, wasn't we. 'Cept you wasn't 'ere, was yer.'

'Clearly not,' I said. 'So what is it you want with me?'

'Whaddya think?'

'I don't know, Ray. Perhaps you could enlighten me.'

His already unattractive features contorted into something between a sneer and a piercing stare of pure venom. 'Our dad, yeah? You fuckin' killed 'im, didn't yer.'

'Course I didn't. Whatever gave you that idea?'

'Yeah, well, that's for me to know, innit.'

There was only one candidate I could think of. 'Wouldn't have been DCI Parkin by any chance, would it?'

'Who?'

'Come off it, Ray. He and your dad seemed very pally when I saw them together in the pub a few days ago. Who else would it have been?'

'So what if it *was* Parkin? Don't make no difference to who did our dad in.'

'OK, listen. I'll own up it was us that took the coffin and the body from your place. The ones you'd nicked from us, yeah? But hand on heart, your dad was already dead when we got there.'

'Says you.'

There was a muffled groaning sound to his left, and he turned towards it. Roy's eyelids were beginning to flicker, so I took the gag out of his mouth – also a sock – as he slowly returned to the land of the living. As he started to raise his head, I saw that there was an impressively large bump and a trickle of blood in the middle of his forehead. Carla must have caught him with a frontal assault with the frying pan.

He blinked several times, and his unfocused gaze roamed around the apartment. 'What 'appened?'

'Crazy bitch from hell got the jump on us and KO'd us both with a bloody frying pan,' said Ray. 'You all right, bruv? How yer feelin'?'

'Not too good, Ray. Not too good at all.'

'Don't worry, mate. She's gonna pay for what she's done big time. Dempsey an' all for what he done to our pop.'

'Admitted it, has he?'

Ray shook his head. 'Not yet, no.'

I was starting to feel like a spectator at my own kangaroo trial.

'Christ, I'm getting sick of this,' I said. 'Roy, as I've already told your brother, I had sod all to do with your dad's murder and nor did any of my... associates. And even if we did, what were you planning to do about it?'

'*Don't be daft*,' said the voice in my head. '*These two dickheads are after revenge, so it's unlikely they'd be satisfied with anything less than your head on a plate.*'

Fortunately on this occasion, the voice had exaggerated – but not by much.

'A shitload of compensation,' said Ray, but after his brother gave him a nudge, he added, 'Oh yeah, and beating the crap out of yer.'

'Tough luck then,' I said, 'because I'm totally skint, and right now you're hardly in a position to beat the crap out of anyone.'

'What, you gonna keep us tied up like this forever?'

It was a good point, and short of killing them, I hadn't got a clue what to do with them. Eleanor had, though.

She hadn't spoken a word since her brief exchange with Carla, but she must have got tired of merely spectating.

'Pass me that frying pan, will you?' she said, and Carla handed it over.

'Be my guest.'

Taking her time, Eleanor closed in on Ray and Roy and stood over them, holding the frying pan by its handle as she rhythmically tapped the base onto the palm of her other hand.

'So, it seems we have ourselves a bit of a conundrum here,' she said, 'but I think I may have the solution. Talking about beating the crap out of someone is what gave me the idea, you see, but don't worry. You're not *both* going to get battered, because us three witnesses will gladly testify that one of you gave the other an extremely nasty whacking with this here pan. And here's the cunning part. From what I've heard, you've each got previous for a bunch of GBH convictions, so whichever of you does the whacking will be looking at a not insubstantial period behind bars. All you have to do is decide between you who's going to jail and who's going to hospital.'

Ray glared up at her and smirked. 'Think you're smart, dontcha? What you've forgotten, though, is you'll have to untie one of us to do that, and I can't promise it won't be you three that end up in 'ospital.'

'Oh, 'cos you've got such a good record on that score, haven't you?' Eleanor said with a sideways nod at Carla. 'But maybe I didn't make myself clear. Neither of you'll be doing any of the actual GBH. That'll be my job, and I have to say I'm really looking forward to it.'

35

Ray and Roy had obviously taken Eleanor's threat seriously and had been arguing with each other about which one of them was going to jail and which one was going to end up in hospital. Eleanor, however, had apparently got fed up waiting for them to make up their minds.

'Maybe I can help,' she said, and pointing at them in turn with the frying pan, started reciting that "Eeny, meeny, miny, moe" thing.

I wasn't convinced that her plan was going to work, and not being of a violent disposition myself, I was also having serious doubts about the ethical justification for beating either of the twins to a pulp. And judging by the increasing volume and intensity in their argument, Ray and Roy weren't too happy about the situation either.

'I ain't doin' any more bird!' Roy shouted. 'Last time nearly killed me.'

'So will 'avin' yer 'ead caved in with a bleedin' frying pan!' Ray yelled.

Eleanor had got to "If he hollers, let him go", so it was now or never.

'Hang on a sec, Eleanor,' I said. 'I think I might have a better idea.'

I hadn't yet, of course, so I needed to come up with something pretty damn sharpish, the urgency compounded by the icy glare she shot me as she broke off from her rhyming and lowered the frying pan to her side.

'Oh yes?' she said. 'And what might that be, genius?'

I got the distinct impression she really had been looking forward to battering one of the twins, but perhaps I was being uncharitable.

'Well, here's what I reckon. The thing is that… in the cold light of day when all's said and done and considering the various options – which I admit aren't exactly in plentiful supply – there is at least one other possibility that springs to mind that I believe may turn out to be a perfectly workable solution and—'

'What the hell are you blathering on about?' Eleanor snapped, understandably beginning to lose patience. 'You going to tell me what this brilliant idea is or what?'

Shit shit shit. I'd got nothing, and was about to admit it and let her get on with the GBH when the voice in my head came to the rescue.

'How about this?' I said, passing on the voice's suggestion to Ray and Roy. 'From what I've heard, your dad had some fairly close connections with a few of the nastier elements involved in organised crime, so I'm guessing you do too. Is that right?'

There was no response from either of them, so I prompted them with some names. 'Billy "The

Butcher" McNally? Jack "Hacksaw" Higgins? Tony "Psycho" Vincenzi? Any of those ring any bells?'

No response again, but I spotted Roy's eyes glance sideways at his brother if only for a nanosecond, which was enough to persuade me that they knew one of them at least.

'So here's what we're going to do,' I said. 'We're going to take a few photos of you trussed up like a pair of dumbass turkeys and send them to each of the scumbags I just mentioned. But here's the kicker. We'll also include a little message explaining that you've been grabbed by a rival gang and – under duress of course – you spilled rather a lot of beans about their operations, safe houses, storage facilities and so on. In fact, anything and everything that would seriously damage their business. Naturally, we wouldn't be able to specify any real details because we've no idea what they are, but I think that would be more than enough to piss them off so badly that they may well want to inflict some particularly unpleasant revenge – possibly even fatal – and I doubt it would involve a frying pan. You with me so far?'

Maybe it was a result of the recent concussion or that Roy was marginally thicker than his brother, but he looked up at me with his mouth hanging open in complete incomprehension. Ray, on the other hand, appeared to grasp the essentials.

'Fuck off. You wouldn't dare.'

I gave him my best smug grin. 'Would you mind doing the honours please, Eleanor?'

'Glad to,' she said, dropping the frying pan and taking out her phone.

We hadn't had an opportunity to discuss my new plan, of course, but her instant compliance told me she was in full agreement.

'Give us a smile then,' I said to the twins as she began clicking away. 'No? Oh go on. Try saying "cheese". The camera loves you, remember.'

Unsurprisingly, Ray and Roy twisted their heads in every conceivable direction as they fought to avoid their ugly mugs being caught on camera, but eventually Eleanor was satisfied that she had plenty of decent shots.

'Bit tricky getting Ray's massive ears in,' she said, 'but I got there in the end.'

Ray was not amused.

'Right then,' I said, clasping my hands together, 'I think that concludes our business for tonight, so in a moment we're going to let you go. However, and it's not that we don't trust you, but I know the first thing you'll do if we set you free is make a grab for the phone. So, what we'll do is just untie your feet, and once you're out on the street I'm sure you have enough brain cells between you to figure out untying your hands. OK?'

I wasn't expecting an answer, but as I bent down to deal with Roy's feet I realised Carla had used plastic cable ties to bind them together. The type that cops sometimes use instead of handcuffs.

'Where'd you get these from?' I asked her.

'Hardware store. I always carry a few with me in case I have to make a citizen's arrest.'

'Uh?'

'Somebody suggested it on one of the self defence videos, so I thought I might as well. Came in quite handy for these two shitheads, didn't they?'

'Absolutely,' I said, having some difficulty processing this new image of Carla as some sort of vigilante street warrior.

Meanwhile, Eleanor had fetched a sharp knife and a pair of scissors from the kitchen, and we each took a twin and set about cutting through the cable ties round their ankles.

Almost inevitably, Ray lashed out with one of his feet as soon as Eleanor had finished, but since she was half expecting it, she dodged the blow easily. In retaliation, however, she gave him a hard whack on the knee with the frying pan, causing him a not inconsiderable amount of pain and a fair bit of swearing. It also meant that I had to support him as he hobbled down the stairs from the apartment while Eleanor and Roy led the way.

Once they were out on the pavement in front of the funeral parlour, though, they were on their own. Ray was limping badly, but given that his brother still had his hands tied behind his back, there wasn't much he could do to help. So, after no more than a dozen yards, they stopped, and back to back, they fumbled to loosen the cable ties from around each other's wrists.

I turned to Eleanor, who was clearly finding the scene as comical as I was. 'You think it'll work?'

'Them getting themselves free?'

'No, the blackmail thing with the photos and stuff. You reckon they'll leave us alone from now on?'

Eleanor shrugged. 'Dunno. Maybe they will, but who can tell with a couple of morons like them?'

This wasn't the answer I was looking for, but she was probably right. Ray and Roy were dense enough not to understand what the consequences would be if we went ahead with our threat, although getting them off our backs, even temporarily, was something to be grateful for.

The twins' continuing struggle to free each other didn't appear to be making much progress, so I suggested to Eleanor that we leave them to it and go back inside. She didn't need any further encouragement, but as I was about to follow her, an all too familiar voice called out from behind me.

'Max, mate. Is Carla still with you?'

Jesus. That was all I needed. Carla's partner Dimitri, and I very definitely wasn't his "mate".

36

My dislike of Dimitri had nothing to do with his having had an affair with Carla while we were still married. Quite the opposite, in fact. In hindsight, he'd actually done me a favour when Carla had packed her bags and gone to live with him because our marriage had been going to shit for months, if not years.

No, the reason I despised Carla's Greek toyboy wasn't simply because he was a dozy twat with only marginally more brain cells than Ray and Roy Ackroyd, but something far more sinister. He'd been heavily involved with his Uncle Nikos's criminal activities that had almost led to having my balls fried, not to mention death, but worst of all, he'd once kidnapped my teenage nephew Toby and threatened to kill him. And since I was as fond of the lad as my own kids, forgiveness was never going to be an option even though Dimitri didn't get to carry out his threat.

This was why I wasn't exactly thrilled by his unannounced arrival at the funeral parlour.

'What the fuck do *you* want?'

Dimitri was struggling to breathe like he'd run all the way from his crappy Acropolis Restaurant, although this was highly unlikely since, along with his other many faults, he was one of the laziest people I'd ever had the misfortune to meet.

'Carla,' he panted. 'She here? Need to talk.'

'Oh yeah? What about?'

I didn't much care why he wanted to talk to her, and I had a pretty good idea anyway. I was just enjoying seeing him squirm.

'None of your... business.'

'Fair enough,' I said and went to shut the door in his face.

'OK, OK,' he bleated, his breathing beginning to return to normal. 'I need her to come back. To the restaurant. I can't cope since she left, and I've got no money to take on more staff.'

'*Good to know that romance isn't dead after all,*' said the voice in my head.

'Busy then, are you?' I said aloud.

'What?'

'At the restaurant. Are. You. Busy?'

Dimitri shuffled his feet. 'Yeah, kind of, although— Listen, Max, is she here or not?'

I was getting bored listening to him, so I told him where to find her and let him get on with it.

'Who was that?' said Eleanor when he'd set off for the stairs up to the apartment and I'd locked the funeral parlour door, taking one last look at Ray and Roy still desperately trying to untie each other.

I explained as briefly as I could be bothered to, then added that I didn't fancy being a witness to Carla and Dimitri's inevitable row and suggested we stayed downstairs till it was all over. I also mentioned that I had a small stock of booze in the storeroom.

'Sounds good to me,' she said, but as I passed the reception desk to get to the storeroom door, my peripheral vision caught sight of something I hadn't been expecting.

On top of the desk and roughly in the centre was the mini cassette player and a handwritten note beside it.

I snatched up the note and read: "MAX. YOU NEED TO LISTEN TO THIS!! NOW!!!"

Sanjeev had been visibly disappointed the day before when I'd told him I didn't have time to listen to the tape we'd got from Edgar Ackroyd's deposit box, but I couldn't fail to spot the sense of urgency implicit in the number of exclamation marks. I'd been meaning to play the damn thing ever since we'd found it, and now at last I had the opportunity.

Eleanor had read the note over my shoulder. 'Go on then. What are you waiting for?'

I hesitated for a moment, half expecting to be disappointed in what I was about to hear, then picked up the recorder and pressed the Play button.

There were a few seconds of fuzzy distortion, and then the unmistakable voice of Edgar Ackroyd.

"So, Ray and Roy, I must be dead then. Otherwise, you wouldn't have read my will and discovered where to find this tape and some rather valuable other items along with it. These, I trust, you will share equally between you, and the same applies to all of my other assets – such as they are. No arguing, eh?

"But let me get to the main reason I decided to make this tape. I suppose it's a kind of insurance in the event that my death is in any way unexpected or unnatural. Murdered in particular, as I don't want the bastard who did it to get away with it.

"And the bastard in question? Well, in the next part of this tape, you'll hear a secret recording I made with the man who is by far and away the most likely suspect. Listen and learn."

There was a faint click, followed by more of the fuzzy distortion before Ackroyd's voice cut in again.

"Tony, as I keep telling you, I need more time."

"You've had plenty." The new voice had a slight hint of an Italian accent. "We're not talking peanuts here. Fifty fucking grand plus a shitload of interest you've run up already."

"I know. I know. But I just don't have that kind of money. Not yet anyway. Another month. That's all I'm asking."

There was a short pause before the other man answered. "You got a week."

"Christ, Tony, I—"

"Listen to me, Edgar. We've known each other a long time, yeah? And it's only because of that I've let you off as long as I have. Do I have to remind you what usually happens to people who cross me? People who don't pay their debts?"

"Course I know. Who doesn't? I mean, you don't get called Tony 'Psycho' Vincenzi for nothing, right?"

The other man grunted. "Yeah, well, it's not a moniker I'm especially fond of, but it is what it is, I guess."

There was the sound of a chair being scraped back and slowly retreating footsteps, and his voice became a little more distant. "*Arrivederci*, Edgar. I'll be seeing you."

"Fucking Eyetie prick."

This was Ackroyd's voice, the words spoken in

barely above a whisper, then a click followed by a second click and he was back again.

"So, there you have it. And as I said before, if I meet an unnatural end, give this tape to the cops so that Vincenzi can get what's coming to him. DCI Parkin would be your best bet. I've bunged him quite a lot over the years to keep him sweet, if you know what I mean." There was a brief chuckle. "I expect he'll want to delete that last bit before he goes public, though.

"Oh, and one last thing. If you stick me in anything but the most expensive coffin we've got, I'll come back and haunt you and make your lives a fucking misery."

There was another click, and we kept the tape running for a few more seconds until we were sure there was nothing else, then I hit the Stop button.

Not long after we'd started listening, Eleanor and I had sat down on opposite sides of the reception desk, and we looked at each other in stunned silence.

'Well, what do you make of that?' said Eleanor after what seemed like a long minute.

'Obviously intended for Ray and Roy,' I said.

'Stroke of luck that we came across it first, though, isn't it? Main thing is it gets you and the others off the hook for Ackroyd's murder.'

'I don't know if it *proves* anything, does it? It's not as if the tape's got this Vincenzi guy actually confessing to the murder.'

'Maybe not, but at least the police will have someone else to look at other than you. And don't forget the last part either. Proof enough that Parkin's bent as a wonky corkscrew, I reckon, so that'll give us a nice little hold over *him*.'

195

This could certainly be useful, of course, but there was also something else about the tape that had got me thinking. Something that we might even be able to use to get our loot back from the lockup.

I rewound the tape to the beginning and hit Play again.

37

Seconds after I'd started to listen to the tape again, Dimitri appeared at the bottom of the stairs that led down from my apartment, so I pressed the Pause button. As he weaved his way through the display coffins, I could see that he was clutching his left elbow with his right hand, and he winced with almost every step.

'Went well then, did it?' I said when he came close enough to hear.

'Some and some,' he said, tilting his head slightly from side to side.

'What's up with your arm?'

Dimitri glanced down at his elbow. 'Carla. She hit me with a frying pan.'

I couldn't resist a snigger. 'She seems to be developing a bit of a habit in that department.'

'It's not funny, Max. Bloody hurts, it does.'

'Yeah, I'm sure. So is there a good part of "some and some"?'

He opened his mouth to speak, but was interrupted

by the sound of a large suitcase being clunked down the last few steps into the funeral parlour.

'You could have given me a hand with this, you know,' said Carla as she wheeled the suitcase towards us.

'Sorry, love. My arm, yeah?'

'Oh, boo hoo. You should've seen what I did to the other blokes.'

It didn't take a genius to read between the lines. Dimitri had presumably pleaded with Carla to come back to the restaurant, which had resulted in a blazing row and Carla giving her toyboy a bit of a battering. Whatever the reason she'd eventually caved, I honestly didn't care. She was leaving, and that was all that mattered.

'Off so soon?' I said to her with undisguised sarcasm.

Carla scowled and shoved the handle of her suitcase at Dimitri. 'Here. You've got one good arm, haven't you?'

I got up from the reception desk to unlock the door onto the street, and Carla swept past me, followed by Dimitri trundling her suitcase.

'You're welcome,' I called out after them but predictably got no response.

I closed and locked the door, having noted that there was no longer any sign of Ray and Roy Ackroyd. Whether they'd finally managed to set each other free or gone off in search of help was something else I couldn't have cared less about. Even if it was only temporary, Carla and the Ackroyd twins were out of my life for now at least. Eleanor was a different matter, however, as we'd already arranged that she'd be spending the night in my flat again.

It was already well into the early hours, so I decided to leave replaying the tape till I'd had some sleep, and Eleanor and I headed up to the apartment. With Carla gone, everything was a lot simpler, but I made a point of pulling out the bed settee before going into the bedroom and closing the door behind me.

Knackered though I was, sleep didn't come easily, however, as I couldn't stop my mind from analysing every word I'd remembered from Edgar Ackroyd's tape. In particular, I couldn't shake the feeling that there was more value to be gained from it than simply shifting Parkin's attention away from me as the chief suspect for the murder.

❖

For some bizarre reason, I'd been dreaming about having a stand-up fistfight with none other than Wolfgang Amadeus Mozart. This was especially odd as most of my dreams tend to be extraordinarily dull and mostly about things like putting the shopping away or filling the car with petrol. I'd no idea what Mozart and I were fighting about either. I mean, I can't say I'm a huge fan of classical music generally, but I certainly wouldn't have started a punch-up over it. Nor had I got anything against Mozart himself or his work, and I've always had a deep-seated aversion to physical violence, so maybe he'd started it. But whatever the reason, Wolfie was just about to deliver what I expected to be the decisive knockout blow when I was reprieved by a knocking on my bedroom door.

'Are you decent?'

It took me a moment or two to recognise Eleanor's

voice. After all, it's not easy to switch instantly from a brawl with one of the greatest composers that ever lived to someone asking me if I was decent.

'Er, yes, I think so,' I said as my brain struggled to make the necessary adjustment.

'You think so?'

'No, I am. I am. Come on in.'

The door swung open, and Eleanor stepped into the room bearing a steaming mug of what I sincerely hoped was ridiculously strong coffee. After what I guessed can't have been more than a couple of hours' sleep, I needed it rocket fuel strength to get me going.

'Thanks,' I said, taking the mug from her and sipping tentatively. Apart from almost burning my tongue, it tasted like it was well up for the job.

'Sleep all right?'

'Not really, no.'

'Me neither. Couldn't stop thinking about that bloody tape.'

'Me neither,' I echoed. 'What time is it anyway?'

'Getting on for eight. I've got toast on the go if you fancy some.'

'That'd be great. Not too well done, though, yeah?'

Eleanor must have realised I was kidding because she smiled and left the room, raising a middle finger at me as she closed the door behind her.

I decided I could do without a shower, dressed quickly and joined her in the living room.

Two hastily gobbled pieces of toast and another half mug of coffee later, we set off down to the shop floor.

Sanjeev and Alice had already let themselves in and were hanging around by the reception desk.

The "good mornings" out of the way – apart from

Alice, who merely grunted and carried on studying her fingernails – Sanjeev asked if we'd listened to the tape.

'Yes, we have,' I said, 'and it's given me the beginnings of an idea how we might be able to use it to our advantage.'

'Getting you and the guys off the hook for the murder, you mean?'

'Maybe, but something else as well perhaps.'

Eleanor raised an eyebrow. 'Oh yeah? And what's that then?'

'I haven't thought it through properly yet, so I need to give it a bit more time. In any case, we ought to go and check up on Alan and Scratch and let *them* know about the tape. See what they make of it.'

Then it occurred to me that the only transport we had was the Polo, which had failed to start the last time I'd tried it.

'I don't suppose you got round to sorting out the Polo, did you?' I asked Sanjeev.

'Yeah, sure. As per your instructions. Turned out to be a flat battery, so I got it charged up and it's running fine now. Well, not "fine" exactly, but you know what I mean.'

'Great. Thanks. You and Alice be all right holding the fort till we get back?'

Given the distinct lack of business, there wasn't much of a fort to hold, so Sanjeev said it wouldn't be a problem, and Alice gave another grunt whilst examining the fingernails on her other hand.

38

As before when Scratch's Aunt Betty had helped us
out by hiding our defecting Russian spy, Oleg
Radimov, I drove into the small car park near the
canal and switched off the engine. The hearse was
parked nearby, as I would have expected, but what I
hadn't expected was the marked police car next to it
and two uniformed cops deep in conversation with
Scratch.

'What the hell's that about?' said Eleanor, sliding
down in the Polo's passenger seat in an attempt to
keep out of sight.

'God knows,' I said. 'Stay here and I'll go and find
out.'

'Don't worry. I'm not going anywhere.'

She slid down even further, and I got out of the car
and walked over to join Scratch and the cops.

'Everything all right, Scratch?'

The two uniforms had had their backs to me and
turned to face me. A man and a woman and both in
their mid twenties.

The female cop was about to say something, but Scratch got there first. 'Yeah, all OK, Max. Just a bit of a misunderstanding, that's all.'

'Well, I'm not sure that misunderstanding quite covers it, Mr…' The male cop faltered as he checked his notebook. 'Mr Bevan. I believe we've already established – and by your own admission – that you have committed a serious breach of the local by-laws.'

'Really?' I said. 'Which one's that then?'

Female Cop looked me up and down, her expression indicating that she didn't much like what she saw. 'And you are?'

I gave her what I believed to be a winning smile. 'Sorry I didn't introduce myself. Jeremiah Forsyth-Dickens. Mr Bevan's lawyer.'

'His lawyer? So what are you doing here? He didn't have a chance to call you.'

'Prior arrangement.'

'To meet him *here*?'

'Correct.'

'What about?'

I feigned an expression of surprise. 'Come now, officer. You should know better than to ask that. Client confidentiality?' Female Cop merely tutted in response, so I carried on. 'And may I ask again which particular by-law Mr Bevan is alleged to have breached?'

It was Male Cop's turn to chip in. 'Camping in this area is strictly forbidden.'

'Camping? In a hearse?'

'The type of vehicle doesn't make any difference. The point is that earlier this morning a lady walking her dog discovered your client sleeping in the back of the hearse and reported it to the police. In fact,

203

originally she believed that your client was a corpse and the hearse had been abandoned.'

I probably shouldn't have laughed, but I did.

Female Cop was clearly not impressed. 'This is no laughing matter, sir. The lady in question was quite traumatised.'

'Yes, of course,' I said, forcing a straight face and scanning the area around the car park. 'So, will you be charging my client or not? As far as I can see, there don't appear to be any signs about camping not being permitted.'

The two officers exchanged glances as if each was wanting the other to make the decision, and it was Male Cop who lost.

'We're going to let your client off with a warning on this occasion,' he said. 'But if we or any of our colleagues find him sleeping here again, he won't get off so lightly.'

'Thank you, officers. I shall be advising my client accordingly.'

I'd no idea why I said that because Scratch was standing right next to me, but it seemed like the right sort of lawyerly thing to say.

'Just make sure you do,' said Female Cop, who apparently didn't think it was odd at all.

She turned back towards the police car, but as she did so, Male Cop pointed to my Polo. 'That belong to you, sir?'

Oh God, now what? As far as I was aware, the tax, insurance and all the other stuff was up to date. 'It is, yes.'

'Bit of an old banger, isn't it?' he said. 'Business can't be going too well then, eh?'

He and his partner had a good old chuckle about

that before climbing into their car and unnecessarily hitting the blues and twos as they left the parking area.

'You should have told them that old one about the Porsche being in the garage for a service,' said Scratch.

'So how come you were sleeping in the hearse?' I said.

'Not much choice really. You know what Aunt Betty's narrowboat's like. Those things aren't designed for people my size. I can barely get inside it, never mind sleep in it, so I kipped in the hearse instead.'

'Fair enough. What about Alan?'

'Not a problem for a shortarse like him. I haven't seen him yet today, but I guess he must still be on the boat. I never mentioned to the cops what I was doing here, though. Didn't want them poking about and finding him in case they knew he was wanted for murder.'

'I doubt those two know anything about it, but we can't be too careful even though Alan and the rest of us might not be in the frame for that any more.'

'Seriously? Why's that?'

'I'll tell you about it in a minute when we're all together.'

Now that the coast was clear, Eleanor had joined us and understandably wanted to know what the cops were after, so Scratch gave her a quick rundown as we crossed the stone footbridge over the canal and down onto the towpath.

There were a dozen or so narrowboats that were moored end-to-end with Aunt Betty's about halfway along the row and by far the shabbiest and least cared-for of all. Where once it must have been a dazzling bright red with a green trim, the colours had now faded to a kind of muddy brown, and the gold lettering on the side was so washed out as to make any words utterly illegible. There were also several large patches of rust on the black hull that were clearly visible above the waterline. But having visited before, I knew that the interior was as immaculate as the exterior was tatty.

As we approached, I saw that Aunt Betty and Alan were sitting on a pair of camping chairs on the small platform at the back of the boat.

'Ahoy there!' I called out. 'Permission to come aboard?'

They both stood and turned in our direction. Aunt Betty was wearing her usual rainbow-coloured knitted hat, and judging by the conspicuous split on the side, it had originally been intended as a tea cosy. Her old army greatcoat that must have dated from the First World War was buttoned to the neck with the collar turned up. Beneath the coat, the bottom few inches of a faded paisley skirt reached down to a pair of heavily scuffed ankle boots.

'Max, my dear. It's been an absolute age. How the devil are you?'

'Not so bad, thanks,' I said, returning but not quite matching the cheeriness of her smile. 'Yourself?'

'Few more aches and pains, but they go with the territory when you're an old biddy like me. Still, it's been such a joy having a bit of company for a change.'

'What, even Alan?' said Scratch.

Alan scowled at him and Aunt Betty told "Michael" to mind his manners and not be so rude.

She never used Scratch's nickname but always called him by his real name, or more often than not, "my little Mikey".

'I see we have even more company today,' she said, her attention switching to Eleanor. 'The more the merrier, I say.'

Introductions over, she asked who'd like a cup of tea or coffee, and when we all declined, she offered a range of almost every kind of alcohol "and some rather nice weed" as an alternative. She seemed disappointed when she again got no takers, but the smile quickly returned.

'Perhaps later then,' she said. 'But in the meantime, I'm afraid there's not really room for all of us on deck, and Mikey's too big to fit inside. Will a picnic blanket on the bank do all right?'

Without waiting for an answer, she disappeared inside the boat to fetch one. By the time she returned, we'd satisfied Alan's curiosity about the police sirens, and I told him we had far more important news to talk about.

'*Good* news, I hope,' said Aunt Betty, catching the tail end of what I'd been saying.

'Kind of,' I said, 'and possibly even better than Eleanor and I first thought.'

39

Aunt Betty and Alan stayed sitting on the small platform at the back of the narrowboat while the rest of us settled ourselves on the grassy bank on the opposite side of the towpath. I tried to ignore the strong whiff of paraffin and diesel coming from the picnic blanket Aunt Betty had given us and summarised everything Eleanor and I had learned from Edgar Ackroyd's tape.

Alan and Scratch reacted in much the same way as Eleanor and Sanjeev had.

'That's brilliant,' said Scratch. 'Surely that puts us in the clear for Ackroyd's murder now, doesn't it?'

'And I don't have to keep hiding out from the cops any more,' said Alan, then quickly turned to Aunt Betty and added, 'Oh, sorry. I didn't mean—'

'That's quite all right, dear,' she interrupted and patted him on the arm. 'I know exactly what you mean, but it'll be such a shame not to have you around any more.'

I didn't want to put a dampener on Scratch and

Alan's relief, but I had to point out – as I had with Eleanor – that the tape couldn't be considered as absolute proof that we didn't murder Ackroyd.

'No, I get that,' said Scratch, 'but what about the part where he says Parkin's bent? We can use that to blackmail him, can't we? Get off our backs or your bosses get the tape.'

'Yeah, that might work,' I said, 'although I may have an idea that could possibly kill two birds with one stone.'

I still hadn't worked out all the details, but I told them all where I'd got to so far.

'The thing is, we might be able to get off the murder charge *and* get our lockup gear back from Mitchell Clayton at the same time.' This certainly got their attention, so I carried on. 'OK, first we tell Clayton we have evidence that it was probably Tony "Psycho" Vincenzi that murdered Edgar Ackroyd. Then we offer him a deal. A copy of the tape in exchange for everything he nicked from Greg, our so-called fence.'

'Just like that, eh?' said Alan. 'From what you've told us, there's nothing about Clayton on the tape, so why would *he* care?'

'Look, I'm only guessing here, but I'd imagine that there's some fairly heavy rivalry between these kinds of people. You know the sort of thing. Gangs poaching other gangs' business, trying to take over each other's territories. We've seen it on the telly often enough.'

'So?'

'So, what if Mitchell Clayton was offered an easy way to get rid of one of his... competitors? No shootouts, no violence, just Tony Vincenzi banged up for murder for what would probably be a very long time. And if he could take over his business as well, that's got to be worth shitloads.'

'There's no guarantee that Vincenzi would actually get done though, is there?' said Scratch. 'It's only a dead man's word against his after all.'

'No, I realise that, but it's the best chance I can think of that's going to get us our gear back. And there's something else too. If Clayton gives the tape to DCI Parkin – including the part about him being bent – he can blackmail him into pulling out all the stops to get Vincenzi convicted. Plus, if Parkin can make it stick, he'd have no reason to go after *us* any more.'

OK, I was hardly expecting a round of applause, but at the very least a few nods of approval and some appreciative mutterings wouldn't have gone amiss. Admittedly, and as Scratch had said, there were no guarantees that the plan would work, although I should surely have got some credit for coming up with the idea in the first place. Instead, all I got was a unanimous round of silent frowns.

'Jesus,' I said when I couldn't stand the silence any longer. 'There's no pleasing some people, is there?'

Scratch reached out and placed a reassuring hand on my shoulder. 'Sorry, Max. I think we're all just working it through in our heads. It's quite a lot to take in really.'

'Max is right, though,' said Eleanor. 'Unless anyone has any better ideas, it might be the only hope we've got. I'm not totally convinced by any means, but it's definitely worth a shot.'

Not that I was jealous or anything, but this time there were the kind of nods and murmurings that I'd been anticipating for myself. Still, at least we all seemed to be in agreement at last.

Aunt Betty, who had been sitting quietly until then and smoking rollup after rollup, suddenly got to her feet. 'Right, everyone. I can't pretend to understand all of what you've been on about – and I missed some of it because my hearing's not what it used to be – but I gather this might be an opportune moment for some form of minor celebration.'

She stepped down inside the boat, and while she was gone, the rest of us discussed my plan in more detail. The first issue to be resolved was how to get Mitchell Clayton to listen to the tape. One suggestion was to start by simply playing it to him over the phone, but we decided that we might be more persuasive if we could arrange a face-to-face meeting and play him the tape in person. A possible sticking point, however, was how to get a high-flying entrepreneur – and gangster – like him to agree to see us at all. In all probability, the closest we'd get would be some minion or other he'd fob us off with, which would defeat the object altogether.

Various implausible strategies were floated until Aunt Betty reappeared on deck carrying a tray with three bottles of spirits and a random assortment of glasses, mugs and an empty jam jar. Whatever strategies anyone came up with from now on were likely to become increasingly absurd as the alcohol began to take its toll.

40

Alan had been getting on so well with Aunt Betty that he wasn't overly disappointed when we all agreed it would be wise for him to stay put on the boat until we were definitely off the hook for Edgar Ackroyd's murder. And as Scratch had pointed out, 'He's such a lazy bastard, he'll be happy as Larry with nothing to do but lounge around drinking Aunty's booze and smoking her dope.' Rather uncharitable, although I couldn't disagree.

He then said he didn't fancy being caught sleeping in the hearse again, and as there was little or no undertaking work to be done, he headed for home.

When Eleanor and I got back to the funeral parlour, Sanjeev was desperate to find out what we were planning to do with the tape. Alice on the other hand appeared to be totally uninterested.

'Sounds good,' said Sanjeev when we'd finished updating him, 'but how are you going to get a meeting with him? People like Mitchell Clayton aren't the sort who'd just let you walk in off the street for a bit of a chat.'

'Yeah, we haven't quite got that far yet,' I said, 'so if you've got any bright ideas, I'm all ears.'

'He's in some kind of building trade, isn't he?' said Alice, even though I'd assumed she hadn't been listening to a word we'd been saying. Clearly, she had.

'Property development,' I said, unable to hide my astonishment that she'd spoken at all.

'Same thing, innit?'

'Kind of, yes.'

'Well, there's this building site I pass every day on my way here. There's bloody great cranes and diggers all over the place. Whole site's fenced off, but there's some boards on it with Mitchell Clayton's name on 'em. "Mitchell Clayton Enterprises" or something.'

Hardly ever had I known Alice to string more than half a dozen words together at a time, so I was momentarily speechless.

'Course, if you're not interested...' she added, misinterpreting my idiotically open-mouthed stare.

'No, no,' I said. 'I'm definitely interested, only I'm not sure how that's going to help us.'

Alice took the gum she'd been chewing out of her mouth and stuck it to the underside of the reception desk. I really wish she wouldn't do that, but I knew from experience that even the mildest of rebukes would end up in a full-scale row. The only occasion when I *had* summoned up the courage to read the riot act – in a quiet, measured tone, I have to admit – was when we found two lumps of gum on the underside of a coffin as we were carrying it into the church.

'OK then,' said Alice, unwrapping another stick of chewing gum. 'Here's the thing of it, see? There's been no work done on the site for the past couple of weeks or so. Complete standstill. And from what I've heard, there's a big fucking problem with some new building regulations, and the council have put the kibosh on it. For now anyway.'

Maybe I was being dumb, but I couldn't see how the council closing down one of Clayton's development projects was going to help us get a meeting with him, and as if reading my mind, Alice filled in the blanks.

❖

Twenty minutes later, after we'd googled the relevant information, Eleanor rang Mitchell Clayton's office number.

'Mitchell Clayton Enterprises,' came a bored-sounding voice over the speaker.

'Hello. I'd like to speak to Mr Clayton, please,' said Eleanor in her posh telephone voice.

'I'll put you through to his secretary.'

There was a brief pause, then another woman came on the line and considerably more chirpy than the previous one. 'Good afternoon. How may I help you today?'

'I'd like to speak to Mr Clayton, please,' Eleanor repeated.

'I'm afraid Mr Clayton is unavailable at the moment. May I take a message?'

'Yes, of course, although it *is* rather urgent. I'm David Henderson's secretary, and he'd very much like to arrange a meeting with Mr Clayton as soon as possible.'

'And would that be David Henderson, chair of the local planning committee?'

'Correct. He has some new information about the suspension of Mr Clayton's development project which might help to circumvent the regulations and allow the work to resume. It's rather a delicate matter, however, so the meeting would have to be in person and in private.'

'I see. Well, I'll need to check Mr Clayton's availability and get back to you.'

'Certainly. I look forward to hearing from you.'

Eleanor hung up, and it was no more than a few minutes before the phone rang, and we got the result we were after.

'Would tomorrow morning at eleven suit?'

'Mr Clayton works on a Saturday, does he?'

'Of course. The whole office does. Mr Clayton insists on it.'

'Mr Henderson often comes in on a Saturday himself, but let me just check his diary,' Eleanor said and tapped a few random keys on the reception desk laptop. 'Yes, eleven tomorrow morning would be fine.'

She hung up again and high-fived me.

'That didn't take long, did it?' I said. 'The guy's obviously desperate. Not surprising, though. Must be losing money hand over fist.'

'He's going to be mega disappointed when us two walk in, isn't he?' Eleanor smirked.

'Yeah, but let's hope he doesn't go totally ballistic and chucks us out before we've had a chance to tell him why we're really there.'

'We'll have to talk quick then.'

I wasn't convinced this was a tactic that was likely to work too well, but we'd just have to wait and see how things turned out, and there wasn't much we could do about it till tomorrow.

'You fancy ordering in some lunch?' I said, aware that my stomach was starting to make some weird rumbling sounds.

Eleanor glanced at the clock on the wall. 'Sorry, I can't. Prior engagement.'

'Oh?'

'Old friend. I've been putting her off for ages, so I can't really get out of it.' She got to her feet. 'In fact, I might end up staying the night at her place, but I'll be back here in the morning in plenty of time for our meeting with Clayton.'

'OK. You wanna be careful, though. The police are still after you, remember?'

'You worry too much. I'll be fine.'

She was out of the door and onto the street before I could say any more, but it didn't stop the voice in my head having an opinion.

'For someone who's supposed to be on the cops "most wanted" list, she seems pretty bloody casual about being seen in public, don't you think?'

I did, and it wasn't the first time this had occurred to me since she'd told us that Chisholm had fingered her for the bank robbery.

41

After Eleanor had left, and with Sanjeev and Alice minding the shop, I'd gone up to the apartment and made myself a sandwich. Then, apart from making a copy of Edgar Ackroyd's tape on my phone, I'd had nothing else to do, so I picked up a book and started to read, but it was impossible to concentrate. After I'd re-read the same paragraph half a dozen times without taking any of it in, I'd put the book aside and switched on the TV. Flicking through the channels, I'd found it similarly difficult to focus on even the most mindless of programmes, and given that it was the middle of the afternoon, there'd been plenty of those to choose from.

The problem, of course, was that I couldn't get my mind to stop thinking about the meeting we'd be having with Mitchell Clayton the next day. What if he *does* go totally ballistic when he finds out he's been conned, as I'd suggested to Eleanor? He'd already have got his hopes up that his building project might be able to start up again, and we'd be bursting that bubble for him as soon as we walked through the door. Christ, the man's a big-time gangster. Never mind not giving us the chance to play him the tape, he'd more likely have us hanging upside down by our feet in some abandoned warehouse while his goons took turns to beat the shit out of us. Whatever the consequences might be, they really didn't bear thinking about. But that was the trouble. How was I supposed to *stop* thinking about them?

With my anxiety reaching cardiac arrest levels, I'd hit the Jameson's, and after a couple of generous measures, opted for an early night. The admittedly vain hope was that a few hours' oblivion would rescue my overloaded brain from its torment. Much to my amazement, however, I'd gone out like a light and slept through till about seven without a single dream involving Mitchell Clayton or being cut into pieces with a chainsaw.

But only moments after the fog of sleep had begun to clear the next morning, the terrors returned, and it was all I could do to fight back the urge to throw up.

❖

I didn't feel much like breakfast, so after a shower and a couple of strong coffees, I made my way down to the funeral parlour. Scratch and Eleanor were already there.

'I've been wondering if we should maybe think this whole plan through a bit more,' I said as soon as I was within earshot.

'A little late for cold feet,' said Eleanor. 'Everything's arranged.'

Without going into too much detail about the

potential consequences as I'd imagined them, I reiterated my fears of how Clayton might respond when he realised he'd been conned. Eleanor agreed that it was certainly a risk but one we'd have to take if we were ever to see our gear from the lockup again.

'*She's right, you know,*' said the voice in my head. '*After everything you've been through, you want to give up now? The business is about to go down the toilet and you're totally skint, remember?*'

It was a fair point, of course, and after some gentle cajoling from both Eleanor and Scratch, along with various reassurances which I didn't find reassuring at all, I decided that the old adage of discretion being the better part of valour was a luxury I really couldn't afford. And besides, if I bottled out now, I'd be letting Alan and Scratch down, and betraying their trust was something I'd never be prepared to do.

And so it was that two hours later, Eleanor and I stood looking up at a ten-storey office block that seemed to be constructed almost entirely of glass. We'd arrived deliberately early for our appointment with Clayton, so we grabbed some takeaway coffees and spent the time rehearsing what we were going to say. Over and over again until we were almost word perfect. Naturally, most of this would go out of the window as soon as we walked into Clayton's office as he wouldn't have read his part in our carefully prepared script, but at least we knew how to start.

'I presume you've got the recording ready to play on your phone,' Eleanor said, the slight tremor in her voice indicating she was almost as nervous as I was.

'All cued up and ready to go,' I said, then added, 'I suppose we ought to be too.'

The reception area on the ground floor of the office

block was spacious, sparsely furnished and gleamingly white. Having checked in at the main desk and been informed that Mitchell Clayton Enterprises was on the top floor, we stepped into one of the three lifts and hit the button.

Neither of us spoke, both staring at the little red numbers above the lift door until the last one was highlighted and we came to a halt with the faintest of bumps.

Another reception area, albeit a far smaller one, and a bored-looking receptionist, who was probably the same woman Eleanor had first spoken to when she'd phoned to make the appointment. She directed us to the end of a brightly lit corridor, and we stopped when we got to a frosted glass door with Clayton's name inscribed in fancy gold lettering. The door was half open, so we walked in to be greeted by a smiling bespectacled secretary.

I cleared my throat and summoned up the most confident "every right to be here" tone. 'Good morning. David Henderson to see Mitchell Clayton.'

We'd been more than a little concerned that Clayton's secretary would instantly clock that I wasn't David Henderson, but we needn't have worried. Either she was new on the job or Henderson had never been here before because she didn't bat an eyelid as she checked her computer screen.

'Certainly, sir,' she said. 'Mr Clayton asked me to send you straight through when you arrived.'

She gestured towards an inner door to her right, and we walked into Clayton's office without knocking.

He was sitting in an enormous leather chair behind a similarly enormous glass-topped desk and poring over a document that appeared to be several pages long.

'Be with you in a minute, David,' he said without looking up.

Even without seeing his face full-on, he was easily recognisable from the many photographs we'd seen of him online, usually presenting a cheque to some charity, accepting an award or standing proudly in front of his latest property development. Always dressed in a dark three-piece suit, his sandy-coloured hair was well groomed and he wore spectacles with a thick black frame. He was also remarkably tall and thin, and overall looked less like the head of an organised crime gang than you could possibly imagine.

He didn't bother inviting us to take a seat, so Eleanor and I stayed standing while we took in our surroundings. It was a corner office with spectacular views through both sets of floor-to-ceiling windows, and close to where the two met was a leather settee and matching chairs either side of a glass-topped coffee table. Not a painting, ornament or pot plant in sight. Minimalist to say the least.

'I hope you've got some good news for me, considering how much I pay you,' Clayton said as he turned another page of the document, and Eleanor and I gave each other a sideways glance.

Finally, he scribbled what was presumably his signature at the end of the document and looked up at us for the first time. His mouth opened, but immediately froze. Whatever he'd been about to say was no longer relevant, and instead he went with: 'Who the fuck are you two?'

42

Eleanor and I took a couple of steps towards Clayton's desk, and I spoke quickly with my phone already in my hand. 'Look, we're really sorry to have to con our way in like this, but there was no other way to get to see you in person, and it's absolutely vital you listen to this recording we got hold of.'

Even before I'd finished gabbling, Clayton had reached for the phone on his desk and yelled at his secretary to call for security.

Knowing that we probably only had a matter of seconds before the heavies arrived, Eleanor took over. 'The thing is, we have evidence that Tony Vincenzi has committed a murder. A man called Edgar Ackroyd. It's all on this recording, so if you hand that over to the police, you'd more than likely get rid of one of your biggest er... competitors for a lot of years to come.'

My hands were shaking as I started to play the recording and placed the phone onto Clayton's desk. To save time, I'd had it on Pause to skip Ackroyd's introduction, but even so, the playback had only got as far as "But let me get to the main reason I decided to make this tape" when the office door flew open. Eleanor and I spun round to see two large men in black suits and ties, each with a hand inside their jacket.

'Trouble, boss?' said the marginally shorter one.

'I don't know who these people are, but I want them out of here. Now!' Clayton barked, then added in a more measured tone, 'And you don't need to be too gentle with them either.'

I could only assume that, having given Eleanor and I the once-over, Clayton's goons had come to the conclusion that neither of us were any great threat because they removed their empty hands from inside their jackets as they bore down on us. Grabbing each of us by the arm, they marched us towards the open door, but just as we reached it, Clayton called out to them to stop.

From what I could hear, he'd reached the part in the recording where Tony Vincenzi is threatening Ackroyd with what he'd do to him if he didn't pay up the money he owed. This had apparently piqued his interest sufficiently to want to listen to the rest.

Still restrained by our well-dressed heavies, Eleanor and I stood motionless in the doorway until Clayton got to the end of the recording.

By now he was leaning forward in his chair, his elbows on the desk and steepling his fingers under his chin.

'You can let our visitors go,' he said after an excruciatingly lengthy silence, 'but wait outside till I need you.'

As instructed, the two goons released their grip on

our arms and exited the office, closing the door behind them.

Once they were out of the way, Clayton beckoned Eleanor and me to approach but raised his palm when he decided we'd come close enough.

'Interesting,' he said, tapping my phone as if to emphasise what he was talking about. 'May I ask how you came by this?'

'Rather a long story,' said Eleanor, 'and it's really not that relevant. We know you're a busy man, so perhaps we should just skip that and get to the main reason we're here.'

'Something about getting rid of one of my competitors, wasn't it?'

'Exactly. Tony Vincenzi. And with him out of the way, you'd have no problem taking over his business.'

'I wasn't aware that Mr Vincenzi was involved in property development *or* the leisure industry.'

'I suppose we had in mind your er... other line of business.'

'Oh, and what would that be?'

This was getting us nowhere. Clayton's criminal activities were pretty much common knowledge, so maybe it was time to stop beating about the bush.

'With all due respect, Mr Clayton,' I said, 'I think it's fairly well known that you're also involved in rather less legitimate businesses than property development and the leisure industry.'

'Is that so?'

Clayton narrowed his eyes at me, and I fully expected he'd be calling for his security people any second now.

Instead, he dropped the icy stare and sat back in his chair with a twisted grin. 'Utter nonsense, of course, but let's imagine for a moment that I *am* involved in some kind of illicit practices. And for argument's sake, let us also imagine that I'd like nothing more than the long term incarceration of Mr Vincenzi, thereby enabling me to "muscle in on his patch", as I believe is the term often used within the criminal underworld. With me so far?'

Eleanor and I both nodded.

'Well then,' he continued, 'what I'd really like to know before we go any further with this fictitious scenario we've created is the age old question of "What's in it for you?". To put it succinctly, you're offering me the opportunity to put Vincenzi behind bars so that I might benefit personally from his absence. Very noble of you, I'm sure, and don't think I'm ungrateful, but I find it hard to believe that you don't want something in return.'

During our detailed rehearsals, Eleanor and I had decided that she would handle this part of the conversation if we ever got this far, and when she spoke, it was as if she was reading from a script.

'We understand that you're acquainted with a man by the name of Greg Murray,' she began, but there wasn't the slightest flicker of recognition from Clayton, so she carried on. 'Well, Greg Murray was in possession of a large quantity of valuable items that he then passed on to you without receiving any payment. And since these items belong to us, we're asking that you return them – or their equivalent in cash – in exchange for the recording.'

Clayton fiddled with his pen, capping and uncapping it repeatedly while he considered Eleanor's proposition.

'I see,' he said at last. 'This is all very interesting,

although there are a number of points that spring to mind. First of all, I have no knowledge whatsoever of this Greg Murray person, and secondly – even if what you say is true – what's to stop me keeping your "valuable items" and using the recording anyway? Or are you going to tell me that the recording will self destruct if I don't do as you ask?'

He clearly found this little witticism highly amusing, but when I started to speak, he stopped smirking and held up his hand to silence me.

'But there are in fact some other matters at play here,' he said. 'And to continue in the hypothetical, if I *did* happen to be some kind of Don Corleone, as you suggest, what if I were to tell you that Tony Vincenzi is a very close friend of mine and I would no more rat him out than cut off my own bollocks? There again, I might add that the later section of the recording vis-à-vis the alleged corruptibility of a certain police officer is pure speculation and should not in any circumstances be shared with his superiors. Besides, DCI Parkin is also an acquaintance of mine, and I would hate to be deprived of his invaluable services in the future.'

'*I might be getting the wrong end of the stick here*,' said the voice in my head, '*but I'm getting the distinct impression he doesn't want to play ball. And not only that but, reading between the lines, I reckon he wouldn't be desperately happy with you if you went ahead and shopped either Vincenzi or Parkin.*'

'So that's it then, is it?' I said aloud. 'You're basically going to keep all the gear you nicked from us and that's the end of it?'

Not a big surprise, but all I got back from Clayton was a supercilious grin and, 'Anyway, as I recall you saying earlier, I'm a very busy man, so I do believe it's high time the pair of you fucked off and let me get on with rather more pressing matters.'

He slid my phone towards me across the desk with such force that I just managed to catch it before it hit the floor. Then he called out to his minders to escort us from the building.

'But before you do that,' he added as the two goons came into the office, 'make sure you search them thoroughly in case they might have been stupid enough to be wearing wires. Oh, and one more thing. It might be an idea to get their contact details in case I need to get in touch... if you catch my drift.'

This last remark was addressed to Eleanor and me, and judging by the accompanying theatrical wink, there was little doubt what he was getting at. Blabbing to the cops about anything on the tape was likely to result in some seriously grave consequences.

43

When Eleanor and I got back to the funeral parlour, I was surprised to see Scratch showing a middle-aged couple around the display coffins. Sanjeev was sitting at the reception desk, tapping away at the computer keyboard and staring intently at the screen.

'Don't tell me we've got customers,' I said.

'Third lot today already. Apparently, the Ackroyds' place is still a crime scene, so they haven't got a lot of choice.'

'Taking their time, aren't they? With the crime scene, I mean.'

Sanjeev shrugged. 'Dunno, Max. Good for us, though, isn't it?'

'I'm not sure Alice would agree, now she'll have actual work to do.'

'I didn't ask her. And you can never tell from her expression whether she's happy or not.'

'Quite.'

'Anyway, how did you get on with Mitchell Clayton?'

'Not great, I'm afraid, but we'll tell you all about it when Scratch is free. Don't really want to go over it twice.'

'Fair enough,' said Sanjeev and carried on with his typing.

I looked up at the clock on the wall. 'You had any lunch yet?'

'Too busy. I was going to nip out when I'd finished processing this coffin order, but I'll have to wait now in case I need to do the paperwork for the people Scratch is showing around.'

'Well, I'm back now, so I can take over if you like.'

Sanjeev didn't need any more persuading, and the moment he'd finished what he was working on, he was off out the door. I asked him to bring something back for me, but Eleanor said she wasn't hungry and disappeared up to the apartment.

Scratch was still doing his sales pitch, so I sat down at the reception desk and did some rummaging about on the internet to pass the time. It occurred to me that I hadn't seen or heard any news for the last couple of days so decided to use the opportunity to catch up. In particular, of course, I wanted to see what the latest was on the bank robbery and Edgar Ackroyd's murder. I was also curious to find out if there was any reason why DCI Parkin hadn't been round to pester us since his last visit the day before yesterday.

It didn't take long to hit on a bunch of articles about the robbery, and the latest – from only a couple of hours earlier – couldn't have come as more of a shock:

DEPOSIT BOX ROBBERY: POLICE STILL CLUELESS

Exactly one week since the audacious theft of cash, jewellery and other valuable items from deposit boxes at the

HMC Bank, the police are still no closer to tracking down the perpetrators. At a press conference this morning, Superintendent Jack Fothergill admitted that there were very few leads to go on.

"Whichever persons committed this crime were clearly highly professional," he said, "and despite a thorough and exhaustive examination of the scene, our forensic team found not a single fingerprint or trace of DNA that might prove useful to our investigation."

Asked whether the manager of the bank, Mr Alastair Chisholm, would be charged with aiding and abetting the robbers, the superintendent replied that he was not at liberty to comment on such aspects of an ongoing investigation.

As readers will no doubt recall, and according to reliable sources, Mr Chisholm was coerced into letting the robbers into the bank when the unscrupulous criminals held his wife and children hostage and threatened to kill them. Given such circumstances, it is hard to believe that the police would have sufficient grounds to charge him with any offence at all.

Before ending the press conference with an appeal to the public for any help identifying the robbers, Superintendent

Fothergill was reluctant to answer a question regarding the total value of the cash and other items that were stolen.

"This is extremely difficult to estimate," he said, "since part of the purpose of deposit boxes is that their contents remain private. Their owners are therefore often reluctant to provide precise details. However, it is believed that the overall value is somewhere in the region of five million pounds and probably considerably more."

I skim read the article again to convince myself that I hadn't misunderstood. But there it was in black and white. Unless the police were lying – and why would they? – Chisholm must have stuck to the original story we'd given him, and his wife must have swallowed the bullshit he'd told her about needing the money to pay off a debt.

What the hell? Eleanor had been adamant that Chisholm had confessed everything to the police, including her own involvement in the robbery. This was why she was on the run and having to keep a low profile. On the other hand, and as I'd wondered before, there'd been occasions when I'd thought she'd been a little too cavalier about the low profile bit. So, had her contact in the police got it wrong about Chisholm's confession or had she made the whole thing up?

But what possible reason could she have had for lying about it? None, as far as I could see, although it *had* given her a way to explain her disappearance after we'd suspected her of running off with the loot we'd stashed in the coffin. And even if we still hadn't trusted her, she'd been quick to point out that she had a hold over us if the cops picked her up: "Of course, I'd never tell them about you being the guys who actually *did* the robbery, but if push comes to shove…". Or words to that effect.

The timing was interesting too. The night that she'd shown up at my flat and begged me to help her hide from the police must have been soon after Greg the Fence had been conned out of all our lockup gear. Maybe that was what this was all about. Make up the Chisholm confession story to get back in with us because she needed our help to recover it. Perhaps she didn't believe she'd manage it on her own, and with five million quid at stake – the first time I'd heard any official figure – she certainly wouldn't have had any intention of missing out on her share.

'*This is bloody ridiculous*,' said the voice in my head. '*You're going round in circles here, and I don't know about you, but you're starting to fry my brain. Why don't you just head up to the apartment and see if you can get some answers out of her?*'

Good advice, although that would have to wait for now. The electronic "bing bong" sound of the funeral parlour door being opened meant that we might have yet another customer, except the three men who walked in didn't seem like they'd come to check out the coffins. Or perhaps they had. The one in front was a couple of inches on the short side and bordering on the rotund. Snappily and expensively dressed with a red carnation in the buttonhole of his suit jacket, he wore a white fedora with a black band and carried a walking stick with a heavy silver top.

'*Blimey.*' It was the voice in my head again. '*Is he*

after winning first prize in the Al Capone lookalike contest or what?'

As for the other two men, they were similarly dressed in suits and ties but minus the fedora and stick. They were also taller and slimmer, and one had an old deep scar that ran diagonally across his cheek to the corner of his mouth.

The first guy tipped his fedora at me. 'Good afternoon. I wonder if you can help me. I'm looking for a Mr Max Dempsey.'

'That would be me,' I said and got up from behind the desk.

'Excellent. Nice to meet you. I'd like to have a little chat if that's possible. Preferably in private.'

'Of course, although we don't really have anywhere that we can—'

Without waiting for me to finish my sentence, he walked over to where Scratch was still busy with the apparently very indecisive customers.

'Pardon me for the interruption,' he said, resting his hand on the edge of the coffin that they were currently examining, 'but I believe this particular model would suit your purposes extremely well. In fact, this is the exact same coffin that I chose for my own dear mother, God rest her soul.' He briefly crossed himself and gave a chuckle. 'Naturally, I don't mean the "exact same" coffin as that would have been turned into ashes long ago.'

According to the blank expressions on the faces of Scratch and both customers, they either didn't get the joke or didn't find it at all funny.

'Splendid,' said Fedora Man and clapped his hands together. 'I think you'll find you've made the perfect choice, but if you'd be so kind as to return at another

233

time to complete the necessary documentation and payment, my men will show you out.'

He waved a hand in the vague direction of his two sidekicks by the main door, and when Scratch started to object, he put a finger to his lips, clearly indicating that he wasn't about to be argued with.

For their part, the two customers made their way between the display coffins towards the door, looking confused if not somewhat shocked.

'Sorry about this,' I said, 'but there's been a rather serious emergency, so I'm afraid we've had to evacuate the building immediately. However, if you'd care to come back whenever might be convenient, I'm sure we'll be able to assist you in any way you wish.'

Even though I was quite pleased with my quick-thinking excuse, the male customer's eye-rolling shake of the head meant that we'd very probably just lost some much needed business. But rather more importantly right now was who this guy in the fedora was. I had a definite inkling, partly from his appearance and the faintest trace of an Italian accent, that we were very soon going to be up to our eyebrows in some very deep and very dangerous shit.

44

After Scratch's customers had been ushered out onto the street, one of the guys with Fedora Man locked the door and flipped the Open sign to Closed.

'What are you still doing here?' said Fedora Man when Scratch came to join me at the reception desk.

'He works here,' I said. 'He's one of my partners.'

Fedora Man gave a faint sigh, took off his hat and placed it carefully on top of the desk, revealing more of his slightly round face, thinning dark hair and thick black eyebrows. He then removed his calfskin leather gloves and used them to flick away any perceived dust from one of the chairs on the customer side of the desk. Satisfied, he sat down, his legs apart with the tip of his walking stick planted between his feet and his hands clasped over the heavy silver top.

'First of all,' he said with a smile that was a long way short of ingratiating, 'please allow me to introduce myself. I am Tony Vincenzi – sometimes referred to as Tony "Psycho" Vincenzi, although this is not a sobriquet I approve of and indeed find it highly inappropriate and utterly disrespectful. Anyway, to get to the point, I trust you'll forgive me for the intrusion, but there's a rather urgent matter I need to discuss with you concerning some disturbing information that has recently been brought to my attention.'

He paused for a moment, presumably expecting some kind of reaction, but all I could manage was 'I see', even though I knew exactly why he was here and had a pretty good idea what was coming next.

'You see,' he went on, 'I had a telephone call earlier today from my very good friend Mr Mitchell Clayton, and he conveyed to me some extremely alarming news regarding a tape recording that I understand to be in your possession. A recording that purports to implicate me – entirely without foundation, I might add – in the tragic murder of a certain Mr Edgar Ackroyd.'

Another pause, during which Vincenzi continued to eyeball me with his unconvincing smile, and my guts did seven kinds of somersault.

At the same time, the voice in my head went into panic overload. *'Jesus, Max, just give him the damn tape before he starts in with the dismemberment threats – or worse.'*

With no reason to hesitate, I began to open the desk drawer that the mini cassette player and tape were in. But the instant I did so, both of Vincenzi's men stepped forward with semi-automatics aimed directly at my head.

'Stop right there!' shouted the one with the scar.

My hand froze with the drawer open by no more than an inch. 'I'm getting the tape. It's what you want, isn't it?'

'Nice and easy then,' said the one without the scar.

Their guns still trained on me, I very slowly took the cassette player our of the drawer and laid it on top of the desk.

Vincenzi raised a thick black eyebrow. 'It's been a while since I saw one of those. Do I take it the tape is inside?'

'It is, yes.'

'Then perhaps you'd be good enough to let me hear it.'

I rewound the tape to the beginning and hit the Play button.

The whole time the tape was playing, Vincenzi had his eyes closed and smiled contentedly as if he was listening to a piece of mellow classical music.

'How fascinating,' he said when the tape reached the end, and he opened his eyes, but the smile remained. 'So thoughtful of Clayton to tip me off about its existence. Wouldn't do at all for this to fall into the wrong hands, would it?'

This was quite obviously a rhetorical question, but I answered it anyway. 'No, I don't suppose it would.'

Vincenzi's smile morphed into a hint of a frown. 'There's something that rather puzzles me, however, because Clayton was a tad parsimonious with the details, so perhaps you might enlighten me. Why did you believe that this recording would be of interest to *him*? Given that it's myself who is incriminated for Edgar Ackroyd's murder, surely you would have been better advised to offer it to me. It's a thoroughly distasteful practice, I know, but why not try to blackmail me in exchange for the tape?'

Scarface and his partner both sniggered at this. Attempting to blackmail a big deal crime boss like

Tony "Psycho" Vincenzi would be the act of a lunatic with a death wish or at least someone who'd decided they no longer had a need for all of their limbs.

'*Yeah, I wouldn't go for that answer if I were you,*' said the voice in my head, but I was struggling to come up with something that was reasonably plausible and within sniffing distance of the truth that wouldn't necessarily get me killed or maimed.

'Well, it's funny you should ask that,' I said.

'*Oh, that's a great start.*'

Vincenzi did the eyebrow thing again – with the other one this time. 'Funny?'

'Er, no, not funny. *Interesting* is what I meant.'

'How so?'

'Because, um…'

Shit, there was no point lying to the guy. He'd only end up beating the truth out of me if I did, so I told him how we'd thought Clayton could use the tape to get rid of him and take over his business.

'And why would you want to do that? Why do Mitchell Clayton such a favour? He a friend of yours, or do you have some grudge against me personally?'

'God, no. I hardly knew who either of you were until a few days ago.'

'So, why?'

'The idea was that we could do a trade. We'd give him the tape in exchange for… something he has that belongs to us.'

'Which is?'

I took a deep breath. I'd got this far, and I didn't see I had a lot of choice but to tell him the rest.

'The HMC Bank robbery? That was *you*?' said Vincenzi when I'd finished, and he seemed to find this highly amusing.

'Me and my two… associates,' I said, casting a thumb at Scratch, who was standing at my shoulder.

Vincenzi's amusement escalated into a roar of laughter. 'I don't believe it. A bunch of undertakers pulling off a heist like that? How utterly wonderful. I really must congratulate you.'

Scratch and I muttered a half-hearted 'Thank you', only because it appeared to be expected, but the voice in my head issued a largely redundant warning.

'Don't be fooled, Max. He's laughing now, but don't imagine he's going to just forget about your attempt to get him done for murder.'

After he'd got his laughter under control, Vincenzi put on his serious face. 'So, if you'll allow me to summarise, Mitchell Clayton has misappropriated the proceeds of your bank robbery due to the incompetence of a fence who turned out to be nothing of the sort. Not unnaturally, you have requested these proceeds to be returned to you, but Mr Clayton refused. However, as part of this negotiation, you provided him with the opportunity to put me behind bars for a very long period indeed. Correct so far?'

I nodded, and Vincenzi leaned forward from the waist. 'Now, this may come as something of a shock to you, or very possibly not, but any act that has the potential to deprive me of my freedom is an act that I have to take extremely seriously and cannot therefore be allowed to go unpunished. As I hope you'll understand, some form of physical retribution is widely acknowledged in my particular field as a *sine qua non* in such circumstances, and I would urge you not to take it too personally.'

I'd been standing ever since Vincenzi and his men had stepped through the door, and I clutched at the edge of the desktop to stop me from falling. It was as if I was in the dock in court and the judge had just pronounced the death penalty.

'Good. That's settled then,' said Vincenzi, getting to his feet and slipping on his calfskin gloves. 'So, without further ado, I would suggest that you and your associate accompany my two chaps to a certain location where—'

'Max, do you know where I might find the—'

Eleanor had suddenly appeared at the bottom of the apartment stairs, but stopped dead in her tracks when she spotted our little group by the reception desk. She came striding over to us, all smiles, and beamed at Vincenzi. 'Well, hello, Leonardo. What on earth are you doing here?'

45

As Eleanor approached the reception desk, Tony Vincenzi's mouth hung open, and his face turned a bright crimson before losing its colour altogether. His reaction and the fact that she'd called him Leonardo rather than Tony or even Mr Vincenzi were all the clues I needed. Surely, he must be yet another of Eleanor's seemingly endless stream of visitors to her S&M dungeon.

'Christ, is there anybody she doesn't have as a client?' said the voice in my head.

Vincenzi's pompous self-assurance vanished in an instant, and he muttered a barely audible greeting.

'Not here because of a bereavement, I hope,' said Eleanor, her faint smile conveying that she couldn't have cared less if he was or not.

'Fortunately not,' said Vincenzi as he visibly fought to regain his composure.

'This is Mr Tony Vincenzi,' I said, seizing the opportunity to force the issue but leaving out the "Psycho" part.

If Eleanor had been surprised, she didn't show it. 'Is that right? Sorry, I always thought your name was Leonardo. Still, we all make mistakes, don't we?'

She gave him a sly wink, which was enough to bring the colour back to his cheeks. Not with embarrassment this time but with rising anger. He yelled at his two men to get the hell out and wait for him in the car, and once they had gone, he glowered menacingly at Eleanor.

'What the fuck are you trying to do to me? Our... arrangement was supposed to be private and confidential. What do you think that would do to my reputation if it ever got out?'

Eleanor paused for a moment as if she was trying to recall what she'd actually said. 'I'm not sure I mentioned anything untoward, did I? Nothing about you being a regular client at my dungeon, for instance, or your rather unusual predilections?'

If this had been a cartoon, there would have been steam blasting out of Vincenzi's ears, and he shot me and Scratch a threatening glare.

'Oh, don't worry about these two,' said Eleanor. 'We're partners, you see, and we know all about discretion – unless of course...'

She let the sentence hang, and Vincenzi was quick to jump in. 'Unless of course *what*?'

'Well, I haven't been party to the conversation you've been having, but if I had to guess, I'd say it had something to do with a certain tape recording that clearly implicates you in a rather nasty murder.'

Vincenzi didn't respond, and I was beginning to get the impression that the tables were about to be turned.

'That's right,' I said. 'Apparently, because Mitchell Clayton is a friend of Mr Vincenzi, he told him about the recording, and he'd like us to hand it over. He also wanted to know why we gave it to Clayton instead of going to him direct and trying to blackmail him.'

'Ooh, blackmail,' said Eleanor. 'Rather an unpleasant business that, wouldn't you say, Leonardo? Oh, sorry, I mean Tony.'

The message was clear from both her tone and the look she gave him, and Vincenzi slumped back down onto his chair, exhaling long and loud like a punctured football.

'Very well,' he said at last after he'd managed to gather his thoughts. 'I shall forego my earlier intention to inflict physical harm on Mr Dempsey and his colleague as an act of vengeance, and as long as he hands over or destroys every copy of the recording he has, that should be an end to it.'

'Oh, I think you can do much better than that, Tony.'

'What do you mean?'

'Well, since we've heard that you and Mitchell Clayton are so chummy with each other, we'd really appreciate it if you could get him to return all the proceeds of the bank robbery that he stole from us.'

Again, Vincenzi took his time before responding. 'Not as easy as you might imagine, but we'll get to that later. There's a couple of things I want to clear up first.'

As long as he *did* get to it at some point, there was little reason to object, but he was obviously in no hurry to start. From the inside pocket of his jacket he produced a fat cigar and sniffed it approvingly along its length before cutting the tip off with some fancy gadget he took from another pocket. Several more seconds passed while he lit the end with a gold lighter and puffed away until he was fully satisfied that the cigar was drawing properly. Only then was he ready to speak, and I decided it would be unwise to interrupt by bringing up the no smoking policy.

'Honour amongst thieves,' he began and blew a series of near perfect smoke rings into the air above his head. 'An admirable sentiment indeed, although in the words of the incomparable William Shakespeare, it is often "more honoured in the breach than the observance". And whereas my good friend Mitchell Clayton has proved himself to be a shining example by alerting me to the existence of the incriminating recording, I myself am infinitely less scrupulous in that regard. That is to say, and if I may resort to the vernacular for a moment, I would have no hesitation whatsoever in dropping my fellow criminals in the shit if I might gain some advantage by it.'

'*Bloody hell,*' said the voice. '*Talk about verbal diarrhoea. When's he gonna stop waffling and get to the good part?*'

'You see,' Vincenzi continued, 'I have been wanting to take over Mitchell Clayton's business for quite some while now, and such an aspiration has been brought to a head more recently as I have also developed a desire to exact a severe revenge upon him for having two of my best men tortured and killed. Oh, and by the by, he's blissfully unaware that I know for a fact that it was he who was the guilty party or he would never have come to my aid vis-à-vis the potential threat to my liberty.'

With a smirk worthy of a Victorian pantomime villain, he leaned forward across the desk and gave the cassette player a gentle tap with his finger.

'But to return to my theme of honour among

thieves,' he said, sitting back in his chair and puffing away on his cigar, 'by far the most unbreakable cardinal rule is "Thou shalt not grass", or more specifically, *omerta*. However, despite Mr Ackroyd's insinuation on the recording, it wasn't I who killed him. It was Mitchell Clayton – or more likely one of his thugs. Clayton has a habit of ensuring that he cannot be directly linked to any criminal act.'

'No disrespect, Mr Vincenzi,' I said, 'but why would—'

'I'll tell you, shall I?' he interrupted, presumably able to read my mind. 'Well, let's clear up the issue of my innocence first. The tape doesn't lie. I *did* threaten Ackroyd, but what use would it have been to me if he was dead and hence in no position to pay me the money he owed me? I knew he'd be good for it eventually, but I felt that a little nudge wouldn't go amiss. It's almost always worked with others who've been somewhat tardy with settling their debts. Of course, there has been the odd occasion when measures have had to be taken that are rather more drastic than verbal threats, although I shan't bore you with the details.'

The rest of us waited in silence while he tilted his head back and concentrated on blowing a few more smoke rings at the ceiling.

'Which brings me to the next important matter of concern,' he said when he was ready to continue. 'Why did Mitchell Clayton murder Edgar Ackroyd?'

'*God, he's beginning to sound like Hercule Poirot now,*' said the voice. '*And ze name of ze murderer iz… Come to think of it, isn't there one of his called "Who Killed Roger Ackroyd?" or somesuch?*'

Because of the voice distracting me, I missed the

next part of what Vincenzi was saying, but it was easy enough to pick up the gist. What it boiled down to was Mitchell Clayton had been hassling Ackroyd for months to sell him his funeral parlour. Not that he wanted to get into the undertaker business. What he *did* want was to pull the whole place down and build one of his chain of restaurants on the site as it was in a prime location with minimal competition. Even though Clayton kept upping his bid, Ackroyd had refused to budge.

'So what did Clayton do?' said Vincenzi with one of his many rhetorical questions. 'He went behind Ackroyd's back and did a deal with the two sons. Twins, aren't they? Ronnie and Reggie?'

For a change, these weren't rhetorical questions, so Scratch corrected him. 'Ray and Roy.'

'Ray and Roy, yes, and the deal was that the sons would sell the funeral parlour the moment they inherited the business. I suppose there's always the possibility that it was they themselves who murdered their old man, although for the reason I explained earlier, it would be infinitely preferable for my purposes if Clayton were found to be the guilty party.'

'But is there any proof that any of them killed Ackroyd?' I said.

'Ah, proof,' said Vincenzi, studying the glowing tip of his cigar. 'I don't think we need worry too much on that score. You'll no doubt recall from the recording that Detective Chief Inspector Parkin is by no means averse to accepting financial rewards for services rendered, and he won't want that part of the tape being brought to the attention of his superiors. And although Mitchell Clayton is certainly one of his major benefactors in that regard, I myself pay him a very considerable amount more. Therefore, I believe that we can rely on DCI Parkin to… do the right thing, as it were.'

'Frame Clayton, you mean?'

'Given that you and your colleagues are prime suspects yourselves, Mr Dempsey, I really don't think you can afford moral scruples at this stage, do you? And besides, whether he killed Ackroyd or not, the man deserves to do time for all of the other murders he has most definitely ordered over the years.'

A particular phrase about pots and kettles popped into my mind, but Vincenzi was right. From what we knew of him, Mitchell Clayton was fully deserving of a few years behind bars, and there was the additional advantage that Scratch, Alan and I wouldn't be joining him any time soon. Maybe for the bank robbery but at least not for murder.

'So if there's nothing else to discuss, I have important work to do,' said Vincenzi and eased himself up from his chair with the aid of his stick. As he did so, he picked up the mini cassette player from the desk and slipped it into his pocket. 'And as I requested earlier, I trust you will dispose of any copies of the recording you might have in your possession?'

'Of course,' said Eleanor, 'but there is one more thing before you go.'

'Oh?'

'What about the loot that Clayton stole from us?'

'Ah yes. Well, once he's out of the way, I should have little difficulty in gaining access to *all* of his assets. And as for the items that belong to you, I'd say that a fifty per cent split would be fair, wouldn't you?' Without waiting for an answer, he was almost at the door when he turned and addressed Eleanor directly.

'And I hope this goes without saying, but such an offer is entirely contingent on your absolute discretion in relation to any of our previous… encounters.'

'Previous encounters?' Eleanor repeated with an overly exaggerated wink. 'But surely today was the first time we'd ever met.'

Vincenzi nodded his satisfaction, then briefly tipped his hat and was gone.

46

There was a collective sigh of relief as soon as Vincenzi was out of the way, and Scratch, Eleanor and I all collapsed onto the nearest chairs.

Scratch was the first to speak. 'Bloody hell, that was a bit of a shock.'

'Turned out quite well in the end, though, didn't it?' said Eleanor.

'Thanks to you, yeah. If you hadn't shown up when you did, Max and I were about to be dragged off somewhere to have God knows what done to us.' Then he added a thought that had already occurred to me. 'Is there anybody round here that *isn't* a client of yours?'

'What can I say?' said Eleanor with more than a touch of pride. 'I ran a very successful business, that's all.'

'For weirdos.'

'Call them what you like, but we all have our little peccadilloes.'

'Our what?'

Before Eleanor had a chance to explain, I decided to inject what I considered to be a rather more pertinent aspect of our encounter with Vincenzi. 'Can we trust him, though? I mean, the guy's a gangster with Al Capone delusions. I'm not sure I believe even half of what he says.'

'I dunno,' said Scratch. 'Yeah, he's a dodgy customer all right, but what have we got to lose? Doesn't really matter what he does about Clayton or Parkin. They're both as bent as he is. But if he can get at least *some* of our gear back and gets us off the murder charge, that's fine by me.'

'A double whammy, in fact,' said Eleanor.

This was the first opportunity I'd had to talk to Eleanor about what I'd seen in the news just before Vincenzi descended on us, so I went for it. 'Oh, and by the way, from what I've heard, our friend the bank manager, Mr Chisholm, has no more blabbed to the cops than I have.'

Scratch's jaw dropped. 'You're kidding. Where'd you get that from?'

'Saw it online just before Vincenzi arrived. According to what I read, the police still don't have any leads, and it seems Chisholm's stuck with the original story we gave him.'

'But that's crazy,' said Eleanor, her face suddenly pale. 'That's not what I was told. My contact was insistent that Chisholm had confessed to everything. That's why I've had to keep a low profile ever since.'

'Not as low as you might have done,' I said.

She rounded on me, her pale green eyes blazing with fury. 'What's that supposed to mean?'

'Only that you've struck me as being a bit too casual at times. Certainly too casual for someone

250

who's supposed to be on the run from the cops.'

'Supposed to be? I had a tipoff, and I didn't have any reason to doubt it. And OK, maybe I haven't always been as careful as I should have been, but sometimes that was unavoidable.'

'You think?'

'Listen, Max, I don't know what this is all about, but if you're accusing me of lying, I'll tell you right now that—'

'Or perhaps your contact was lying,' said Scratch, possibly deciding to play peacemaker before the escalating row got even more out of hand. 'Either that or they got the wrong end of the stick somehow.'

Eleanor's tone softened a touch. 'Could be, Scratch, but I don't know why he'd lie to me. He's been pretty reliable in the past. So, yeah, it's quite likely he just got it wrong.'

'And whichever way you look at it,' said Scratch, warming to his role as peacemaker, 'if Chisholm really hasn't ratted you out, that puts the rest of us in the clear as well – for now anyway.'

'There's something else too,' said Eleanor. 'If the cops aren't after me, I can go wherever the hell I like, so that's exactly what I'm gonna do.'

'Where you going?' I asked as she stomped off towards the door.

'What do you care?' she snapped and would very probably have slammed it behind her if Sanjeev hadn't turned up at the same moment.

'Not a happy bunny, that one,' he said, depositing a carrier bag of pre-packed sandwiches on top of the desk. 'What's been going on?'

'Quite a lot,' I said, and filled him in on the more essential details of Vincenzi's visit and the dust-up I'd had with Eleanor.

'Just another normal day at the office then,' he said when I'd finished, and unwrapped one of the sandwiches from the carrier bag. 'Seriously though, most of that's good news, isn't it?'

I guessed it was, although the part about Eleanor having had to go on the run from the police was disturbing to say the least. We'd had good reason to believe she'd been lying about the gear we'd hidden in the coffin and the break-in at the lockup, and now this. Whatever trust we'd placed in her when she first came up with the bank robbery plan had been chipped away at, almost to the point of evaporating completely. But what the hell was she up to?

And as for Vincenzi, we'd just have to wait and see if he did everything he'd promised or he'd taken us for a bunch of mugs and all of it was bullshit.

I grabbed a sandwich from the carrier bag on the desk before Sanjeev and Scratch had managed to scoff the lot.

47

There wasn't a lot we could do after Tony Vincenzi's visit except wait for news, and two days went by before we heard anything from him, although what we heard wasn't at all what we'd expected.

Well, I say there hadn't been a lot to do, but we'd been busier than ever at the funeral parlour, mainly due to the fact that we were the only remaining option in the area. Even though the Ackroyds' funeral parlour was no longer an active crime scene, Ray and Roy still hadn't re-opened. This could have been because they were a pair of lazy bastards, or more likely because they were intending to go ahead with selling to Mitchell Clayton, so what would have been the point?

We hadn't seen or heard from Eleanor since she'd stormed out after the row about the Chisholm news. Where she'd got to or what she was up to was anyone's guess, but I have to say I was glad to get the flat back to myself for a change. And even though she may well have lied about Chisholm spilling the beans to the cops, if the police weren't after her any more, she wouldn't have had any need to put us in the frame for the bank robbery. Every cloud and all that.

As for Alan, we'd obviously been in regular phone contact to keep him updated with everything that had been happening, but we'd decided it wasn't safe for him to come out of hiding until Vincenzi had had his quiet word with DCI Parkin. Alan hadn't been too happy about that, and when Scratch had somewhat surprisingly admitted he was actually missing the "malingering little twat", we went to visit him on Aunt Betty's narrowboat.

It was mid morning when we'd got there, and Aunt Betty and Alan were already both pissed. And if the strong aroma of dope smoke was anything to go by, they'd also been making quite a dent in Betty's seemingly endless supply of weed. When she'd disappeared down inside the boat to fetch another bottle, Scratch had asked Alan why he was so hacked off about having to stay there.

'You've got as much booze and ganja you could ever have wished for and sod all work to do. I'd have thought that would be your idea of heaven.'

'Yeah, I know,' Alan had said, 'and don't get me wrong. Your aunty's an absolute diamond, and I love her to bits, but if I stay here much longer, this kinda lifestyle's gonna kill me.'

'You could always say no, I suppose.'

'Come off it, Scratch. You know what's she's like better than any of us. Turning down a drink or a spliff when she offers it – which is pretty damn often – is never an option. I learnt that very early on when she went all teary-eyed and started on about not having many pleasures left in life and how great it was to have someone to share them with.'

It was at that point that Aunt Betty had re-emerged from inside the narrowboat clutching an almost full bottle of green liquid.

'Right then,' she'd said. 'Who's for a drop of absinthe?'

Following Alan's advice, Scratch and I hadn't felt able to refuse, but after one glass we made our genuine excuses that we were needed back at the funeral parlour because of the sudden upturn in new business. And as we left, Alan had pleaded with us to let him know as soon as there was any news from Vincenzi.

In fact, this had come sooner than we could have predicted since our arrival back at the funeral parlour was when we got the unexpected news that I mentioned earlier.

Tony Vincenzi was sitting behind the reception desk, smoking one of his fat cigars while his two minders hovered nearby.

'There's been a development of the not especially fortuitous kind,' he said before we'd even closed the door behind us. 'Our mutual acquaintance Detective Chief Inspector Parkin is no more.'

'No more what?' I said, although I had little doubt what he meant. I guess it was the shock that made me hesitate to believe it.

'As in no more living. Dead.'

'Dead? Jesus, how did that happen?'

In between frequent puffs on his cigar, Vincenzi explained that he'd contacted Parkin and "persuaded" him to stitch Mitchell Clayton up for Edgar Ackroyd's murder. But instead of that, the slimy little bastard had gone straight to Clayton's office and told him everything. It was no great surprise that Clayton had gone totally apeshit, but that wasn't the end of it. When Parkin had said he could get him off the hook if he bunged him double what Vincenzi was paying him, he'd lost it completely. And bearing in mind that this took place in Clayton's legitimate place of work, there were plenty of witnesses who'd seen him chase Parkin down the corridor with the cricket bat he kept in his office and smash it repeatedly over the DCI's head until his face was almost unrecognisable.

'So much for Clayton always making sure he could never be directly linked to any of the crimes he was actually responsible for,' Vincenzi added through a haze of cigar smoke. 'And seeing that all these witnesses were legitimate, honest employees rather than his hired thugs, none of them were slow in coming forward when the cops arrived. For the first time in years of trying, they finally had Mitchell Clayton bang to rights, as I believe the expression goes. Not quite how I'd planned to get him out of the way, although a lengthy spell behind bars is definitely on the cards, so all's well that ends well, I guess.'

Vincenzi sat back in his chair and grinned the grin of the eminently self-satisfied.

Scratch and I remained silent for several seconds as we both began to get our heads round this latest bombshell. No wonder that Vincenzi was happy about the way things had turned out. With Mitchell Clayton gone, he'd have little problem taking over his business, which had always been his intention, but where did that leave us? OK, maybe he'd stick to his promise and we'd get at least some of the gear back from the bank robbery, but we were still left with Edgar Ackroyd's murder hanging over our heads. Getting Clayton done for that was a big part of the original plan, but with Parkin dead, that was presumably out of the window now. And just because Parkin was off the scene, it didn't mean the police were simply going to drop the investigation. Obviously not. This was a murder that they'd be desperately keen to solve, so all that would happen is there'd be a different cop taking over the case.

'*And don't forget the bank robbery*,' said the voice in my head. '*There's no way you're in the clear for that either.*'

I hadn't forgotten, of course, and our only ray of hope was if Vincenzi came good with our loot. In the article I'd read, the police had estimated the total haul from the robbery to be about five million quid. If that was true, and after Vincenzi had taken his fifty per cent, that left two and a half million to share between Scratch, Alan, Eleanor and me. We'd agreed from the beginning that Eleanor would get half of whatever we got, which left the rest of us with a smidge over four hundred grand each. Sanjeev and Alice deserved a decent cut, for sure, but would Scratch, Alan and I have enough to do a runner to some country with no UK extradition treaty and start a new life? Probably. But not as bloody undertakers.

Scratch was maybe of a similar mind because it was at that point in my pondering that he asked Vincenzi when he might be able to get back what Clayton owed us.

He blew a few smoke rings while he considered the question. 'Well, naturally there are a few matters to deal with before I can make that happen, but for the sake of argument, let's say…' He took another heavy drag on his cigar. 'Two to three weeks?'

'Not before that?' I said, aware that if we were

going to do a runner, the sooner was most certainly the better.

Vincenzi pushed back his chair and got to his feet. 'I could write you a cheque right now if you'd prefer.'

Even though he made a show of reaching inside his jacket, the wry smile made it clear he was joking. I almost took it as a compliment that he didn't think we were complete idiots.

'No, that's OK,' I said, and opened the door for him.

'I'll be in touch,' he said, and his two minders trailed after him and out onto the street.

'You think we can trust him?' Scratch said after they'd gone.

'Christ knows,' I said, 'but we've still got Eleanor's threat of blackmail which might help to persuade him.'

'Wherever the fuck *she* is.'

'Quite.'

48

'Jesus Christ, tell me this isn't gonna be an open coffin job,' said Alice. 'I mean, I'm one of the best there is at what I do, but I'm not a bloody miracle worker.'

She and I were down in the mortuary and standing over the body on one of the cadaver tables. Mitchell Clayton had certainly gone to town hitting quite a few sixes on DCI Parkin's head with a cricket bat. If I hadn't known who it was, I'd never have recognised him.

There was a particular irony that it was us who'd been tasked with carrying out his funeral arrangements, but I suppose it wasn't unexpected, given that the Ackroyds weren't in the game any more.

As in the case of all murders, there'd been a mandatory autopsy, even though the cause of death was pretty obvious to the average layperson. These things usually took a while, but since Parkin was a cop, he'd been swiftly moved to the top of the list, and the autopsy had been completed in record time.

'No, I shouldn't think it'll be an open coffin,' I said to Alice. 'But just do whatever you can, yeah?'

She snorted and lit a cigarette. 'OK, but I'll tell you now. He's still only gonna end up lookin' like Frankenstein's much uglier brother. Mind you, that's not a million miles from how he was when he was alive.'

A touch unfair, perhaps, but I wasn't about to argue with her, and I also wasn't going to point out that what she really meant was Frankenstein's *monster*. Nor would I have had the chance, because at that same moment, Sanjeev called to me from the top of the mortuary steps.

'Max. Somebody to see you up here.'

'Who is it?'

'Didn't say.'

I assumed it was one of our many recent customers who wanted my personal attention, so I didn't hurry on my way up the steps.

There were two women waiting at the top. One was familiar. Parkin's sidekick, DS Hibbert. The other was new to me. Mid to late forties, she had blond hair tied back in a ponytail and wore a pale grey jacket over a matching blouse that was buttoned up to the neck.

'Max Dempsey?' she said with one of those fake have-a-nice-day smiles like she was about to try and sell me something.

Without waiting for an answer, she thrust out a hand that I politely shook before she withdrew it almost instantly as if fearing some kind of contamination.

'Allow me to introduce myself,' she said. 'I'm Detective Chief Inspector Paula Montague, and I believe you already know Detective Sergeant Hibbert?'

It was framed as a question, and although it didn't seem to require an answer, I nodded anyway.

'I'm sure you're aware of DCI Parkin's recent tragic passing?'

Was this another question? 'Yes,' I said. 'He's down below on one of the cadaver tables as we speak.'

'Indeed,' said the DCI, a hint of surprise filtering through the smile. 'Well, to put you in the picture, I've been appointed to take over DCI Parkin's caseload, which happens to include the murder of a Mr… er…'

'Edgar Ackroyd,' said DS Hibbert.

Montague clicked her fingers. 'Edgar Ackroyd. Precisely.' Then she lowered her voice to not much more than a whisper. 'Not too good with names, I'm afraid. Bit of a disadvantage in my line of work, but we muddle by, don't we, Hibbert?'

'Yes, ma'am,' said the detective sergeant, but not with any great conviction.

'As you might expect,' Montague went on, her volume back up to a normal level, 'I have been attempting to familiarise myself with the facts of the case in as much detail as possible, even though I have had only a limited amount of time since DCI Parkin's unfortunate demise. I have also been hampered by the rather sketchy notes that he left behind regarding the progress of his investigation, but DS Hibbert's assistance in filling in some of the gaps has been invaluable.'

'*God almighty*,' said the voice in my head. '*Here's another one who likes to waffle. Is she ever going to get to the point?*'

In many ways, though, I was almost glad that the

261

DCI was delaying what I was beginning to believe was the inevitable punchline. She'd found something that Parkin had missed, and "getting to the point" meant charging me or Alan or Scratch with Ackroyd's murder, or maybe all three of us. But how she could possibly have come to that conclusion was a complete mystery. We were all innocent, so what evidence did she think she'd unearthed that told her we weren't? Or perhaps she was as bent as Parkin and planted some.

'And from what I have been able to ascertain,' Montague was saying, 'it appears that DCI Parkin was convinced that you or one of your associates – and primarily the chap with the neck brace – were the party, or parties, who were directly responsible for Mr Ackroyd's murder.'

'*OK, here we go then,*' said the voice, and I had to send an urgent message to my knees not to buckle.

DCI Montague's smile had hardly slipped during her entire monologue, and I now found it more irritating than ever coming from somebody who was just about to read me my rights.

'Judging from what there were of his notes, and from what DS Hibbert has informed me, it was clear that DCI Parkin was struggling to find any hard evidence to link you to the murder, and a particular stumbling block was the CCTV footage from the Ackroyds' funeral parlour. Or rather, it was the *absence* of any footage of the area where the murder took place. Indeed, this was one observation in his notes that he clearly wished to emphasise. Naturally, I devoted a good deal of the time I had available to study everything that the cameras had captured, but there was one section of the footage that got my attention almost immediately. The section that showed the actual murder being committed.'

I don't know if Montague paused for effect or simply to get her breath back, but either way, it wasn't quite long enough for me to figure out all the implications before she began to join up all the dots.

'Of the two persons involved, the first came up from behind Mr Ackroyd and hit him over the head with a cremation urn. The blow was not sufficient to render the victim unconscious, but he was obviously stunned, and as he staggered forward, the second person grabbed him by the shoulder and stabbed him several times in the chest and abdomen with what appeared to be a large kitchen knife.'

'Bloody hell,' I said. 'So who—'

'Who were the guilty parties?' said Montague, finishing my question, although not in the exact words I would have used. 'Well, ordinarily I wouldn't be at liberty to divulge such information as this is an ongoing investigation. However, since their identities will be made public at a press conference in a couple of hours or so, I see no harm in telling you that it was the victim's own sons, Ray and Roy Ackroyd. Having been shown the CCTV footage, they had little option but to confess, and in so doing, were quick to explain that they were paid handsomely by a Mr Mitchell Clayton to carry out the murder.'

'Really not very bright those Ackroyd twins, are they?' said the voice in my head. *'Anyone with half a brain would have destroyed the CCTV evidence, but not those two dickheads.'*

'Furthermore,' the DCI continued, 'we have been led to understand that Clayton had already done a deal with Ray and Roy to buy the Ackroyds' funeral parlour once their father was "out of the way".'

263

She did that air quotes thing with her fingers, which normally makes me cringe, but on this occasion I couldn't have given a toss. The point was that Scratch, Alan and I were finally in the clear for Edgar Ackroyd's murder, which was then confirmed by DCI Montague herself.

'Anyway, once I had discovered the truth, I decided to come and apologise personally for the trauma you must have suffered as a result of DCI Parkin's unforgivable actions. And I have to say that alarm bells should have been raised when he steadfastly refused to let anyone else view the footage, and that included his colleague DS Hibbert here.'

Hibbert opened her mouth to speak, but her boss was having none of it.

'As for Parkin's motives, it is our belief that he had been accepting bribes from a number of sources for quite some time, with Mitchell Clayton being one of his most generous benefactors. If Parkin had done his job, Ray and Roy Ackroyd would have been arrested very early on, and Clayton – correctly as it turned out – would have been afraid that they would waste little time in naming him as ultimately responsible for the murder.'

'Yes, that would make sense,' I said, suppressing the urge to punch the air in celebration. That would have to wait.

Montague thrust out her hand for another cursory handshake. 'Still, no hard feelings, I trust?'

'*You know that's a warning not to try and sue the cops for harassment or whatever, don't you?*' said the voice. '*Not that you'd have much of a leg to stand on, though.*'

'Not at all,' I said. 'I'm just grateful to you for

letting me know.'

Her fixed smile broadened. 'Least I could do, Mr Dempsey. But I'd best be making tracks. As I mentioned earlier, I have a press conference to prepare for. Then there's the rest of DCI Parkin's caseload to deal with, not to mention the so far unsolved mystery of the deposit box bank robbery that you've no doubt heard of. No rest for the wicked, eh?'

Shit, was that a wink that went with that last remark, or was I just being paranoid? We were off the murder charge at last, but maybe it was a bit too soon to start the celebrations.

49

OK, we did have a celebration after all. Nothing major, although as Alan had said when we'd brought him back from Aunt Betty's narrowboat, 'Fuck's sake, Max. Not only can I finally come out of hiding, but we've just got off a murder charge. Sure, we've still got the bank robbery hanging over us, and it sounds like Parkin's replacement might be a lot more on the ball than he was, but let's forget about all that for now and sink a few bevvies.'

And that's exactly what we did, although not so excessive that we all ended up with hangovers the next day, which was probably a good thing as we all needed to be on our toes when Eleanor turned up at the funeral parlour with a small suitcase. It was the first time we'd seen her in days, and our questions about where she'd been and what she'd been up to were met with a frosty 'None of your business.'

She even refused Sanjeev's offer of tea. 'I won't be here that long. I've just come to pick up a couple of things I left upstairs in the flat – if that's all right with you, Max.'

It was perfectly clear from her tone that she didn't care whether it was or not, and she set off through the display coffins on her way up to the apartment. I should maybe have followed her to make sure she didn't take anything that didn't belong to her, but even though I'd lost all trust in her, I doubted she'd stoop as low as petty thievery.

'What's got in to her?' said Alan, and I reminded him about the row we'd had when I'd pretty much accused her of lying about having to go on the run because Chisholm had confessed to the cops.

'Which he hadn't,' Scratch added.

Alan grunted. 'Yeah, you told me, but that was no great surprise, was it? She's been lying to us all along. And if you ask me, I reckon we need to keep a bloody close eye on her at least till we've got our share of the gear from Vincenzi.'

'Follow her, you mean?'

'You got a better idea?'

'No, but how are we gonna do that without being spotted? It's not as if she doesn't know all of us.'

'You could always try using this,' said Sanjeev, who'd been rummaging around in one of the drawers of the reception desk until he found what he was looking for.

It was a small black disc of about two and a half centimetres in diameter, roughly the same as a ten pence coin and the same thickness.

'What's that then?' said Scratch.

'GPS tracking device. Oleg Radimov left it behind with some of his other spying gadgets.' He turned the disc over to reveal a QR code on the other side. 'All you do is scan this into your phone and the app will show you wherever the tracker is.'

Alan took the disc from him and inspected it for himself. 'So all we have to do is drop it into her bag or pocket or somewhere before she leaves.'

'Correct. But her bag would probably be best. She's much less likely to spot it in amongst all the other stuff, and she always seems to have it with her.'

'Better get on with it then. She could be back down here any second.'

Alan was right. No sooner had we scanned the QR code into each of our phones and checked that the tracker was working than Eleanor crossed the floor towards us with her suitcase.

'I think that's everything,' she said, stony-faced, and put the case down next to the desk.

I couldn't help thinking it felt like she was saying a final goodbye, but that was absurd. We'd have to meet up again at some point to share out the loot, and there was no way she was going to miss out on that.

'We'll let you know if we hear from Vincenzi before you do,' I said.

'I'd better give you my new number then.'

She took her phone out of her pocket and jabbed at the screen until my own phone began to ring. I glanced at the display, then ended the call.

While Eleanor was distracted, Sanjeev had sidled round behind her, and as he passed, he dropped the tracker disc into the tan-coloured faux leather bag slung over her shoulder.

Eleanor put her phone back in her pocket and picked up her suitcase. 'I wouldn't hold your breath about Vincenzi, though. I spoke to him yesterday, and he reckoned it might not be till the end of next week. Still, patience is a virtue, or so they say.'

Moments after she'd gone, we all checked the tracking app on our phones. According to the little red dot on the map, she was making relatively slow progress along the street, but after fifty yards or so, she stopped.

'Bollocks,' said Scratch after the red dot had remained motionless for a good thirty seconds. 'She must already have found the tracker and dumped it.'

No-one else spoke, presumably fearing the same thing, but after another twenty tense seconds, the dot was on the move again, and this time at speed.

'She must be in a car,' said Alan. 'I didn't think she had one.'

'Must have rented one,' said Sanjeev. 'Or somebody's picked her up.'

'Or a taxi,' I said. 'But whichever it is, we need to get after her and see where she goes. Maybe she's just going straight back to her place now that she doesn't have to hide from the cops any more, but what if she doesn't? We have to know where she is every minute of the day until we get our hands on the goods from Vincenzi.'

50

We were still fairly busy with customers, but there were no actual funerals happening that day, so Alan and I were free to follow Eleanor while the others stayed behind.

I'd recently shelled out a small fortune to get the Polo a long overdue service, and the engine started at the first time of asking. The acceleration was as sluggish as ever, though, but that hardly mattered since we weren't expecting a *Bullitt*-style car chase. The tracking device in Eleanor's bag meant that we could hang well back and take our time. The only risk of her spotting us was wherever she happened to stop off and we needed a closer look. Otherwise, from what Sanjeev had told us, the device's range was virtually limitless.

Alan was in the passenger seat, his eyes glued to the map on his phone and giving me directions.

'Looks like she's stopped,' he said, about ten minutes after we'd left the funeral parlour.

'Where?'

'Dunno. Take the next right and then hang a left straight after.'

I did as instructed and pulled up as close as I dared to where the little red dot was. As far as we could tell, Eleanor was either just outside or gone into a four-storey office block that was almost identical to several others in the street.

I squinted through the windscreen at the large glass frontage and the wording printed above it.

'I can't make it out from this angle,' I said.

Alan had already started to open the passenger door. 'Me neither. I'll go and check it out.'

'OK, just make sure she doesn't see you if she's sat outside or when she comes out.'

'Oh really? Good thing you're here or I'd never have thought of that. Pity I didn't bring my Boris Johnson mask I used for the bank job.'

'Yeah, very funny, but at least you're not wearing your "Hello, my name is Alan Wilkins" neck brace like you did at the Ackroyds' place.'

Muttering a 'Fuck you, Max', Alan got out of the car, closed the door and set off along the pavement on the opposite side of the road to the office building. After only a dozen or so yards, he stopped and came back, his heavy frown difficult to read. Bewilderment or a sudden bout of indigestion.

'Well?' I said as he slipped back into the passenger seat.

'Transcontinental Freight Solutions, apparently.'

'What the hell's she gone in there for?'

'I s'pose she might not have, but I didn't see any sign of her outside.'

'We can't be certain either way. We don't even know what vehicle she's in.' Alan didn't answer, and I

271

glanced to my left to see he was busily tapping away on his phone. 'What you doing?'

'Googling the company,' he said without looking up. 'Keep an eye on the place in case she— Oh, hang on. Here it is.'

'And?'

'"Transcontinental Freight Solutions. Established in 2012, and with thousands of satisfied customers, TFS has an exemplary record for delivering all kinds of freight, however large or small, both safely and securely to destinations all over the world. In fact…" Blah blah blah. "You can rest assured that…" Blah blah blah…'

'Yeah, that's really helpful, Alan, but it still doesn't explain why—'

'Wait. Wait. Here's the interesting bit. "With many years' experience in the business, our chairman and CEO Mr Antonio Vincenzi"…'

He didn't need to read any further, and I leaned across to check the name for myself. There was even a picture of him, all smiles and with his customary cigar.

Alan zoomed in on the photo. 'Bit of a coincidence, wouldn't you say?'

'But what's she going to see *him* for? She told us she only spoke to him yesterday.'

'God knows, but I doubt it's got anything to do with shipping freight.'

I was still staring at the image of Tony Vincenzi when Alan grabbed my arm. 'Look. She's coming out.'

I switched my attention back to the office block. It was Eleanor all right, a big smile on her face and carrying the small suitcase she'd had with her when she'd dropped by the funeral parlour earlier. She seemed to hesitate for a moment as if trying to make up her mind, then crossed over the road and got into a dark red Kia hatchback. At least we knew what vehicle she was in now, and she was obviously on her own.

Instinctively, Alan and I had both ducked down in our seats when she'd stepped out onto the pavement. Pointlessly, though, because she'd have recognised the Polo straight away whether we were in it or not. But since she hadn't so much as turned her head in our direction, there was no chance she could have clocked us.

We gave her time to get out of sight and waited till the little red dot was well on its way. It led us for several miles to a park outside the town, where it stopped again for a few seconds before moving off at walking speed.

I slowed down when we could see where Eleanor had left her car, and I drove on past until I found a space for the Polo and switched off the engine.

'There she goes,' said Alan, twisting round in his seat and looking over his shoulder. 'What, she planning on having a picnic now?'

The park was no more than about four or five acres in size, consisting mainly of well mown grass that sloped gently down to a small duck pond at the bottom. Dotted here and there were a variety of well-established trees and a smattering of randomly placed wooden picnic tables.

'She's heading for the pond,' I said as Alan and I got out of the car.

Alan grunted. 'Not the duck-feeding type, I wouldn't have thought.'

'Any idea who that is?'

There were half a dozen benches that lined the edge of the pond, and Eleanor had sat down on the only one that was already occupied.

'Can't tell from here. Obviously a man, but he's too far away and got his back to us. How about we try and get a closer look?'

'Course, it might not be anyone we know anyway.'

'True, although it has to be somebody she's arranged to meet, or why didn't she choose one of the empty benches if she just wanted to sit and watch the ducks for a while?'

I couldn't fault Alan's logic, and even though we might not recognise the guy, it was well worth finding out who it could be.

Fortunately, there was only a handful of people in the park to take any notice of two grown men bent low and scurrying down the slope, taking cover every so often behind a conveniently large tree. The nearest of these to the duck pond was an old oak, and peeking around its trunk, we still couldn't identify who the man was that Eleanor was deep in conversation with. But even from behind, there was something familiar about him, although this may have been my imagination working overtime.

It was only when he finally stood up to leave and gave Eleanor a quick peck on the cheek that I immediately recognised the profile.

'Fuck me. What's *he* doing here?'

51

Scratch's eyes nearly popped out of his head. 'You're having me on.'

'It was him all right,' said Alan. 'No doubt about it.'

Back at the funeral parlour, the three of us were standing around the reception desk, which seemed to have become the equivalent of an office water cooler over the last few days, and we'd filled Scratch in on Eleanor's movements.

'Alastair Chisholm? The bank manager?'

'The very same,' I said.

'But why the hell would… Surely he…'

His brain understandably flooded with questions, Scratch was obviously struggling to decide which one to start with, so I helped him out.

'We've no idea about any of it, Scratch. After Chisholm left, Eleanor hung around for a few minutes and then went off in her car. That's all we know so far.'

'And they actually kissed, you say? Wouldn't have

thought he was her type.'

'Well, it was more like a quick peck on the cheek really, but there's no accounting for taste, I suppose.'

It took a moment for Scratch to digest the image that had presumably entered his head. 'So where's Eleanor now?'

'Back at her flat. We kept a watch on it for a couple of hours, but after that, we guessed she was probably there for the night and came back here.'

'Er, sorry, Max,' Alan chipped in, 'but in the interests of accuracy, that's what *you* reckoned. Not me.'

I stifled a sigh. 'And as I told you at the time, as long as we keep an eye on the tracking app, we'll know straight away if she makes a move. She's not that far away, so we can be after her in minutes.'

'Yeah, well, on your head be it if she does a runner in the middle of the night. And what if she finds the tracker and destroys it before she leaves the flat?'

This time, I didn't even bother to suppress the sigh. 'OK then, so somebody'll have to sit outside and watch the flat all night. You volunteering?'

'Am I bollocks. I've done my bit for today. How about Scratch taking a turn?'

'Or Sanjeev,' said Scratch, quick as a flash.

'Great idea,' I said. 'If you both go together, there'll be less danger of you falling asleep on the job.'

Whatever excuses Scratch might have had remained unspoken, very probably because he failed to come up with anything that sounded even vaguely plausible.

Instead, he grudgingly agreed. 'All right then, but you can tell Sanjeev I'll need to vet any snacks he's planning to bring with him. I'm not having him sat next to me all night chomping on peanuts or anything else that's gonna set off one of my allergies.'

'Christ,' Alan smirked, 'the poor bloke'll starve to death if that's the case. You've got more bloody allergies than LeBron James has got followers on Twitter.'

'Who?'

'Famous basketball player.'

'Never heard of him. And anyway, it's called X now, not Twitter.'

'Yes, I know that, but I thought you wouldn't know what I was talking about.'

'Excuse me for interrupting, guys,' I said, realising that this could easily develop into one of their interminable and generally pointless arguments, 'but if we're going ahead with Alan's brilliant plan, you might want to be on your way sooner rather than later, Scratch.'

'Yeah, OK. I'll give Sanjeev a shout.'

'Where is he?'

'Down in the mortuary.'

'What's he doing down there?'

'Supervising?'

'He's a braver man than me then. I can't imagine Alice will be too happy about that.'

And right on cue, Sanjeev appeared at the top of the mortuary steps and stomped towards us. 'Bloody woman's impossible. All I said was I thought the body she was working on could do with a little more makeup, and she went totally berserk. Throwing stuff at me and all sorts.'

'Might be an idea if you kept out of her way for a while,' I said, 'and luckily for you, that's exactly what you'll be doing for the next few hours.'

'Eh?'

While Scratch explained about staking out Eleanor's flat – including his strict rules about the consumption of snacks – I suggested to Alan that he should kip down in my apartment in case we were called upon at a moment's notice.

When Scratch had finished laying down the law to Sanjeev, I handed him the keys to the Polo and told him that if nothing happened during the night, Alan and I would take over about eight the next morning.

'And just make sure at least one of you stays awake,' I called after them as they were almost at the door.

'May as well lock up,' said Alan after they'd gone. 'It's well past closing time, and I seem to remember you've got a rather nice single malt up in your apartment.'

'What about Alice, though?' I said. 'She's still down in the mortuary.'

'Fine. You can go and tell her we're closing up if you like, but personally I wouldn't go within a million miles of her when she's in a mood and probably still raring for a fight.'

It was a fair point, and Alice could let herself out and lock up again when she was ready, so Alan and I climbed the stairs up to my flat with slightly more haste than usual.

52

As so often lately, I'd barely slept. Too much shit rattling around in my brain and fruitlessly trying to make sense of whatever it was that Eleanor was up to. Nothing good, that was for sure.

Anyway, my insomnia meant that I was already half awake when my phone went off soon after six in the morning.

It was Scratch.

'Hi, Max. First thing is, you gotta promise not to lose your shit.'

I sat up in bed, already prepared to lose my shit over whatever came next. 'Why? What's happened?'

'Well, according to the tracking app, she's left the flat and on the move. Eleanor, that is.'

Of course it was bloody Eleanor. Who else were they supposed to be keeping tabs on? Still, I hadn't heard anything yet that was going to make me lose my shit except...

'Hang on. What do you mean "according to the tracking app"? Did you actually *see* her leave the

279

flat?'

'Er, not exactly, no. The thing was, there was a bit of a misunderstanding between me and Sanjeev about whose turn it was to stay awake and—'

'Christ almighty, Scratch. If you remember, the whole point of sending *two* of you to—'

'I know. I know. And I'm really sorry we screwed up, but the good news is that the tracking gizmo in her bag is still working, so we can see where she's going.'

OK, maybe it wasn't a complete disaster, so I did my best to calm down and keep hold of my shit. For now anyway.

'All right, Scratch. No real harm done, I guess, but you're on her tail now, right?'

There was a worrying silence, and come to think of it, I couldn't even hear any sound from the Polo's normally clanking engine.

'Scratch? You still there?'

'Yeah, but we ran into a bit of a problem, see?'

'Problem? What sort of problem?'

'Er, like the Polo breaking down on us kind of problem.'

'You gotta be kidding. I only just had it serviced.'

'We'd almost caught up with her too, but that's when the engine sort of spluttered and died. Not to worry, though. Sanjeev'll be back any minute now and we'll be on our way again.'

'Back from where?'

'Sanjeev?'

By now I was hanging on to my shit with little more than my fingertips. 'Yes. Sanjeev.'

'We passed a garage about a mile back, so he legged it back there.'

'What, he's gone to fetch a mechanic to come and

fix it? How long's that gonna take?'

'No, not a mechanic. Petrol.'

I bade a not so fond farewell to my shit. 'Fuck's sake! How could you have run out of fucking petrol?'

'Well, it's not my car, so I'm not used to—'

'It's got a fucking fuel gauge right there in front of you. How hard can it be?'

Scratch started babbling more apologies, but I cut him short and told him to keep a better eye on the tracking app than he had on the fuel gauge and get going again as soon as Sanjeev got back with the petrol. Then I hung up.

I was already dressed and out of bed by the time Scratch had got to the part about the Polo "breaking down", and I charged into the living room. Alan was fast asleep on the bed settee, so I shook him awake rather more roughly than was strictly necessary.

'Jesus, Max. What the—'

'I'll explain on the way,' I said and tore the blanket off him in one swift movement.

❖

It wasn't the first time our speeding hearse had turned a few heads as we raced through the town, but we had no choice if we were ever going to catch up with Eleanor. No doubt we'd be picking up a fair few fines, thanks to all the speed cameras, although they'd be a piss in the ocean compared to the loot we might be about to lose for good. It was pretty obvious by now that she'd somehow managed to grab at least a good chunk of it for herself and hadn't the slightest intention of sharing it. Where she was heading for, though, was still a mystery.

281

Or a mystery, that is, until Alan suddenly took his eyes off the tracking app he'd been directing me from and turned towards me.

'Bloody hell,' he said. 'She's not quite there yet, and it might not be where's she's aiming for, of course, but from what the little red dot's telling me, I'd lay odds she's on her way to the airport.'

'What, Gatwick?'

'Uh-huh.'

I dropped down a gear and floored the accelerator.

53

Even at the speed we were travelling at, we were struggling to catch up with Eleanor until we had an all too rare stroke of luck. The tracking app told us she'd stopped off not far from the entrance to the airport and stayed where she was for about twenty minutes.

'I'd say the car she was in is a rental and she's dropping it off at the hire place,' said Alan, still staring at the map on his phone.

But whatever the reason, we were able to pull into the airport drop-off area soon after she'd entered the terminal building on foot. I knew from past experience that the drop-off parking charges were extortionate even for a few minutes, but as with the speeding fines, however much we'd have to pay wasn't worth stressing about.

The little red dot on Alan's phone had come to a halt again, but the tracking app didn't work in three dimensions, of course, so we had to check each level on the way up until we found her. She was sitting at one of the few vacant tables of a busy bar-cum-restaurant, wearing a broad-brimmed, navy blue hat and oversized dark glasses and idly flicking through the pages of a glossy magazine.

'Going somewhere nice?' I said as Alan and I stood over her.

She looked up from her magazine, seemingly unsurprised at our sudden appearance. 'Hello, guys. What brings you here?'

'Well, it wasn't to wish you *bon voyage*.'

'No, I didn't imagine it was.'

'You want to tell us what the fuck's going on?'

'In respect of...?'

'Christ, Eleanor, don't play games. You know exactly what I'm talking about.'

She slowly removed her sunglasses, and with an incredibly irritating sardonic smile, said, 'Not to put too fine a point on it, Max, I'm afraid you've been well and truly had.'

'Yeah, I think we've already got that far, but maybe you'd like to go into a little more detail.'

The heavy sigh was a clear enough indication that she really couldn't be bothered, but she went ahead anyway. 'OK, I'll keep it as brief as possible. The main bullet points, if you like. First off, I'd planned this whole thing right from the start, although there were one or two unfortunate hiccups along the way. My biggest mistake was doing a deal with that utter bellend, Greg Murray. I can't believe I was stupid enough to think he was a proper fence, but hindsight is a wonderful thing, as they say. We'd had an agreement that he'd break in to the lockup and we'd share the loot, but when I didn't hear back from him, the obvious conclusion was that he'd screwed me over, and I was right. The little fucker tried to pull a fast one and went straight to Mitchell Clayton. Thought he'd do better than the eighty-twenty split I'd offered – the eighty being mine, of course – and we all know how that ended up, don't we?'

'We'd pretty much figured out that's why you'd disappeared. You and the fence had come to some arrangement and buggered off with everything from the lockup. But what I don't understand is why you decided to bring *us* back in when you found out that Greg had stitched you up.'

'Because I still had no idea he was a fraud, and if he really was a fence, it was perfectly possible he'd have his own little private army of minders. I didn't fancy facing him on my own if things turned nasty, so I realised I might need your help. That's why I lied about Chisholm squealing to the cops and me having to go on the run. As I told you at the time, if I'd got caught, I might have been tempted to do a deal and give the police all your names as being involved in the robbery.'

'So you basically blackmailed us into being your backup when you went to confront Greg.'

Eleanor shrugged, and there was that annoying smile again. 'Funny, isn't it? A bunch of wussy undertakers as my personal heavies, but I didn't have a lot of choice at the time.'

Even without looking, I could sense Alan's fists clenching and unclenching at my side. 'Wussy, eh? Scratch is built like a brick shithouse, and in case you didn't know, I used to be a bloody weightlifter.'

'Aww, I've offended you,' Eleanor said with blatantly mock sincerity. 'But how is your poor neck these days? I see you're not wearing the brace for a change.'

285

Before Alan could come back at her, I jumped in and asked her about the gear we'd stashed in the coffin.

'Me again, I'm afraid. If you recall, I'd already been to the Ackroyd place and sussed everything out. I also knew exactly when you were intending to break in, so it was a simple case of getting there before you did. And with what I thought was a touch of real genius, and as a bit of an insurance, I went in wearing a neck brace almost identical to our friend Alan's here. Course, I'm a few inches taller, but I doubted the CCTV cameras would have picked that up. Oh, and by the way, if it's of any interest at all, old man Ackroyd was already dead by the time I got there.'

'So what did you do with it?' I said, again before Alan could mouth off at her. 'The stuff from the coffin. Ackroyd's diamonds and all the cash.'

'Huh. What do you think I came back to your flat for yesterday?'

'It was in my flat all this time?'

'Since the night I came to stay, yeah. Loose floorboard near the TV. Bit of a gamble you didn't know about that little hidey-hole, but unless you're into peddling cocaine – which I doubt – I assumed you didn't.'

'Cocaine? What are you talking about?'

'I guessed that's what it was, although I don't know much about that sort of thing. It's lucky Carla stopped the cops searching the flat or you'd be facing some serious jail time if they'd found it.'

'How much was there?'

'Dunno. Kilo? Something like that. Didn't you tell me the guy who owned the place before you was a big-time dealer?'

Maybe I had. I couldn't remember, but I made a mental note to get rid of the coke the moment we got back. In the meantime, though, there were far more pressing matters.

'So the coffin loot was in the suitcase you took to Vincenzi?'

She seemed genuinely taken aback. 'How'd you know about that?'

'We followed you.'

'Oh, now I'm really hurt,' she said with a phony pout. 'Makes me feel like you didn't trust me.'

It was a remark I had no difficulty ignoring. 'And you flogged all that lot to Vincenzi, did you?'

'He was actually quite generous, given that all the cash would have to be laundered, and I got more than I was expecting from the lockup gear too.'

It was all I could do to stop myself yelling, but even so, there were a few of the nearby punters who took a sudden interest. 'Fuck's sake, Eleanor. He's already paid you? But he told us it wouldn't be till—' And that's when the penny finally dropped. Why it had taken me so long, I'd no idea. I mean, what the hell else would she be doing at the airport? 'So you went behind our backs and did your own private deal with Vincenzi, right?'

'Laid it on thick about being urgent, so he paid me himself even though he hadn't yet got hold of what Clayton nicked from us. Course, it didn't do any harm to remind him about the little blackmail threat I had over him.'

'I'm sure it didn't.'

'To be fair to the man, though, he didn't know I was going to keep it all for myself. In fact, he said something about sending you his regards when I gave you your cut. Bit odd for a gangster like him to give a shit about that, but maybe there is such a thing as honour amongst thieves.'

'Apparently not in *your* case,' said Alan, spitting the words out like he was getting rid of a bad taste in his mouth.

'So how much did you get?' I said.

Eleanor tapped the side of her nose. 'I think that's for me to know, don't you?'

'And he paid you all of it in cash?'

'No, all went direct into Alastair's account, and he's transferred it into some offshore account. Untraceable, apparently.'

'Alastair? Chisholm, you mean?'

'He knows how to do that sort of thing, so I left it to him. He *is* a bank manager after all. Or was anyway.'

'Did I hear my name taken in vain?'

Alan and I had our backs to the voice, and we both turned to see the man himself holding a disposable coffee cup in each hand.

54

Alastair Chisholm was wearing a similarly smug grin as Eleanor and appeared to have undergone quite a transformation. Nothing major, but it looked like he'd lost a pound or two in the waistband area, and what I guessed must have been a few sunbed sessions had taken the edge off the deathly pallor of his complexion. In place of his dark bank manager suit, he had on a light blue polo shirt under a cream linen jacket. Gone too were the rimless glasses. Contact lenses perhaps? He also had a new-looking leather briefcase hanging from his shoulder by a long strap and the initials A.J.C. embossed in gold lettering on the flap.

'Prince Andrew and Boris Johnson, I presume. Or is one of you Donald Trump?' He leaned forward between Alan and me and handed Eleanor one of the coffees. 'There you go, darling.'

'*Darling*?' said the voice in my head. '*Seriously*?'

'I take it you two are an item then?' I said aloud.

Chisholm raised an eyebrow at me. 'You find that

surprising?'

'None of my business, but I did start to wonder when we saw you in the park together.'

'They've been following us,' Eleanor said in response to his puzzled glance.

Chisholm nodded and took a sip of his coffee.

Besides the physical changes, it was as if he'd had a personality transplant as well. His confidently upright bearing and way of speaking were in complete contrast to the mouselike nerd we'd known before.

'I assume you can get your pervy S&M kicks for free now,' I said, urged on by the voice in my head to take him down a peg. 'Do you still have to call her "Mistress" though?'

'God no. And for your information, I never was one of Ellie's clients. In fact, I find all that sort of thing utterly abhorrent, and I'm only glad that she's now free of all that herself.'

'So if you weren't a client, how did—'

'How did we get together? As you were saying earlier, none of your business, and anyway I don't have the time. We have a plane to catch.'

While he was speaking, he set his coffee down on the table and opened the flap of his briefcase. Taking out a single sheet of paper, he passed it to Eleanor.

'Boarding pass, darling. In case we get separated. But I'm desperate for a pee right now, so I'll meet you at the entrance to security. Don't be too long, though. You know what those queues can be like.'

'I'll be there in a minute,' said Eleanor. 'I think we're almost done here.'

'*No "darling" from her, I notice,*' said the voice.

And with a sarcastically cheery 'Lovely to see you both again', Chisholm scuttled away from the table.

His odd way of walking was one of the things I'd registered about him the first time we'd met. His legs too short in proportion to the rest of his body. There are some things you just can't change, I guess.

Eleanor perched her sunglasses on the top of her head, got to her feet and picked up her shoulder bag from the floor next to her chair.

'Funny,' I said, 'but I wouldn't have thought he was your type.'

'Oh, he isn't at all. Not that I have a "type" as such, and however hard he tries, he's never going to be a looker. But if that makes me sound a bit too superficial, I'd also much prefer somebody who wasn't so incredibly boring. And if you really want to know how we got together, it was through one of those online dating sites.'

'Really? So what the hell was *he* doing on there? He's married with kids.'

'Honestly, Max, I never realised you were such a puritan.'

'I'm not. It's just that—'

'I'm joking,' Eleanor said with a broad grin, 'and him being married was a positive bonus.'

'How so?'

'Well, I wasn't looking for a relationship at all. What I *was* looking for was somebody exactly like him. Somebody with access to vast amounts of money who didn't have the looks to attract too many clicks on the "Let's Date" button. Of course, he didn't mention anything about him being married on his profile, and I didn't find that out till later, but he did say he was a bank manager, so I decided to give him a go.'

'But if he was never one of your S&M clients and

you couldn't blackmail him over that, how did you manage to persuade him to help us with the bank job?'

Eleanor put on her hurt face. 'What? Don't you believe in my feminine charms?'

Before I could answer – and I didn't know quite how I would answer – she carried on.

'No, that was the real clincher when I eventually found out about him being married. Threatened to tell his missus about us, of course.'

'OK, that makes sense, but how come you're acting like a pair of lovestruck teenagers now that you've got all the cash?'

'Truth is, I needed him to do all the dodgy transfer stuff, because I didn't have a clue. But never fear. I'll be dumping him as soon as we get where we're going and I've got my hands on all the lovely moolah. And speaking of which, I'd better get my skates on or I'll miss the flight.'

Alan and I kept either side of her as she made her way through the concourse to security, firing questions at her all the while.

She was distinctly cagey when we asked her where she was flying to except that it was a country that didn't have an extradition agreement with the UK.

'It won't be long before Alastair's wife realises he's left her,' she added, 'and it's a racing certainty she'll rat him out to the police when she does. A woman scorned and all that. She'll tell them everything about hubby's involvement in the robbery, but by then it'll be too late. But look on the bright side. As long as the cops can't get to me – which is highly unlikely – I'd have no reason to drop you guys in it, so you shouldn't have any worries on that score. Same applies if you call the cops now to try and stop me leaving.'

'No worries and none of the cash either,' said Alan.

Eleanor shrugged. 'Yeah, I'm sorry about that, but I'll see what I can do when we get to… our destination. Maybe send you some of the dosh. Not your full share, I'm afraid, but every little helps, eh?'

By now, we'd reached the security area, but there was no sign of Chisholm until I spotted him just beyond the boarding pass check-in.

'Looks like he's gone through already,' I said, and pointed him out to Eleanor.

He was tapping his watch and beckoning to her to hurry up.

'Yeah, keep yer wispy hair on,' she muttered as she gave him an acknowledging wave, then switched her attention back to me and Alan. 'Well, it's been nice knowing you, guys, and at the risk of repeating myself, I'm really sorry for how it's turned out for you, but I never have been much of a team player.'

If she'd been expecting even a hint of forgiveness from either of us, she was shit out of luck, and we watched in silence as she walked over to one of the boarding pass scanners. I remembered from the last time I'd flown that the process should only have taken a few seconds, but Eleanor was clearly having problems.

Even from where we were standing, we could tell she was becoming increasingly flustered, and giving up, she spoke to a nearby member of staff. Stepping over to a different scanner, he tried the boarding pass himself – several times. Then he picked up the pass and examined it closely before shaking his head and apparently explaining something to Eleanor.

Whatever he'd said, Eleanor responded by flapping

her arms around, and Alan and I caught most of the expletive-ridden tirade she was yelling at the poor bloke until he gave her back the pass and made his retreat.

In desperation, Eleanor called out to Chisholm, who was still in the same place just beyond the bank of boarding pass scanners.

Oddly enough, he seemed totally unconcerned and was actually smiling at her – smirking even – and the next moment he was joined by a fortyish woman in a floral cotton dress and two young children, one of whom began pulling at the sleeve of Chisholm's linen jacket. We couldn't hear what he said to Eleanor, but after blowing her a kiss, Chisholm, the woman and the two children disappeared amongst the throng of people trying to find the shortest queue to have their hand luggage checked.

55

After all her lies and devious plotting, Eleanor had been screwed over herself and ended up with bugger all. Not that Alan, Scratch and I were any better off, of course – and that was entirely down to her – but even so, I couldn't help but feel a little sorry for her. Alan was considerably less sympathetic, but he'd grudgingly come with Eleanor and me when we went back to the airport bar we'd only recently left.

Eleanor was getting stuck into a large gin and tonic, cursing Chisholm to hell and back while now and again having to fight back the tears.

'Bastard must have tampered with my boarding pass. Insisted on printing it out because he said he didn't trust the ones you have on your phone. Said he'd had problems with them before.'

'How'd you mean he tampered with it?' I asked.

Eleanor took another swig of her G and T. 'QR code thing didn't work, so I'm guessing he used a black pen to add a few extra dots or marks or whatever. And when the security guy checked, he told me that the flight number printed on the boarding pass didn't exist. He must have fiddled with that as well. I dunno. Changed the 3 to an 8 or something.'

'But surely they'd have picked that up before you even got to security. Don't you have to show your pass when you check in your luggage?'

'Didn't have any luggage. Decided I'd travel light. I was starting a whole new life and wanted to leave the old one behind me. And what with all the money that was coming my way, I could afford to buy whatever I wanted when we got where we were going.'

'Which is where?' said Alan, somewhat irrelevantly at this stage, I thought.

'You asked me that already, but it really doesn't matter now, does it? In any case, I wasn't around when he booked the flights, and I never got to see *his* boarding pass. For all I know, he probably even lied about which country we were supposed to be flying to. One thing I'm sure he didn't lie about, though, was the no extradition part.'

The voice in my head was wondering if all might not be lost after all, and Scratch, Alan and I might still get a cut of the loot.

I knew it was a long shot, but I asked the question anyway. 'I don't suppose you'd be able to access the account he paid the money into, would you?'

Eleanor almost choked on her drink. 'You serious? Kept all that to himself, didn't he? Account numbers. Passwords. All of it. Told me it was "all in hand" and I didn't need to worry about it.' She set her empty glass down on the table and slapped her palm to her forehead. 'God, how could I have been so stupid? Never occurred to me for a moment that he'd have the guts or the brains to be able to fool me like this.'

'I guess we might say the same about you fooling *us*,' said Alan, 'and to be perfectly honest, you've got what you deserve. Fuck all, like the rest of us.' He pushed back his chair and stood up. 'You coming, Max? I don't know about you, but I've had more than enough of this bullshit.'

'I'll be right there,' I said as he hurried away like his arse was on fire.

Eleanor reached across the table and placed her hand on top of mine, her eyes moist with tears that may or may not have been genuine. 'I'm sorry, Max, I really am. And I don't mean just about the money. If things had been different, maybe you and I could have—'

'Yeah, maybe,' I said, not wanting to hear the rest, 'but somehow I doubt it. If things had been "different", as you put it, you'd have been somebody I knew I could trust, and I'm not convinced that's in your nature.'

'*Harsh but fair*,' said the voice in my head as I left Eleanor alone at the table, staring into her empty glass.

I caught up with Alan at the drop-off parking zone. He was leaning against the side of the hearse and chatting to Scratch and Sanjeev.

'Good of you to join us,' I said.

'Yeah, sorry, Max,' said Scratch. 'Had all sorts of problems getting here, not least of which was Sanjeev bringing back diesel instead of petrol from the garage, so he had to go back again.'

Sanjeev coughed and dropped his chin to his chest.

'Anyway,' Scratch went on, 'Alan's been telling us all about Chisholm stitching Eleanor up and all that stuff. Didn't see that one coming.'

'Nor did anyone except Chisholm, apparently.'

297

'What a fucker, eh?'
'Never a truer word, Scratch. Never a truer word.'

56

So, that was that. We were back to business as usual, except "Max Dempsey and Partners: Funeral Directors" was doing better than ever. As expected, Tony Vincenzi had taken over all of Mitchell Clayton's businesses – legit and otherwise – and bought up the Ackroyds' funeral parlour with plans already in place to turn it into a restaurant. With no competition in the area, the bereaved were now flocking to us to take care of their recently departed loved ones. The dramatic increase in our income was more than enough to rescue us from the brink of bankruptcy, but it still smarted that we'd ended up with sod all from the bank robbery.

Smarted? Now, there's the understatement of the century. Scratch, Alan and I had had some notable and occasionally spectacular disasters when we'd tried our hands at robbing banks in the past, although this one had been an outstanding success. But we'd still ended up with the same result. Zero return for all the effort and planning we'd put in and all because we'd been stitched up by our very own *femme fatale*. The fact that she'd been screwed herself was hardly any consolation, of course, but her failure to benefit from her treachery did at least take a sliver of an edge off the pain that the rest of us had been suffering. Presumably, she'd started up her old S&M business again, although we really couldn't have given a toss where she was or what she was up to.

The only positive outcome for us was that there was now only the slimmest of chances that we'd ever get done for the bank robbery. Chisholm's sudden exodus from the country with his wife and kids had not gone unnoticed by the police, and since they had then discovered additionally incriminating evidence, he'd now become their prime and only suspect. So, as long as his whereabouts remained unknown and he managed to evade extradition even if they did eventually catch up with him, Scratch, Alan and I were in the clear.

We'd also got Ray and Roy Ackroyd off our backs for many years to come. Having confessed to their dad's murder, the twins had done a deal with the cops and provided them with evidence that Mitchell Clayton had paid them to do it. This had earned them a reduced sentence of twenty years, and even with time off for good behaviour – which, knowing those two, I found highly unlikely – they could be safely forgotten about.

As for Clayton himself, he was banged up on remand in a top security prison, awaiting trial, and according to media reports, his charge sheet was one of the longest the British police had ever put together. Given the evidence against him and a queue of witnesses who were ready and willing to testify for the prosecution, the cops were supremely confident he'd be convicted of most, if not all, of his crimes. And since his brutal murder of a serving – albeit bent – DCI was among several other horrific offences, there was every possibility that he'd be looking at a life sentence without parole.

One of the few things that Eleanor hadn't lied about was the cocaine she'd found hidden under a loose floorboard in my apartment. It was about the first thing I checked when we'd got back from the airport. Probably about a kilo, as she'd guessed.

'That's gonna be worth a few quid,' Alan had said. 'May as well try and sell it, so at least that would be some compensation for having lost everything from the bank robbery.'

'You out of your mind?' Scratch had said. 'Remember the last time we got involved with that shit? We nearly all wound up dead, so I'm never going through that again, that's for sure.'

For once, this was one of their many arguments where I had no trouble taking sides, and so it was that a two to one majority resulted in every last grain of coke being unceremoniously flushed down the toilet.

But no sooner had I finished than Sanjeev shouted up from the shop floor of the funeral parlour.

'Max, you'd better come down here. I think we might have a problem.'

I took my time going down the stairs, my imagination already running wild. Christ, what now? Handcuff-wielding cops? Heavily armed irate gangsters?

The voice in my head wasn't helping either. '*What if it* is *the cops? That new DCI is obviously a hell of a lot brighter than Parkin, which isn't saying much,*

301

admittedly. Maybe she's found new evidence linking you to the bank robbery, or worse still, the cops got it wrong about Ray and Roy doing their old man in and for some reason got you down for it instead. And even if it's not the cops come to arrest you, how about a bunch of Mitchell Clayton's goons? OK, he's safely locked away right now, but he's bound to still have people working for him on the outside, and sure as shit he'll be pulling out all the stops to wreak revenge on anyone he thinks was responsible for putting him behind bars.

'On balance, though, I think if I was you, I'd prefer it to be the cops. At least then you won't be beaten to a bloody pulp or have a limb or two removed with a rusty chainsaw by some half-crazed gangster thugs. Sure, if it's the cops and you're facing a lengthy prison stretch, it's a fair bet that you'll still get beaten to a pulp now and again by some of your psychopathic fellow inmates, but looking on the bright side, it's fairly unlikely they'll have easy access to a chainsaw, rusty or otherwise.'

I reached the bottom of the stairs, my knees by now barely capable of keeping me upright, and I scanned the whole of the coffin display area.

No sign of any handcuff-wielding cops or heavily armed irate gangsters. Just Sanjeev hovering nearby with a stainless steel electric kettle in his hand.

Scarcely registering his presence, my eyes darted in every direction for any threat that might be lurking in the shadows. 'What is it, Sanjeev? You said there was a problem.'

'It's this bloody kettle,' he said, waving it in front of me to get my attention. 'Switched it on and it blew a fuse. We've had it for ages, so I guess we might

302

need a new one. Can't make tea without a kettle, can I?'

'Oh, for f—'

EPILOGUE

I suppose you might call this a kind of "STOP PRESS", but I've just had some late news from Eleanor. It was about three weeks since we'd had any contact with her, and I really hadn't expected to hear from her at all – probably never again, in fact. But that was the name that flashed up on my phone when it rang one afternoon when I was taking care of business at the funeral parlour.

I was half tempted not to pick up, but my curiosity got the better of me. 'Eleanor? What's up?'

'I've had some information you might be interested in.'

From the flat coolness in her tone, I got the impression that she'd maybe been in two minds about calling me in much the same way that I'd hesitated before answering.

'It's about Chisholm,' she went on when I didn't respond. 'He's dead.'

I'd no idea what I'd been expecting, but this particular piece of news would never have occurred to me. 'What happened? Heart attack or something?'

'No, Max. He was murdered.'

'Murdered? Holy shit. Who by?'

There was an audible sigh from Eleanor, like she almost couldn't be bothered to go into the specifics, but she did anyway.

'Vincenzi. Well, not him personally, although he was the one who ordered the hit. Not that surprising in his line of business, but he's got some rather nasty contacts in all sorts of countries around the world, including Venezuela.'

'Venezuela?'

Another sigh. 'Venezuela, yes. And if you stop keep parroting everything I say, I'll tell you the rest.'

'OK, sorry. Go on.'

'I'd told Vincenzi that Chisholm was heading for some country that didn't have an extradition treaty with the UK, which narrowed the search down a fair bit when he put the word out among his organised crime pals. And it didn't take too long before one of the Venezuelan gangs tracked him down to Caracas, and that was that. Didn't kill him straight away, though. Tortured him first to find out the account details of where he'd stashed all the money.' She gave a little chuckle. 'From what Vincenzi told me, he coughed up pretty quickly.'

It took me a few moments to process all of this, and there were parts that I needed clarifying. 'So this organised crime gang got all of our dough, yeah?'

'That was part of the deal apparently. Vincenzi called it their "finder's fee".'

'Quite a generous one, I reckon.'

'What can I say? Perhaps Vincenzi took a cut for himself, but a deal's a deal, and I suppose he thought a big financial incentive would help to speed things up.'

'Speed things up? Why? What was the hurry?'

'Yeah, that was me really. Like I told Vincenzi, revenge isn't always a dish that's best served cold. It was seriously messing with my head the way that fucker stitched me up. I could hardly sleep thinking about it, so I knew I wouldn't get anywhere near any peace of mind till he got what was coming to him.'

'It wasn't just you he stitched up, though, was it?'

'So you got your revenge as well then, didn't you?'

To be honest, the idea of revenge had never really crossed my mind. Nor Alan and Scratch's either. Sure, we were mightily pissed off with the guy to say the least, but then again, we felt much the same about Eleanor. I could have pointed that out to her, but I didn't. Instead, I asked her what had happened to Chisholm's wife and kids.

'Dunno,' she said, 'but I do know that Vincenzi made it very clear when he issued the hit order that they were not to be harmed in any way. Maybe they're still in Venezuela, 'cos I doubt the wife would risk coming back to the UK for fear of getting nicked for aiding and abetting or whatever. And even if she did, it's highly unlikely she'd be able to finger any of us for the robbery.'

Well, that was a relief, but there was one thing that was puzzling me. 'What I don't understand is why Vincenzi would go to all that trouble just so you could get your revenge on Chisholm?'

'Oh, that wasn't too difficult as it turned out,' she said with what might have been a hint of pride in her voice. 'For starters, I gave him all the video footage that showed he'd ever been a client of mine. And to add a little icing on the cake, I said he could take his pick of what I had on some of my other high profile clients in case he might want to expand the blackmail side of his business.'

'And that did the trick, did it?'

'Uh-huh. Probably also helped that he seems to have a bit of a crush on me as well.'

'Really?'

'Find that hard to believe, do you?'

'No, not at all. It's just—'

'*You* did, after all.'

'Yeah, I don't think that's—'

'Anyway,' Eleanor interrupted again, 'I thought I'd let you know the news, but now I have to dash. I'm meeting Carla for a coffee, and I'm already running late.'

Then she hung up.

I sat back in my chair behind the reception desk, staring at the screen on my phone as if this would somehow help me to get my head around everything she'd told me. I didn't give a toss whether Eleanor and Carla had become best buddies or not, but the Chisholm stuff was something else altogether. There was a time when Alan, Scratch and I could cheerfully have wrung the bastard's neck, although that was all in the heat of the moment, and we'd never have carried it through even if we'd managed to catch up with him. And besides, Eleanor was just as much to blame for how we'd ended up with sod all from the robbery, and probably more so, given how she'd wormed her way into gaining our trust whilst plotting her treachery from the very beginning. But Chisholm being tortured and murdered by some South American organised crime gang? That was definitely a step too far.

'Excuse me.'

The voice had come from the customer side of the reception desk, and I looked up to see a smartly dressed man and woman who must have been in their early sixties.

'Hello,' I said. 'How can I help you?'

'Do you do sale or return?' said the man.

My brain was still fuddled from my conversation with Eleanor, so I wasn't sure if I'd heard him right. 'Sorry. What was that?'

'Sale or return. Do you do sale or return?' the woman repeated with a slightly frosty edge to her tone.

OK, I *had* heard right, but I was at a complete loss what they were on about. 'I'm afraid I don't know what you mean.'

'It's actually quite simple,' said the woman, taking the frost level up another notch. 'All we're asking is if we buy a coffin from you, can we bring it back and get a full refund if it's the wrong size.'

'Er…'

The man presumably realised that further explanation was necessary. 'You see, our aunty is – how shall I put this? – a rather *large* lady, and we want to make certain she'll fit in whatever coffin we choose. Might be a tad embarrassing otherwise.'

'Ah, now I understand, but that's not really how it works. What we do is collect the deceased from their residence and then bring them here so that—'

'Deceased?'

'Yes.'

'But she's not dead yet. Not far off, though, from what the doctors have told us, and we thought we'd save a bit of faffing about if we got some of the practicalities out of the way in advance.'

'*You know*,' said the voice in my head, '*one way or another, you're gonna have to get out of this undertaker lark, and the sooner the better if you ask me.*'

And I couldn't have agreed more.

THE END

DEAR READER

Authors always appreciate reviews – especially if they're good ones of course – so I'd be eternally grateful if you could spare the time to write a few words about *Grave Expectations* on Amazon, Goodreads or anywhere else you can think of. It really can make a difference. Reviews also help other readers decide whether to buy a book or not, so you'll be doing them a service as well.

MAILING LIST

If you'd like to be kept informed of new posts on my website, my new books, special offers on my books and other relevant information, please use the link below and add your details.

Don't worry, any emails I send you will be few and far between, and I certainly won't be sharing your details with any third parties. You can also easily unsubscribe at any time.

http://eepurl.com/cwvFpb

AND FINALLY...

I'm always interested to hear from my readers, so please do take a couple of minutes to contact me via my website at **https://rob-johnson.org.uk/contact/**

ABOUT THE AUTHOR

'You'll have to write an author biography of course.'

'Oh? Why?'

'Because people will want to know something about you before they splash out on buying one of your books.'

'You think so, do you?'

'Just do it, okay?'

'So what do I tell them?'

'For a start, you should mention that you've written four plays that were professionally produced and toured throughout the UK.'

'Should I say anything about all the temp jobs I had, like working in the towels and linens stockroom at Debenhams or as a fitter's mate in a perfume factory?'

'No, definitely not.'

'Motorcycle dispatch rider?'

'You were sacked, weren't you?'

'Boss said he could get a truck there quicker.'

'Leave it out then, but make sure they know that *Grave Expectations* is the eighth book you've written. And don't forget to put in something that shows you're vaguely human.'

'You mean this kind of thing: "I'm currently in Greece with my wife, Penny, seven cats and two rescue dogs and working on a new novel and a couple of screenplays".'

'It'll have to do, I suppose, and then finish off with your website and social media stuff.'

'Oh, okay then.'

- visit my website at http://www.rob-johnson.org.uk
- follow @RobJohnson999 on Twitter
- check out my Facebook author page at https://www.facebook.com/RobJohnsonAuthor
- follow me on Amazon at http://viewauthor.at/Rob_Johnson_Author

OTHER BOOKS BY ROB JOHNSON

LIFTING THE LID
(Book One in the 'Lifting the Lid'
comedy thriller series)

"The twists and turns kept me on the edge of my seat, laughing all the time." – San Francisco Review of Books

http://viewbook.at/Lifting_the_Lid

**Also available as an audiobook
from Amazon and Audible**

**Read on for the opening chapters
towards the end of this book.**

HEADS YOU LOSE
(Book Two in the 'Lifting the Lid'
comedy thriller series)

"Masterfully planned and executed... It tickled my funny bone in all the right places." - Joanne Armstrong for Ingrid Hall Reviews

http://viewbook.at/Heads_You_Lose

DISHING THE DIRT
(Book Three in the 'Lifting the Lid'
comedy thriller series)

"Once again, Rob Johnson entertains his readers with distinctive characters, credible and lively dialogue, and unique plotting." - Pamela Allegretto (Author of *Bridge of Sighs and Dreams* and *Ashes to Ashes, Diamonds to Dust*)

https://viewbook.at/Dishing_the_Dirt

LIFTING THE LID - BOX SET

All three books in the 'Lifting the Lid' series in one box set.

https://viewbook.at/LTL_BOX_SET

CREMAINS

(A comedy crime caper.
Book One in the 'Cremains' series)

"A hilarious comedy that keeps you on the edge of your seat... and there are loads of twists and turns as the story hurtles towards an explosive ending." - Anne-Marie Reynolds for Readers' Favorite

http://viewbook.at/Cremains

THE UNDERTAKING

(A comedy spy caper.
Book Two in the 'Cremains' series)

"Just when they think they have things under control and have figured out how to deal with it, something else happens, with the pace of these wild twists coming faster and faster as the story progresses." - Books and Pals book blog.

https://mybook.to/The_Undertaking

QUEST FOR THE HOLEY SNAIL

(A comedy time travel adventure)

"Fans of Douglas Adams' *Hitchhikers' Guide to the Galaxy* will enjoy *Quest for the Holey Snail*." - Awesome Indies

http://viewBook.at/Quest

A KILO OF STRING

(Non fiction: A British expat in Greece)

"Witty and very funny. I really enjoyed this book. The author clearly has a love for the country and the people." - *USA Today* bestselling author Kathryn Gauci

http://viewbook.at/A_Kilo_of_String

**Also available as an audiobook
from Amazon and Audible**

"LIFTING THE LID"
OPENING CHAPTERS

I hope you've enjoyed reading *Grave Expectations* and that you might be interested in reading one of my other novels.

To give you an idea what to expect, these are the opening chapters of *Lifting the Lid*, which is the first in my comedy thriller series. It's similar in style to my *Cremains* series but with completely different characters.

LIFTING THE LID
CHAPTER ONE

Trevor stood with his back to the fireplace like some Victorian patriarch but without a scrap of the authority. Although the gas fire wasn't on, he rubbed his hands behind him as if to warm them. His mother sat in her usual chair by the window, staring blankly at the absence of activity in the street outside.

He knew exactly what her response would be. It was always the same when he told her anything about his life. Not that there was often much to tell, but this was different. This was a biggie. Almost as big as when he'd told her about Imelda's—

'It's of no concern to me.'

There we go. And now for the follow-on. Wait for it. Wait for it.

'I'm seventy-eight years old. Why should I care? I could be dead tomorrow.'

Trevor screwed up his face and mouthed the words of his mother's familiar mantra, but it became rapidly unscrewed again when she added, '...Like Imelda.'

'Don't,' he said. 'Just don't, okay?'

'No concern to me,' said the old woman with a barely perceptible shrug.

In the silence that followed, Trevor became aware of the ticking of the pendulum clock on the mantelpiece behind him. It had never been right since his father had died, so he checked his watch instead. 'You won't be... ' and he hesitated to say the word, ' ... lonely?'

If his mother had had the energy or inclination to have laughed – derisively or otherwise – she would have done, but she settled for the next best option and grunted, 'Hmph.'

Trevor knew from experience that the intention was to pick away at his already tender guilt spot, and he looked around the room as if he were searching for the nearest escape route. His mother still referred to it as "the parlour", perhaps in a vain attempt to attach some kind of outmoded elegance to a room which, to Trevor's eye at least, was mildly shabby and darkly depressing even on the brightest of days. It was festooned with fading photographs of people who were long since dead, interspersed here and there with pictures of his more recently deceased brother and his very-much-alive sister. Of Trevor, there was only the one – an unframed snapshot of him and Imelda on their wedding day.

He became aware of the clock once again and cleared his throat. 'So... er... I'll be away then.'

This time, the shrug was accompanied by the slightest tilt of the head. 'No concern to me,' she said.

Again, he glanced at his watch. 'It's just that I have to—'

'Oh get on if you're going.'

Trevor stepped forward and, picking up his crash helmet from the table next to his mother, kissed her perfunctorily on the back of the head. For the first time, she turned – not quite to face him, but turned nevertheless.

'Still got that silly little moped then,' she said, repeating the comment she'd made when he had first arrived less than an hour before.

'Scooter, mother. It's a scooter. – Anyway, how

could I afford anything else?' He was thankful she couldn't see the sudden redness in his cheeks or she would have instantly realised that he was lying.

He kissed her again in the same spot, and this time she seemed to squirm uncomfortably. For a moment, he followed her line of vision to the outside world. – Nothing. He tapped his helmet a couple of times, then turned and walked towards the door. As he closed it behind him, he could just make out the words: 'Your brother wouldn't have gone.'

Out in the street, he strapped on his helmet and straddled the ageing Vespa, eventually coaxing the engine into something that resembled life. He took a last look at the window where his mother sat and thought he saw the twitch of a lace curtain falling back into place.

'Oh sod it,' he said aloud and let out the clutch.

At the end of the road, he turned right and stopped almost immediately behind a parked camper van. Dismounting the Vespa and still holding the handlebars, he kicked out the side stand and was about to lean it to rest when he decided that some kind of symbolic gesture was called for. Instead of inclining the scooter to a semi-upright position, he looked down at the rust-ridden old machine, tilted it marginally in the opposite direction and let go. With the gratingly inharmonious sound of metal on tarmac, the Vespa crashed to the ground and twitched a few times before rattling itself into submission. Trevor took in the paltry death throes and allowed himself a smirk of satisfaction.

Pulling a set of keys from his pocket, he kissed it lightly and walked round to the driver's door of the van. The moment he turned the key in the lock, a lean-looking black and tan mongrel leapt from its sleeping position on the back seat and hurled itself towards the sound. By the time Trevor had opened the door, the dog was standing on the driver's seat, frantically wagging its tail and barking hysterically.

'Hey, Milly. Wasn't long, was I?' said Trevor, taking the dog's head between both hands and rocking it gently from side to side. 'Over you get then.'

Milly simply stared back at him, no longer barking but still wagging her tail excitedly.

'Go on. Get over.' Trevor repeated the command and, with a gentle push, encouraged her to jump across to the passenger seat. Then he climbed in and settled himself behind the steering wheel. 'Right then,' he said, rubbing his palms around its full circumference. 'Let's get this show on the road.'

LIFTING THE LID
CHAPTER TWO

The lift was dead. The grey-haired guy in the expensive suit wasn't, but he looked like he was. Lenny had him pinned against the wall by leaning his back into him as hard as he could to keep him upright – no mean achievement since, although built like a whippet on steroids, Lenny was little more than five feet in height and well into his fifties.

'Come on, Carrot,' he said. 'What you messin' about at?'

Carrot – so called because of his ill-fitting and very obvious ginger toupee – jabbed at the lift button for the umpteenth time. 'Lift's not working. We'll have to use the stairs.'

'You kidding me? With this lard-arse?'

'So we just leave him here, do we?'

Lenny's heavily lined features contorted into a grimace. 'How many flights?'

'Dunno. Couple maybe?'

'Jesus,' said Lenny, taking a step forward.

The laws of gravity instantly came into play, and the Suit slid inexorably down the wall and ended up in a sitting position, his head lolled to one side and his jacket bunched up around his ears. Not for the first time, Carrot wondered why he'd been paired up with a dipshit like Lenny and even why the whining little git had been put on this job at all.

'Well you'll have to take the top half then,' Lenny said. 'Back's playing me up.'

Carrot snorted. Here we go again, he thought. The old racing injury ploy.

Lenny pulled himself up to his full inconsiderable height and shot him a glare. 'And what's that supposed to mean? You know bloody well about my old racing injury.'

'Doesn't everyone?' said Carrot.

Although Lenny's stature – or lack of it – gave a certain amount of credibility to his countless stories about when he used to be a top-flight steeplechase jockey, nobody in the racing business ever seemed to have heard of him. It was certainly true that he knew pretty much everything there was to know about the Sport of Kings, and most of his tales of the turf had a ring of authenticity about them, so he must have been involved in some way or other but more likely as a stable lad than a jockey. Hardly anyone bothered to doubt him to his face though, probably because his vicious temper was legendary and so was his ability with both his fists and his feet. For a little guy, he could be more than handy when it came to a scrap.

He looked like he was spoiling for one right now, so Carrot diverted his attention back to the Suit.

'Grab his ankles then,' he said and manoeuvred the man's upper body forward so he could get a firm grip under his armpits from behind.

Halfway up the first flight of concrete stairs, Lenny announced that he'd have to have a rest. Even though Carrot was doing most of the work, he decided not to antagonise him and eased his end of the body down onto the steps. Truth be told, he could do with a short break himself. He was already sweating like a pig and, besides, he needed at least one hand free to push his toupee back from in front of his eyes.

Lenny leaned back against the iron handrail and started to roll a cigarette.

Carrot's jaw dropped. 'Lenny?'

'Yeah?'

'What you doing?'

'Er…' Lenny looked down at his half completed cigarette and then back at Carrot. 'Rollin' a fag?'

His expression and tone of voice rendered the addition of a "duh" utterly redundant.

'We're not in the removal business, you know.' Carrot nodded towards the Suit. 'This isn't some bloody wardrobe we're delivering.'

Lenny ignored him and lit up. He took a long drag and blew a couple of smoke rings. Putting the cigarette to his lips for a second time, he was about to take another draw when he hesitated and began to sniff the air. 'What's that smell?'

'Er… smoke?' Two can play the "duh" game, thought Carrot.

'It's like…' Lenny's nose twitched a few more times and then puckered with distaste. 'Ugh, it's piss.'

'Dumps like this always stink of piss.'

'No, it's more…' Lenny carried on sniffing, his eyes ranging around to try to identify the source of the smell. 'Oh Jesus, it's him.'

Carrot looked in the direction he was pointing and, sure enough, the dark stain which covered the Suit's groin area was clearly visible despite the charcoal grey of the trousers. 'Oh for f—'

'Bugger's wet 'imself.'

'I can see that.'

Lenny took a pull on his cigarette. 'Fear probably.'

'Don't be a prat. The man's out cold. He doesn't know if it's Christmas Day or Tuesday.'

'Maybe it's like when somebody has their leg cut off – or their arm. They reckon you can still feel it even though it's not there any more.'

Carrot stared at him, unable to discern any logical connection between amputation and pissing your pants.

'You know,' Lenny continued, apparently aware that further explanation was necessary. 'It's like your subconscious, or whatever, doing stuff behind your back without you realising.'

'I think it's far more likely it's a side effect of the stuff we injected him with.'

'Could be,' said Lenny, and he took a last drag on his cigarette before lobbing it over his shoulder into the stairwell.

'Ready now?' Carrot made no attempt to disguise the sarcasm in his tone.

'I'm not taking the feet this time though. My face'll be right in his piss.'

Carrot squeezed his eyes shut and counted to three. 'You want to swap?'

'Not necessarily. We could try taking an arm each.'

Because of the substantial difference in their heights, Carrot knew that this meant he would be taking most of the weight again, but he also realised there was no point in arguing. The priority was to get the guy up the stairs and into the flat before somebody spotted them.

LIFTING THE LID
CHAPTER THREE

The time wandered by, and the miles slid comfortably under the tyres at a steady fifty-five. Battered though it was, the converted Volkswagen Transporter was only twelve years old and could have gone faster, but Trevor was in no particular hurry. He was enjoying the ride, happy to be away and with the road stretching before him to an unknown destination. Milly seemed equally contented and alternated between sitting upright on the passenger seat, staring fixedly ahead, and curling up to sleep in the back.

It was Trevor's first real trip in the camper, and he liked the idea of having no fixed itinerary. After all, he reasoned, wasn't that the whole point of having one of these things?

To say that he had bought it on a whim would have been a gross distortion of the truth. Trevor didn't really do whims. His idea of an impulsive action was to buy an item that wasn't on his list when he did his weekly shop at the local supermarket. Even then, there would have to be a pretty convincing argument in favour of dropping the quarter-pound packet of frozen peas, or whatever it might be, into his trolley. Half price or two-for-one were minimum requirements.

The camper van hadn't fulfilled either of these criteria, and to begin with, he'd toyed with the idea of a motorbike. Something a bit flash, like a Harley. He'd have needed a halfway decent tent of course. A simple bedroll and sleeping out under the stars were all very well in Arizona or wherever but totally inadequate over here – unless you were one of those rufty-tufty outdoor survival types with an unnatural fixation about the SAS. He'd never understood the attraction of deliberately putting yourself in a situation where it was more than likely you would either starve or freeze to death or be attacked by a large carnivore or stung by something so venomous you'd have seconds to live unless you applied the appropriate antidote in time or got your best friend to suck out the poison. No, Scottish midges were about as much as he was prepared to tolerate, but even then he'd make damn sure he had a plentiful supply of insect repellent with him.

A hermetically sealable tent and a good thick sleeping bag would be indispensable as far as Trevor was concerned and, if space permitted on the Harley, an airbed – preferably with a pump which operated off the bike's battery. It had all started to make perfect sense until a small problem finally occurred to him. What about Milly? She was too big to ride in a rucksack on his back, and as for the only other possible option, the very idea of a Harley with a sidecar made him squirm with embarrassment.

A car was far too ordinary for his purposes, so a camper van had seemed to be the next best thing if he couldn't have a Harley. It still had a kind of "just hit the open road and go where it takes you" feel to it, and he'd once read a book by John Steinbeck where he set off to rediscover America in a camper with an enormous poodle called Charley.

The whole decision-making process had taken months of what Imelda would have called "anally retentive faffing", but which Trevor preferred to consider as an essential prerequisite to "getting it right". In his defence, he would have argued that it wasn't just about buying a van. There had been much greater life choices involved, such as whether to pack in his job at Dreamhome Megastores.

As it turned out, that particular decision had almost made itself for him. The company was in a bit of financial bother and was having to make cutbacks, so he and several of his colleagues had been offered voluntary redundancy. Although not exactly generous, the severance package was certainly tempting enough to cause Trevor a run of sleepless nights. But it wasn't until his annual staff appraisal that he'd finally made up his mind.

He had sat across the desk from the store manager and studied the thin wisps of hair on top of the man's head while he read out a litany of shortcomings and misdemeanours from the form in front of him.

'This simply won't do, Trevor. Really it won't,' Mr Webber had said, finally looking up and removing his glasses. 'I mean, there have been more customer complaints about you than any other member of staff.'

'I don't know why. I'm always polite. Always try and give advice whenever I—'

'But that's exactly the problem, Trevor. More often than not, the complaints are *about* your advice. We've had more goods returned because of you than... than...' The manager had slumped back in his chair. 'Good God, man, have you learned nothing about home maintenance and improvement in all the... What is it? Fourteen years since you've been here?'

'Fifteen.' And in all those long years, he'd never once heard Webber use the phrase "do-it-yourself", let alone its dreaded acronym.

'Quite honestly, I'm at a loss to know what to—'

This time, it was Trevor who had interrupted. He couldn't be sure that he was about to be sacked, but he'd already had his quota of verbal and written warnings and thought he'd get in first with: 'About this voluntary redundancy thing...'

And that was that. Decision made and not a bad little payout. Added to what he'd squirreled away over the last couple of years or so, he could buy the van and still have enough left to live on for a few months as long as he was careful. He'd have to look for another job when the money did run out of course, but he was determined not to worry about that until the time came. At least, he was determined to *try* not to worry about it.

'What the hell, eh, Milly? This is *it*,' he said and shoved a tape into the cassette player.

He caught sight of the dog in the rear-view mirror. She briefly raised an eyebrow when the opening bars of Steppenwolf's *Born to be Wild* bellowed from the speakers above her head. Then she went back to sleep.

Trevor tapped the steering wheel almost in time with the music and hummed along when the lyrics kicked in. A song about hitting the open road and just seeing where it took you seemed particularly appropriate for the occasion, and when it got to the chorus, he'd begun to lose all sense of inhibition and joined in at the top of his voice.

Moments later, the van's engine spluttered and then abruptly died.

LIFTING THE LID
CHAPTER FOUR

Carrot and Lenny hauled the Suit to his feet and, with an arm slung around each of their shoulders, half carried and half dragged him up to the first floor landing. As Carrot had predicted, Lenny's contribution amounted to little more than providing a largely ineffectual counterbalance, and by the time they'd lurched and staggered to the top of the second flight of steps, every muscle in his neck and back was screaming at him to stop whatever he was doing.

'I'm gonna have to... have a break for a minute,' he said, fighting for breath as he altered his grip and lowered the Suit to the ground.

'Come on, mate. We're nearly there now,' said Lenny, but his words of encouragement were meaningless, given that he did nothing to prevent the Suit's descent.

Carrot groaned as he sat him down against the frame of the fire door and so did the Suit.

''Ang on a sec. He's not coming round, is he?' Lenny squatted like a jockey at the start gate and brought his face to within a few inches of the Suit's. 'He is, you know.'

The muscles in Carrot's back grumbled as he crouched down to take a closer look and spotted the faintest flicker of the eyelids.

'You can't have given him enough,' said Lenny.

'What?'

'The injection.'

'Yeah, stupid me,' said Carrot, slapping his palm against his forehead. 'I should've allowed extra time for all your fag breaks.'

Even though he resented Lenny's accusation, he'd worked with him on several other jobs and was used to getting the blame when things went wrong. Not that this was surprising since Lenny always avoided making any of the decisions, so any cockups were never his fault.

'We'll have to give him another shot,' said Lenny.

"We" meaning "you", Carrot thought and shook his head. 'Stuff's still in the van.'

'Jesus, man. What you leave it there for?'

Carrot bit his lip, aware from his peripheral vision that Lenny was staring at him, but he had no intention of shifting his focus to make eye contact. The Suit's eyelids were twitching more rapidly now and occasionally parted to reveal two narrow slits of yellowish white. Maybe the guy was just dreaming, but it was two hours or more since they'd given him the shot, so—

'Better bop him one, I reckon,' said Lenny.

It was Carrot's turn to stare at Lenny. 'Bop him one?'

'Yeah, you know…' He mimed hitting the Suit over the head with some blunt instrument or other and made a "click" sound with his tongue. 'Right on the noggin.'

Carrot continued to hold him in his gaze while he pondered which nineteen-fifties comedian Lenny reminded him of, but he was shaken from his musing by a strange moaning sound. The Suit's eyes were almost half open now.

END OF FIRST FOUR CHAPTERS OF 'LIFTING THE LID'

To read on, please go to:

http://viewbook.at/Lifting_the_Lid

Printed in Dunstable, United Kingdom